D0433958

HORSES THEY RODE

RODE

A Novel

SID GUSTAFSON

RIVERBEND
PUBLISHING

As with life, so with words.

Published by Riverbend Publishing, Helena, Montana.

Printed in the United States.

1 2 3 4 5 6 7 8 9 0 MG 11 10 09 08 07 06

ISBN 13: 978-1-931832-74-8
ISBN 10: 1-931832-74-9

Cataloging-in-Publication data is on file at the Library of Congress.

Riverbend Publishing
P.O. Box 5833
Helena, MT 59604
Toll-free: 1-866-787-2363
www.riverbendpublishing.com

Chapter 1 of *Horses They Rode* originally appeared in *Montana Crossroads Magazine,* October 1997, as the short story "Brakeman."

Front cover art
"The Blue Horse" is a pastel by Marietta (Mari) King, NI-NAM-SKIYI-INII-MAKI (The Woman Who Catches the Thunder Medicine), a member of the Blackfeet Nation, Browning, Montana. A college instructor, King has a master's degree in criminal justice. She serves as the Senior Blackfeet Honorary Advisory Council Coordinator (HC) for the Blackfeet Tribe and is the author of Native American Food is Medicine. Her oil and pastel paintings are available at the Blackfeet Heritage & Art Gallery and the Blackfoot Art & Cultural Center, Browning, Montana.

for Nina

Also by Sid Gustafson
Prisoners of Flight, a novel
First Aid for the Active Dog, a guidebook

Acknowledgements

I wish to thank my children, Connor and Nina, as well as my parents Rib and Patsy, and my siblings Kris, Erik, Barr, and Wylie for their devoted and patient support of my creative endeavors. My Grandfather Errol Galt began my thoughts of writing by gifting with me with a collection of autographed books by James Willard Schultz, chronicler of the Blackfeet.

Billy Big Springs, Sr., fullblooded Blackfoot, artist and storyteller, knower of a world past, proud and savvy horseman and keen dogman, took me under his wing long ago. We rode the summer foothills together under the glint redness of Rising Wolf Mountain all through the sixties. He taught me what it could be like to be an Indian in a land of grass and cattle. The two of us rode long and hard, him atop his painted pony, three Montana cowdogs at his horse's heels, me atop my white-stockinged sorrel with my dog alongside. Billy was not big on fixing fence, nor was I, and in the end that was my failing as well as his, but with our two horses and four dogs we could move two thousand cattle from the log cabin where Billy was born to Big Rock pasture, a river and a day away. They weren't buffalo, but they were close.

Additional thanks to Brad Okerlund and the Forever Scholarship Fund, Kristen Juras, Grandma Pat, Wylie, Svenni, Randy Scott, Connor Patrick, Loren Miles, and many others for their friendship and financial assistance in lean times. Special thanks to Beth Boyson and the Bozeman Public Library for providing diverse writerly resources.

Without these people and all the animals that have informed my life this story could never have been written.

Chapter 1

BRAKEMAN

Wendel Ingraham slumped in the Spokane Amtrak station. Waiting for the eastbound *Empire Builder* to take him to his longlost home in Montana, he gauged his life with that of the hobo and homeless riffraff strewn under and upon the worn wooden benches. He too was now homeless, a drifter no better or worse than they. With this company he found pitiful consolation. His wife of six years had just given him the boot. No longer did she appreciate his thoroughbred ways.

Locked out of his home, he felt no urge but to leave this town, something he'd always considered anyway. Earlier in the day, in her increasingly disillusioned mood, she'd allowed him into the house one last time to pack his old leather bag. That, and to give his five-year-old daughter a hug good-bye. There wasn't much to pack. She'd made short work of it, shoveling his scant belongings together for him. "Here," she said, gnashing her teeth to knee the grip of crumpled clothes out the door.

As Wendel embraced his little one he had looked his wife in the eye. "Please, Willow, come on. Try to remember the good times. Let go of the bad. Do that for our daughter, do it for Trish, please."

"Good times? What good times?" She whisked their child out of his snuggle, pushed the door in his unshaven face, and opened it a crack to bid a last farewell. "We'll maybe see you in some other life." Clunk.

His daughter shrieked "Daddy" through the heavy wood. He pinched the bridge of his nose and lifted his head to the colorless sky. The deadbolt to which he had no key sounded a discordant endnote.

And that was that for the family life he'd always dreamed.

The oldtown station reeked of stale smoke, bitter body odors, and pissed pants. Welcome to scuzzville, Spookaloo's underbelly. The lobby—the waiting-for-a-train-to-carry-you-away atmosphere—jogged the memory of Wendel Ingraham. Remembrance of train, clamor of travel, the acrid smell of transience. Echoes of lobby and squeal of metal. Soon it would be the same cars, the same stations, the familiar clunk CLUNK clunk CLUNK clunk CLUNK. Running, running from one misfortune to the other. Again. A life fraught with travel—a fate too recurrent to explain.

He pulled himself upright, rose, and walked to the ticket window. Clack of dust-hardened soles. Iron bars of the teller window, like some frontier bank. Money passed, change made, the ticket pocketed—the same ageless clerk adorned in the same company shirt, his starch shoulders pinched by the same ying-yang suspenders. A black visor shadowing rheumy eyes, a pursed mouth mumbling departure times. A tarnished gold tooth. The man looked up, eyeing Wendel as he might a child, "Please wait and be ready."

Wait and be ready. "Wait and be ready?"

"That's right, sonny. Wait and be ready to board."

Wendel submerged to a distant reincarnation of his younger self chinned to the same cage alongside a dad he was once so proud, a father lost to these same rails to never return. Frozen in front of the window staring at his ticket, Wendel felt a tap on his shoulder. He excused himself and stepped back. The next pilgrim took his place.

Wendel walked along immersed in the massive architecture of the train station. His boots sang off the warped marble of the long room inciting an echo pleasant to his ear. He retrieved a crinkled *Spokesman Review* that had been used as a blanket, or maybe a bed, and sat down. Snapping the sports page taut, he revived the crinkled print. He checked the Playfair horseracing results. Oh yes, his horses had run well last night despite his absence, Dharma Bum winning wire to wire, Corporal Trim coming off the pace to nip the fave by a nose. The apprehension of departure seized Wendel's guts. A passage of people began.

Wendel's thoughts had few places to go other than the depths of regret and recapitulation. It was clear relief when the *Empire Builder* chimed in, people shuffling to and fro, folk rushing to board. Others stood empty-handed, waiting with bent expressions for their train-traveling ilk to disembark, praying time had not disfigured them beyond recognition. This *Empire Builder* had arrived to whisk Wendel away. He marched down the gangway and jumped into the last passenger car. Striding down the aisle, he felt dizzy, weak-kneed. He stopped and racked his bag, stooped to pull down a window, and fell into the seat of an empty compartment. He breathed methodically, waiting for motion to tender its relief. Freight and luggage banged aboard, tossed from an iron-wheeled dolly into the baggage car behind. Then came the snap and hiss of brakes releasing, a kinetic thrum lurched the train ahead, movement Wendel Ingraham welcomed.

A stop soon after the departure took his breath, and the train rocked back and forth, maybe taking on another car. It then resumed forward progress and soon accelerated to speed, carrying him back to a life he once knew, the sway fine and familiar. Wendel reckoned if he couldn't find happiness in Montana, he wouldn't find it anywhere. He hadn't found it in Spokane and nor had his wife, not with him around. Trish seemed happy enough, too young to know the true drear of father-daughter separation. Someday he prayed she would seek him out to know herself. He wished for her to be older, to understand and share more thoughts with him—to know his love for her. He thought of his vanished father. The last time he had seen him he'd arrived unexpectedly at the ranch and hauled Wendel off in the same *Empire Builder*—his last trip with his father. He felt himself becoming that same vanquished dad.

He hadn't ever tracked his father down, why would his daughter ever try to seek him out? Wendel pledged to make himself available, to let her know his every whereabout, or to at least know her's. He promised to no god in particular to be there for his little girl, hanging his head, rubbing his temples with bony-knuckled thumbs. He looked up to a spotty Spokane River fog. He made a pillow with his coat, closed his eyes and let the train do its work.

The trip up and through the Idaho panhandle seemed short enough. By the time they reached Montana sunshine heated the landscape. As the train whizzed along the Kootenai River Wendel rose in rhythm with the train and ambled down the aisle to the door, a balance unforgotten. He entered the cage between cars. He stood in the uncertain box, watching through a gap. The girders of a long bridge went by, went by, went by. Wendel took a deep breath, inhaling the air from a budding Montana, the green world thinning by. He went through car after car until he found the observation car. He climbed into its dome. With the world flying below, he fell asleep.

The train shucked over the trestle into Whitefish. Bells clanged, waking him. Everyone clamored to unload, stranding Wendel in the *Vista Dome*. He caught his breath from a dream unremembered and lowered into an empty passenger compartment and sidled through to the bar car—quiet and empty, a black man smiling as he wiped down the mahogany. "Have a pleasant journey," the man said. Wendel debarked and walked down the street toward the closest lounge, a drink to soften the final leg home. All that remained between Whitefish and his former home was that sweet ribbon of Great Northern rail straddling the Continental Divide. Ingraham had ticketed himself to Cut Bank, Montana, an oil town wilting on the plains below the Walking Box Ranch, where he hoped they would welcome him back to work and ride. The thought of arriving unexpectedly worried him. He stopped, reconsidering his flight. The tang of conifer air gripped him, begging him to stay in Whitefish, at least for awhile. Instead of continuing on, he decided to catch the next eastbound over the mountains, whenever that might be, early tomorrow he surmised. He sprinted back to the station, tripped aboard, and grappled his way through the awkward cars to his baggage. Breathless, he skidded the sorry sum of worldly belongings off the mumbling train and into the depot. He hefted the grip onto a high shelf. Before he knew it he found himself spinning on a barstool in the Great Northern Saloon.

"What'll it be, cowboy," the bartender snarled, looking at Wendel's curly blond hair springing from under his stable-rumpled Stetson.

"What do you have?" Wendel asked.

The bartender spouted off a list of beers Wendel had never heard of before and ordered the local microbrew called Great Northern, a mountain goat on the label. He looked at himself through a pyramid of liquor stacked in front of a great mirror. The après ski crowd chatted and gestured in reflection, milling about like sheep. From ski bums to gandy dancers, the town had its share of characters. Out of the collection of afternoon drinkers a familiar face flashed, a woman he hadn't anticipated seeing ever again.

"Wendel, is it you?" Nancy said.

"It's me, darling" he replied, standing to hug her.

"Well I'll beeee. The powder hound returns. Just look at yooou!" The young lady betrayed her joy with feminine twinges of excitement, lips like licked candy, lips that entranced Wendel, lips pursing and stretching through each wonderful word.

Wendel offered her a stool. Nancy was a fine-looking woman, ever more svelte with time, her sculpted facial features softening with age, her hair the same dirty blond as his, but long and sleek. Steely eyes that radiated a certain blue. She smiled and sat down beside him, Wendel savoring the moment. He'd surprised himself calling her darling and hugging her, such a welcome presence, friendship he needed.

"Let's take a walk after it gets dark," she said. "Whitefish is a fine town by night."

"You live here still, then?" Wendel asked.

"Yes, I do. Seems I always have and always will. It's been

12

that sort of town for me, you know, the place you can't leave."

She ordered a drink from a bartender she seemed to know, and stood up to take off her cashmere coat. Nancy stepped back to take Wendel in. She put her hands on her sway hips and looked him up and down. "You look great! Tell me about your life."

He tried to add something up to tell her before bringing the words to his lips. He couldn't imagine that he looked great. He didn't feel so great, not just yet. Nancy had been his teammate from the *gelundesprung* days of too many years back, limberlost days when the two of them had concocted a ski jumping and aerial play off The Big Drift on top of The Big Mountain, the good ol' days. The little lady could get more air than any woman on the hill. They would fly off the drift together in high slung fashion, freeing themselves of the surly bonds of earth, twisting their bodies, flailing their skis—back scratchers and daffys to relieve the rigors of downhill training. Wendel had nearly forgotten the thrill of those flights, the sight of her flush face sailed him back into that whiteness.

"Well. Aren't you going to tell me?"

"Horses mostly," he said. "Back to being a bum right now, though."

"No, never." Nancy jerked her head back, appalled at the whim. "Don't talk about yourself that way!"

"Nothing wrong with bumming from time to time."

"No? I'm not sure it fits your bill. I've heard the news of your good horsework from here and there."

"My good horsework?"

"Yes, you're a famous trainer some say."

"Former trainer is more like it."

The bartender showed up with Nan's drink, a tall gin and

13

tonic, the frosted glass sweating. Wendel dug a wad of crumpled bills out of his pocket, flattened them out and set them on the bar. Wendel and Nancy giggled and visited into the night, trading out the superficial details of lost years. Wendel had always wanted Nancy, but she'd always been involved with one or the other of the stud-duck downhillers on the ski team. He'd so tried to gain her favor, but she spun his fragile heart around back then. He remembered giving up on her love, and love in general—the rejected feeling a young man never forgets when first love fails. His presence was needed back across the mountains at the Walking Box Ranch, then as now it seemed. He was expected to break the colts each spring as he had every spring of that boyhood life.

It had been a long twisted time ago when he kissed her goodbye from the top of that lonely mountain, kissed her on the forehead as she tucked her lips into her turtleneck to avoid his lips—his lips wanting, hers unwanting. She skied down the groomed side of the mountain, he the backside—the powder deep and untracked, the turns sweet and lonely… but that was then, and this was now, vanished desire was soon restored. When the lounge closed she offered him her flat across town. Out in the street Nancy put her arm through his, pulling him close. Train whistles worked delicious song through the Whitefish fog. The two reunited skiers sauntered along, waltzing through the chill. She danced Wendel all the way to her cozy bed, and all the way beyond—her tender womanliness rendering him delirious…

"Oh, Wendel, I'm so sorry," she said in an interlude of loving.

"Sorry for what?"

"For not loving you like you loved me. No one's ever admired me like you did back then."

"You knew?"

"I knew."

"Thanks," Wendel said. He was glad she knew.

After the passionate loving that comes to those whose lives have gone astray, Nancy drifted into a swoon. For Wendel sleep would not come, not enough Nancy to bestow the calm his heart needed to sleep. Remembrance engulfed him as he lay spooned to her, his eyes open, his chest feeling her breathe. After an hour listening to the clack and hump of railyard freight Wendel became restless. He disentangled himself from his lover's meld and slipped out of bed to shower off the love. The hot water gave him energy, needed energy to move on. He quietly dressed and spent a long while looking for a missing sock he never found. Before departing he leaned over Nancy, gently jostling her. "Nancy," he said, "I'm leaving." With his little finger he outlined the contour of her nose, curling his knuckles to stroke her cheek. He stood and backed away. "Goodbye, Love." Maybe she would feel his words in the morning, perhaps the way she'd felt his body snuggled to her through half the night. Sleep had her, yes it did, sleep and not him. He stepped out into the cold crank of railroad night.

He jogged to the train station and pulled his awkward baggage from its perch. It landed with a thud that wrought no echo. The readerboard bore disappointing news. The eastbound *Empire Builder* wouldn't be through until late afternoon. Out the door of the empty station Wendel limped his wiry frame through the street light, hipping his luggage down the main line. The marrying of cars dizzied him, metal shifting in the darkness, switching and more switching. Beyond streetlights the moon hovered, a jaundiced ghost, a moon no help at all.

Hiking along he hoped for an eastbound freighter. He

located a pod of Burlington Northern engines heating up and chased down the waiting cars looking for a hole. There was only one car with open doors. Ingraham lugged his bag up and grunted it aboard, scrambling after the grip as if there was an impending urgency to not to let his life be separated from the skimp belongings it contained. A strange stink greeted him, the boxcar littered with the unfrozen decay of fermenting corn. He waited for his eyes to adjust to the dimness and swept out a space in the back corner. He sat, breathing deeply, praying the train roll east. His body throbbed, mind afflux—the wife, his daughter; Nancy, no home—his life rotting with the turning corn. Now and then thoughts of Nancy soothed his boxcar blues, her attentive breasts and curved flanks, but the thoughts soon drifted cold, seconds ticking all too slowly to minutes. The night passed in mixed-up thought and worried wait. He laid his head on his baggage to doze with the trembling car. Time vanished into a fashion of sleep. When the wet night penetrated every measure of his existence he clicked awake—hungover and sick… a cold world inside and out.

Finally the jerk came. Eastbound it was. Up he snapped to the glory of freight car roll. He stood to the door and braced himself across the opening. Whitefish passed by, dead in the moony fog. The train chopped through Columbia Falls befuddled by the stink of its aluminum mill. Beyond, a hearty night air streamed down Badrock Canyon and into Wendel's car, restoring a needed order to his central nervous system. The Flathead flowed, a great undertow of water, a seamy surface intimating turbulence below.

The moon and stars and Wendel Ingraham witnessed night pass over this great draw of water as the train picked up steam, skimming the banks, the clickety-clack a pleasure. Rollicking and rolling they shot into Glacier Park, wending upward, a fine passage of midnight forest. At Nyack Flat the engineers poured the coal to her, gaining momentum to rise over Marias Pass. Wendel figured he was as good as home and wandered to his querencia at the back of the boxcar. He laid his spent body on the floor and resigned himself to the womb of transit. He savored the passage of every tie, each spike a happy day of life to come. The security of movement lulled him into a knotted sleep.

Suddenly, a westbound freight thundered past, gyrating Ingraham's dream, snatching him from a place he could not recall. His train had stopped, perched on a siding under an avalanche tunnel on the tip of Glacier Park's heart. The passing westbound freighter shattered time. Then, without warning, night fell quiet and still. An eerie air hovered as the freight dopplered off distant, abandoning Wendel. He waited for his train to start moving again, but instead—as if a nightmare—there was a clattering and scratching at the open door. A moonlit creature swept an armful of corn out of the car. Feeble light struggled its way through the avalanche timbers, allowing Wendel to see a pink tongue flicking the kernels into a dark mouth. After devouring all the corn in reach, a bear leapt into the car with the ease of a mountain lion. The animal stood up and with harrowing eyes inspected Ingraham. Satisfied, she casually dropped to her forepaws and lapped at some corn in the middle of the floor. She continued feasting, stopping occasionally to sniff in Wendel's direction. After a small eternity, the silver-haired griz waddled to the other end of the car where most of the corn remained and sat down, her back in the diagonal corner. From this position *Ursus arctos horriblis* considered her fellow passenger at length, and then, as if secure with his company, proceeded to devour corn like there was no tomorrow. Between slurps and chomps the bear occasionally huffed at Wendel to protect her stash. Sometimes she would vocalize unpronounceable sounds, but she never offered to move in for a closer inspection. The bear stank, the corn stank, the whole night stank, stink embossing the dark murk Wendel's life had all too suddenly become. He felt hollowed by cold and fear. His life flashed before him for the tenth time since bailing out of Spokane.

Down the line of freight cars the canyon echoed cha-clang cha-cling as the domino of pull yanked them into motion. By the time the train chuffed out of the tunnel Wendel could clearly see the bear eating away and felt right glad of the vegetarian preference. Its paws swiped handful after pawful of corn into its mouth—the Medicine Grizzly, a sacred reality. Wendel tried to calm himself down. Languid words began to dent the night, half-words, a cadence to them—praying, Wendel Ingraham was, of all things, praying. The only catechism prayer he could remember spilled off his tongue. "Oh, Blessed Virgin Mary, never was it known that anyone who fled to thy protection, implored thy help, or sought thy intercession was left unaided… Save me, hear me, please, my daughter doesn't know me, please, oh Blessed Mother, please."

Repeated incantations tranquilized the bear enough to allow movement toward the open door. Wendel pushed himself out of the corner as his travelling partner slurped up more of the cidered corn. The train pulled on, grinding and canting—*growling* through the towering mountains, Wendel's prayers in rhythm with the wheeling train. Mama steadfastly enjoyed her inebriating binge and did not appear to care what Wendel did. He moved, inches at a time, deliberate and entreatingly.

At the door Wendel considered jumping, but not for long. The train moved through the world at a breakneck clip, passing in and out of tunnels, racing along cliffs, moonlight vanishing as the freighter careened into a bible black gorge. Empowered by a strength he had never before realized, he shimmied to the top of the door and wrested himself atop the car. Speed seeped through him, night. He looked ahead, the cusp of tunnel approaching low and fast. "Whoa cowboy," he gasped, dropping flat his head, groping at cold metal. The tunnel timbers passed inches from his scalp. Diesel smoke billowed thick and harsh in the underground passage. His throat burned. His muscles burned. His eyes burned. He shut them and waited. When the train cleared the tunnel Ingraham gathered the last of himself and stood up on the whistling freight. He stumbled toward the end of the long train leaping between cars, grabbing at nothing to grab. He looked back toward the front of the long winding train. Morning copper rimmed the horizon, silhouetting the mountains of his childhood.

The trestles stopped coming, the landscape flattened, giving Wendel a breather—time to think. Ten years ago his friend Oakie had been a brakeman riding high in the caboose of this same Hi-line train. Ingraham's flummoxed mind figured maybe Oakie was on this very train this very morning. He would tightrope the remaining line of corn cars until he arrived at the caboose and tell Oakie, or the brakeman in charge, about the vagabond bear. That and warm up.

Another tunnel nearly decapitated Ingraham. Things were not getting any simpler. Flattened, he peeked over the writhing cars to the angry puff of drilling diesels. "Come up, sun," he urged, his throat parched, his words frogged. A quivering sun hummed at the lip of the Continental Divide. It had taken

Wendel forever reaching the end of the train, forever as the agglutinated sun. The daybreak freeze of Glacier Park took its toll. Time was not helpful. He vaulted to the last car—crawled to the end expecting to see the Great Northern caboose lolly-flopping behind waiting to dislodge his misery. He looked over the edge. No caboose. A little box with a blinking red light sat on the hitch at the end of this last freighter, computer caboose of slipstream time. Old friend Oakie wasn't there for him as Nancy and the Blessed Virgin had been earlier that night. Looking down over the back of the car, his body trembled. Ties skittered under, rails streaming. He lay poleaxed.

He closed his eyes to recount the events leading up to this inflicted condition. Yes, his wife was a tough woman to love—Spokane Indian that she was, he'd tried his very best. Crosswise to this Nancy was too nice, too easy, ten years after too easy, no effort at all, a falling more than anything. Beyond all this and worst of all, his daughter was gone, separated from him, he from her. Nothing would ever be easy again. His mind began to blank, teeth chattering to couplings of rail. He worked open an eye. The blinking red light of the cyclops stopped blinking and glared back at him.

Nearing the summit the pulling train relaxed, allowing a stark realization—it wasn't his wife that mattered so much, nor Nancy; it was his life—someday he would need to be there for his little girl.

Bellowing engines echoed, mountains moaned, the train crested Marias Pass. Chuffing released to glide. Boxcars worked the downhill drift. Wendel held tight, lifted his head, and mustered a wail: "There's no brakeman on this train."

Chapter 2

THE HORSE MEDICINE MAN

The lords of freight train night and the Medicine Grizzly reserved a mercy for Wendel Ingraham. The locomotives eased the long string of iron bison into the Blackfeet Reservation depot, piling them to a halt. Wendel's moribund posture reflected his tortured trip over the pass.

Fortunately, his old friend Bubbles Ground Owl relaxed along the tracks, his secret escape from town. Wind leapt through the boxcars, bending into trills and caterwauls. Bubbles took a swig of wine from his bottle and carefully beheld the arrival. The past few days he'd seen many visions, most abetted by wine or the rollercoaster lack thereof. From the corner of his native eye he spotted the train's only passenger—a vague silhouette of memory. Indian of the prairie, Bubbles was not surprised by unforeseen arrivals.

Bright flowers blew past the Blood Indian as he lay with his wine—the green of their plastic leaves too emerald to be real, the faded pinks and blues of the petals too counterfeit to represent the bright hope of life after death. Chinook wind carried them off the midtown cemetery recently defrocked of its winter snow. Cogitation drifted to Bubbles' mouth, mumbling his lips. He recognized things about the passenger's sprawl, the blond curly hair springing in the wind, the lank bowlegs, those Wellington boots. HorseMan? Is that my horseman riding freight? Ah hah. The HorseMan has returned.

"HORSEMAN," Bubbles bellowed, vocalizing his stream of thought. No answer. "Oh, boy," he said, rising onto his knees. "Here we go." Wendel's vacuous appearance concerned him. The contemplative Canadian Indian took a moment to align the situation. He stood and gazed west by southwest, facing the cemetery's brisk wind, hoping it might clarify his wine-weary mind. He looked back to Wendel. What a frazzled sight, that blowsy bright hair of his the only hint of life.

This wouldn't do. Something must be done. Wendel had not moved since he'd spotted him. Bubbles had no idea how long he'd been entranced by the vision. He set aside his bottle of wine and hopped to the train. No stranger to freight, the swart man scrambled up and jerked Wendel off his roost. He strung the HorseMan down the boxcar ladder dangled by his belt. Safely grounded, he slapped Wendel around a little, then a lot, bullying him into consciousness. Rocks gave way under Bubbles' feet. Unbalanced, he slipped and fell down beside his torpid friend. The body emitted a groan, as Bubbles figured it eventually would.

"Hey, Wendel, you're a sick puppy. Some sorry HorseMan riding to town frozen atop the IronHorse." He pushed the bottle of fizzie wine at him. Overflowing foam splashed Wendel in the face. "Here, this'll fix you up. Have a sip," Bubbles urged, trying to be as helpful as the situation allowed. He nudged Wendel with a gout-riddled knee. A few more slaps and pokes incited Wendel to repel Bubbles' advances. HorseMan shoved off, sat up and grabbed the wine. He imbibed three choice gulps, before spitting out the last swallow.

"Rot gut," Wendel blurted, suddenly alive, the wine the magic potion Bubbles knew it to be. "You drink rotgut, Bubbles. I'll call you RotGut Ground Owl, no?"

Bubbles didn't reply, he only looked at Wendel.

Wendel licked his lips and took another drink, swilling for the relief as he had swilled ten years ago. The screwtop beverage dizzied him, followed by a surge of well being. He looked out across the prairie; conscious, shivering, painfully alive— barleycorn comeuppance levying a bitter toll. He shook his head and tried to limber his jaw with his palm. Last night's journey floated about the rough sea of ale his mind had become, bounced around. Tongue swollen, it hurt to talk. He tried to sputter out a thought and gagged, wine boiling out his nose. He grabbed his face in his hand, and pushed the bottle toward Bubbles.

"Enough, eh?" Bubbles chided, grabbing the bottle. "Ha, ha, my boy. Ha ha. Your world has become mine. Now you know, yes. Now you know what it is like to live with a burdened soul such as mine."

Wendel smiled feebly and looked at the round-faced Indian. His dark black hair had thinned over the years, and now the braids that hung over his shoulders were pencil-thin. Wendel dropped his head between his knees waiting for the qualm to pass. It was true enough, it wasn't about being Indian or White, life was about Time. Tears swam out of his eyes, the wind rolling one across his face and into his ear. He shook his head, looked up and motioned for the bottle with his hand. Bubbles laughed, retracting the sparkling wine. "Any more 'll just make you sicker."

Wendel spotted Bubbles' satchel. He grabbed it and rummaged through the scant contents. "I was hopin' for a little sip of Jim Beam."

"You won't find whiskey in that bag. This is all the wine I have left Mister HorseMan. If you want more wine, we'll just have to hoof it on into town." He felt around his pockets. "You didn't happen to make it out of Spokane with any spare change, now did you?"

Wendel retched.

"Good then. We jog us in to Napikwan's and get something on your good credit. They take credit cards now, you know. Yes man. We'll put the fun on your Visa card, init?" Bubbles asserted, laughing. He stood and pulled Wendel to his feet. "Thunderbird Red, drink of our people," he roared. He held Wendel by the biceps and slapped his back, spilling him forward and holding him up at the same time. "You still my people, aren't you HorseMan?" Bubbles asked. Wendel took a deep breath. "We're still brothers, right? You buy the sweet wine like old days?"

"Street wine, you mean?"

"Sweet wine, street wine, whatever you say. We're still brothers, no?" Bubbles asked, letting go of Wendel.

"We're brothers alrighty, just like we always have been. Your retrieving my frozen soul off this train is brother enough for me." Wendel put his hands on his knees to steady himself, holding the Thunderbird in his belly, coaxing it to stay calm. "Whatever you need, Bubbles, we'll get. I guess. Any chance we could head ourselves back to the ranch? Maybe detour around town?"

"You don't want to go back to the ranch," Bubbles said. "Wouldn't like what you might find."

"What might I find?"

"Well, let's just head to town and talk that over," Bubbles said, throwing his arm around Wendel's shoulder. "Times have changed, I'm telling ya." They steadied one another, and moved along. Indians aren't afraid to hug a man, and Bubbles hugged Wendel. Wendel needed it. "We'll get a bit more wine, a case say. Two bucks a bottle, 24 dollaire. You've got 24 dollaire credit on the plastic, don't you HorseMan, twenty-four hundred dollaire?"

Indians knew everything, Wendel thought. Bubbles correctly intuited he carried credit cards, although he'd carried none when he left. All white men out there in the netherworld carried credit cards.

An especially inclement blast of wind toppled Bubbles to the ground. A new covey of cemetery flowers team-tagged by. A black rose slapped onto Bubbles' neck and held there, hissing like a grasshopper. Wendel bent over and dislodged the flower, freeing it to tumble along its prairie way. More wine, he thought, my man needs more fizzie wine. Sugar as much as the alcohol, sad sugar and sadder alcohol. Wendel looked down to Bubbles. The decade had taken a heavy toll. Bubbles made no attempt to rise. Wendel looked at his old friend, his aging old friend. What'd happened to his earthboy life?

Wendel rolled Bubbles onto his back. "I didn't come back to start our drinking thing anew, Bubb. I managed that fine without you in Spokane."

"I can see you did."

"Came to recapture my life. You told me to come back if things didn't work out."

"I did?"

"You did, and guess what?"

"I'm not a guessing man."

"Well, things didn't exactly work ou—" Wind hamstrung his utterance, taking him down beside his hooched brother.

He grabbed at the knot twisting his gut, the wine working along, finding its way to his central nervous system. Maybe. "I returned hoping…," retch, "hoping to rid myself of the trouble my life has become."

"Trouble," Bubbles said, plainly. He carefully built himself up to a tripod posture and looked Wendel over, poking and prodding at him with his free hand. "Ya, you look like trouble all right. Come here to rid yourself of trouble. Riddled you are. Of all places you come here to kick trouble?"

"Seems so," Wendel said, his throat hot with bile, his physiology hammered. He bellied to the ground, waiting for his blood to drop the wine into his depleted synapses. Wendel closed his eyes and gritted his teeth… things calmed down. And there Wendel lay, fetal, Chief Bubbles Ground Owl sheltering him from the reservation wind he had all but forgotten.

Chapter 3

OUTDOORSMEN

"You okay, HorseMan?" —the sad, sure voice from the last corner of Native America graced Wendel's ears. He felt better. Some time must have passed. He lay beside the wheels of a great boxcar. He was back in Bubbles' world, a world he'd yearned to return for ten long years. The warm smell of the Chinook wind slogged his memory. He tried to rise, but the gale kept him down.

Bubbles surveyed Wendel's plight. "I see you pack no baggage, HorseMan. Always good to travel light, eh? The Indian way?"

Wendel tried unsuccessfully to respond, his tongue dry and swollen.

Bubbles grabbed onto the bottom rung of the boxcar ladder, and pulled himself up. His big belly bulged out of his untucked shirt, its tails flapping in the wind.

Wendel rolled to his back. Words moved through his blue lips. "Bubbles," he implored, "we've got to get that life back."

"What life is that?"

"That life we journeyed when I was a kid."

"Pretty hard to journey with a feller in your shape, init? You're no kid no more."

"I journeyed here with the bear, Bubbles."

"What bear?"

"The realbear." Wendel sat up, his memory mad with the thought—the train ride, last night's chaos. "I came with the bear. Rode in with the Medicine Griz herself. She's watching my luggage, in fact."

"Ha. Medicine Griz. Looks to me you rode in on the whiskey griz."

Wendel stood out from under the jovial Indian. Perfect recall sobered him to action. A rush of wind swayed Bubbles backward, sending his arm ajib, ballast to temper the gust. "Ya, Ya. That's a fine one HorseMan, real good dream. You betcha. Good medicine to dream up ol' grizzz…" He hung onto the word, not quite able to spit the Z off his tongue, "…zizz." A namesake bubble appeared on his lips, salivary trouble. "Vizzion," popped the bubble. "You've had a vision. You return to your homeland and find your power on the way." Bubbles waved a wine bottle across the sky as he spoke, gesturing to the Sun, a supplication on Wendel's behalf.

"No vision, Bubbles. Griz was not a vision, no more than you're a vision to me." Wendel shouted the words into a howl of wind, the effort pinning pain through his head.

"I wouldn't count on me being too real, Wendo. Things haven't been so well inside. I could be dead."

"You'll never die. You told me yourself Indians never die."

"Yeah, 'cause we're already dead." Bubbles poked the wine bottle into Wendel's chest. "If you saw Griz, she'll take care of you. I'm too weak to take care of you this time around. Your other people will have to help you out."

"Other people? I have no *other* people, no blood of mine around these parts."

"Sure about that, are ya?"

"Sure as my Spokane woman kicked me out and kept my

daughter. Not one lick of Indian or sense left in me. I feel like a friggin' ghost ... all emptied out." The wind blew every other word away. "I ... too much," Wendel shuddered.

Bubbles said something and tried to slap him on the back, but missed and fell over. He toppled into the right-of-way scree and rolled to a stop. He quickly shot up his arm as if to rewind time while he took a moment to stand upright. Bubbles rose irregularly, fazed by the nasty fall. Took a deep breath, and another, gathering himself. "You'll feel alright soon enough, Wendel. If this Griz is real, you'll fill back up with hope." Bubbles blundered up the railbed rock, grabbing Wendel to steady himself. "Don't doubt my wisdom."

"Follow me," Wendel said, anxious to show his reeling mentor the bear.

He led Bubbles between two cars and pushed him under the hitch and across the tracks. The Wind God kept the hurricane from pushing the train downwind and slicing them in two, eastern front wind that in its iron horse anger blows railcars off the tracks—train-derailing, metal-twisting wind, wind Wendel and Bubbles knew.

"This was no dream, my friend. I tell you, I rode here with realbear herself."

"Let's hope so," Bubbles put in.

Wendel knew he had, but the long journey and hangover fog made him doubt the memory. He squatted to catch his breath. Bubbles sat beside him. "I don't... don't know much anymore. Maybe the whole shebang's all been a dream. Wife, kid, horses, maybe it's all a long bad dream."

"Kid? A kid is never a dream HorseMan. A son, eh?"

"A daughter," Wendel said. The wind wearied him. His head throbbed, his bladder swollen. He stood and tried to pee. The blow whipped urine into his face. Bubbles watched sorrowfully. The wanderer had forgot how to piss in the wind. Too long gone, too long gone from his home. Bubbles tipped up his bottle. He too, long gone— far too gone.

"You ride with either a bad hallucination or a sacred vision. Too much hop whiskey," Bubbles said, before coaxing a last drop out of the bottle.

Bubbles' tongue reminded Wendel of the bear's tongue lapping the cidered corn of last night's boxcar. Wendel looked away and closed his eyes, the moonlit flicking of a pink tongue flashed in his head, a flashback reflecting the realbear night, confirming it. He breathed wind through his nose, and gathered his strength.

"Follow me Chief Thunderbird. You'll see. You'll think hallucinate. I'll show you. We'll find the bear an' have us all one big brotherly vision."

Bubbles shook his head, jowls shaking, eyes squinting. The spindly Wendel led the way, the round Indian behind, his braids blowing in the wind. The odd couple headed down the line, the tailwind shaping them along. They stubbled down and clambered along the right-of-way talus making their way from boxcar to boxcar. Wendel pounded each freighter with a horse's femur he'd found along the tracks. Bubbles chanted some ancient song. They floundered south one car at a time, marionettes of the wind. Bubbles stopped and watched Wendel hammer the next car with the sun-bleached bone. "Don't remember which car, eh, HorseMan?" Every other utterance seemed to be HorseMan, the word sprinkling Bubbles' talk. The reference pulled Wendel to a strange, almost forgotten consciousness of his former life; a life and time where Bubbles exerted his power as the last Horse Medicine Man, owner of the last horse medicine bundle. A life and time unlike this railing madness.

An especially angry gust wavered the line of freight. A yellow car with hiphop graffiti swayed over them, springs screaming, a smell leaking. "The rotten corn—I smell it," yelled Wendel. "You watch. This is the car. The bear's inside."

"If realbear comes forth, then you *are* a lucky man," Bubbles proclaimed. "If indeed you hop freight with the Medicine Grizz we may have to change your name to RailBear. HorseMan RailBear. You'll go far with a handle like that." Bubbles chuckled his first laugh of the day, roundhousing a bottle to emphasize Wendel's convergence with the spiritual.

"You don't believe me?"

"I believe." Bubbles said. Despite intemperance, Bubbles believed. He stepped toward HorseMan.

Wendel bonged the car some more, then dropped an ear to listen. The wind eased and the car echoed a firm thump thimp thump. He looked to Bubbles. "Stand back, Bub, here she comes. Big Medicine herself." Wendel gave the car a last gong with the thighbone. Out poked she-bear's conical nose, sniffing.

Bubbles stopped in his tracks. Empty wine dropped out of his grasp. Fingernails smooth and yellow curled over the ends of his plump fingers. One of the bottles rattled down the flinty incline, jinking a quick music. Realbear flopped out of the corn car as if to chase the tune. The blond animal rolled down the grade, a silvertipped comedy of errors. She plopped into the wind-pressed bunchgrass, a sprawled beauty of a beast. Neither man said a word, becoming as sober as the alcohol floating in their plasma would allow. Realbear lolled. She had trouble rising. Determined, she gathered herself and stood two-legged to examine the clowns. Satisfied they were not a threat, she dropped to all fours and circled a certain spot before squatting to shit like a manx cat. After some sniffs to the wind, she moved off, her gait improving with each step. She soon found her balance and sauntered over the foothills toward the mountains.

"See there, HorseMan. Mama Griz knew not to shit her bed like you musta shit yours in Spookaloo." Bubbles Ground Owl found native philosophy in all natural activity, especially in regard to horses and realbears. For his people grizzly represents an incantation of life—an animal part man, their Sasquatch of sorts, the only creature they knew to walk on two legs like man himself. Bubbles began singing a flowing canto. Seeing realbear shitting was right up there in the realm of spiritual experience, as it well should be. The only higher sacrament would to have witnessed realbear fucking.

Wendel thanked the shining sun that he wasn't a portion of the steaming pile of sacred scat. The bear moved over the horizon in a soft lope. When she fell out of sight Bubbles stopped his singing. "Better git to town, get something to drink to celebrate your good medicine." He crawled between the tracks and sat under the train. The wind had diminished markedly. He waited for Wendel, who stood entranced, hoping for his bear to reappear in some imagined distance.

"Did you touch her?" Bubbles asked from under the train.

"Touch her?"

"In the boxcar with her?"

"Didn't think to try."

"Too bad," Bubbles said. "Too bad for you. Big opportunity to have it all touching realbear."

"Like counting coup?"

"No, not like counting coup. Realbear is not the enemy."

32

Wendel thought of touching realbear.

"Let's go get something to drink," Bubbles said.

"Drink?" Wendel asked. He crawled under the boxcar and sat with Bubbles. He threw his arm around the horse medicine man's shoulder. "Is drink how realbear helps these days?"

"How it works today," Bubbles said, crawling out of Wendel's hold.

"Looks like that's how its been working everyday."

"Everyday is right."

Wendel followed Bubbles as he limped it on into town. In light of his peculiar drift of rail and celebration of life, Wendel purchased a nice tight cardboard case of T-Red, the great vision enabler. In addition to the wine, he picked up two mickeys of his 'lover,' as his wife referred to Jim Beam. The two found the same Browning Montana alley that had cushioned different rodeos years ago. They seated themselves on a rock deposited by another ice age, a rock sat on by the many that came before them. Bubbles twisted the screwtop off a bottle and leaned back to tope down a long draw of the red substance. Wendel sipped his Beam. Two horses grazed the vacant lot next door. One eye of each horse measured the meager green growing before them, which they nipped precisely, while the other eye watched the distempered men mud themselves back to an unforgotten synthesis.

Wendel lapsed into the same hole he'd climbed out of a split-second decade before. Bubbles wasn't so much sucking out of the bottle as the bottle sucked out of him. Each quaff brought them beyond their broken dreams, Bubbles' dream broke over a century ago, Wendel's not yet a week past.

A crowd of smiling men showed up to greet HorseMan, good prairie folk misplaced and fallen behind. Bubbles depicted

Wendel's journey home. The Indians hallowed the realbear who escorted their whiteman home. His wine eased their sorrowed memory of buffalo. They toasted the horses who hung their heads over the fence waiting expectantly for the men to someday be horsemen again and ride them on to greener pastures. Not this day.

The case of wine and a mickey of Jim were tipped dry by mid afternoon. Sun softened the earth. A balm April gale erased the cold memory of snow. The wine faded and the men tired. They slept. Everyone dreamt the same dream—a never-ending pursuit of buffalo, horses after the buffalo, men upon the horses.

Wendel Ingraham napped with his adopted people in the Browning Montana alley, his dirty blond hair betraying his roots. At the edge of the mountains nestled in an aspen grove realbear slept curled atop winterpressed leaves.

Chapter 4

RED MAN

The comfort of outdoor sleep is short-lived in Glacier County Montana, no matter the season or century. Realbear moved into the forest. Wendel Ingraham woke to physical pain, sleep giving way to shivering, shivering to want, want to the full effect of withdrawal without the benefit of food and fluids. It took him more than a few moments to assimilate an awareness of himself thus afflicted. Once sensate, Wendel wanted out. "Better head for Ripley's," he announced.

Bubbles Ground Owl grunted at the feeble notion. He had awakened earlier preoccupied with need. He rubbled through scattered bottles searching for any remaining wine. "Screw Ripley, nothing but a money-blundered whiteman." He was not a happy Indian as the sun buckled out of the sky. The Chinook warmth had failed. A gloaming pressed cool wind off blue mountains. Wine no longer held its morning glimmer.

"His wife's your people," Wendel countered. "She'll nurture your burdened soul into shape. She knows your need."

"Knows my need is right, no goddam wine on the whole goddam outfit. Not my idea of nurture. Her cattle make me sick." Bubbles heaved a wine bottle at the last fist of sunlight. Want crazied the horse medicine man.

"Give it up, Bubbles. It's time to go back."

Bubbles did not give it up. He examined bottle after bottle, his jones intensifying with each drop found. Pariah dogs sniffed about, they too seeking maintenance. Dusk blanketed the town.

"Time we get back and heal up," Wendel said, pushing out the words.

"Hell with healing. Indian never heals," Bubbles shouted. He organized a row of bottles in preparation to rinse them with water from a handwell in the middle of the lot. He pumped until rusty water flared from a tarnished nipple. More pumping, abrasive metal sucking water out of a stubborn cistern, a mangy she-cat slinking in with the hungered hope the noise was a dying rat. The Blood Indian persevered until he drew water. He filled each of his bottles with a splash and swirled the mixture about, gulping down the deluded pinkness.

Wendel shook his head. If the water didn't give him cholera it should do Bubbles some good. There was a time not so long ago when he could have never imagined this scene. "I'm heading to Rip's. Best you sally along," he declared. "Calving. He always hires during calving."

"Calving is nearly over," Bubbles replied.

"A good time to start then, no? Ease back into the prairie life." Wendel was Walking Box family of the by-association sort, he still felt the need to be hired anew each time he returned to the ranch. He strolled across the lot to the backyard pasture, nightfall upon the horses. They stopped their grazing and came to him. He rubbed their heads, calming himself with the slick feel of hair under their forelocks. In the lot beyond Bubbles persisted with his alchemy, brittled by need. He wheezed and coughed, bottles bumped and clinked about.

"There's Chief Mountain back at the ranch. You claimed time spent under that great eye meant living the good life," Wendel shouted back at him.

"'Once good life,' I should've said. Today it's more life than one can handle. You'll see if you make it back there." He caught his breath enough to manage another swallow.

Daylight lost itself behind the mountains, fallen below the edge of the world. Wendel walked over and started tossing Bubbles' bottles into a barrel. "Quit this shit. You're coming with me."

"Ha."

Wendel grabbed Bubbles by the shoulders and looked into the depth of his dilated eyes. He gave the Indian a little shake. Bubbles, brought into a brief reality, grabbed his lower teeth. He tried to stabilize his breathing by pulling down on his jaw. Fresh wind swirled a cold twilight. He closed his eyes and emitted a wail, a wail curiously answered by a faraway drumming. He opened his eyes, canted his head so. Yes, a drumming listed through the night. Bubbles sat cross-legged to pray. The drumming intensified—drumming now accompanied by background singing.

Mendicants crossed the vacant lot moving in a certain motion toward the drumming, natives emerging from the shackles of prairie night to dance under the wolf moon. Mange-brindled dogs and tapewormy cats chased along the edges of the people, a hope in the drumming that even the animals sensed. In the unlit streets beyond, adumbrated dogs joined in the song, the links of their chains rolling and clacking through the darks of government housing, their howls rising above it all. Bubbles sat in the weeds, people flowing past him as if he were invisible.

"We are a proud people, Wendel," he said. "Bust down this reservation and our culture ends."

"Who said anything about busting anything down?"

"They once tried to make us stop drumming, you know."

"They?"

"Your people."

"My people?"

"You Americans."

"You're protesting your past treatment with me? What? Because I've been out there? Ha."

Bubbles stopped and closed his eyes. He cleared his throat and hummed with the drum-DRUM beat, winter in his blood. When a pause came he spoke: "Okay, we'll try the Walking Box. One last chance."

"You'll come, then?"

"Let's go to the drumming, first."

"Drinkers aren't allowed at the drumming, you know that," Wendel said.

"That's right. No drinking at the drumming," Bubbles said evenly. "And no drinking at the ranch. Worlds apart and no drinking either end." He postured to make a point about the drinking and drumming and ranching, but didn't have the wherewithal to put anything together. He dropped his arms to the ground and waited a few minutes. He licked his lips and prepared to speak. "The ranch is not so true to my culture as it to yours, HorseMan. You understand I have trouble going back there?"

"You think your culture is all that different from mine these days?"

"I wouldn't say your culture personally, Wendel. But your people's."

"Fair enough," Wendel said.

"My horse medicine doesn't heal so well at the Walking Box anymore."

"Oh, and it's healing everything up here just fine, I suppose?"

"No. The only place it still works is up Palookaville way with Frenchy." Bubbles smiled his first smile since sundown. "French has some nice horses up Mitten Lake way."

"Let's go ride Frenchy's horses, then. Let's go heal."

"He's not there, yet. Not 'til summer."

A scabby moon reared a tired eye over the plains east of town. Its light silvered the distant hills to the north and in that distance a truck with one headlight crawled toward town.

In time the vehicle plodded through the backstreets of manifest despair and bounced down Wendel's street. When the headlight flashed over Bubbles' wine predicament it pulled over and stopped. A merle-blue dog peered out of the back of the pickup and wagged his fluff tail.

The truck's rear view mirror had been knocked loose by an itchy bull and swung back and forth upside-down. The motion had ground a semicircle through the paint on the lower door. The crescent provided the only sense of symmetry anywhere on the vehicle. An ocher-skinned man sat in the vehicle, waiting easy. The moon, fishcolored now, lit his asymmetrical face (a horse hoof to the jaw as a child). A torn-pocket smile hid under the brim of his range-weary Stetson. Sweatstain wicked up the crown of his hat gauging the toil of the Walking Box cycle. Maternal Blackfoot/Cree blood pulsed through his crook nose, a nose once finely shaped by his Métis/Blackfoot pa, a nose later broken by horseplay. Jesse James had Blackfeet blood on both sides—blood split and brought back together, thinned on his mother's side with Cree and on his father's by English, a genetic remix that reddened his skin.

The drinking men writhed in his spotlight. Jesse shut off the diesel engine and quelled the headlamp. His cowdog barked, once. The drumming resurfaced: dum-DUM, dum-DUM,

dum-DUM... a round-dance beat. Jesse James sat and meditated, envisioning harmony in the midst of turmoil, an attribute that helped him run the Walking Box. Wendel and Bubbles were Jesse's friends, as close to the Walking Box land and cattle as Jesse himself. He needed their help (and they, his). He waited easily. Time was nothing to Jesse James, in fact it was said he did not believe in time.

His slouch told of a bitter winter past, something fallen apart. Rocky Boy peyote tingled his eyelids... He was in no hurry and would wait until his men were ready to come home with him if home was what the Walking Box had become for any of them. If they wanted to sleep in the lot, he surely could sleep in his pickup cab. He stretched his fingers and rolled his head about and laid back. Earlier in the day, Mrs. Diana Ripley had informed the mixed-blooded Jesse James that Wendel and Bubbles were on a tear in town. She'd gotten word from Mabel Old Coyote's second cousin, Arlene Pipe Weasel, who'd stopped by the ranch to drop off some buffalo hump for souping the commodity lima beans. She'd witnessed the pair chasing the railroad bear out of the railyard early that morning. Big news, man and bear, bear doing man things, man bear.

When Jesse James intercepted this moccasin telegraph, he forewent his afternoon nap and hit the road to town to retrieve his two longlost men. He would have arrived earlier and perhaps intervened before the winefest, but it was not meant to happen. He became sidetracked with the church man in Babb, who had bestowed upon him wisdom to complete this quest, wisdom and peyote.

Wendel stared at Jesse in disbelief. He'd been five times rescued in one day: first Nancy, then realbear. The Virgin Mary and Bubbles. Now the Métis Blackfoot Jesse James, said to be related on his father's side to the American/Irish/British novelist Henry James. Henry's uncle was Jesse's great-grandfather, a Hudson's Bay fur trader who married a Northern Blackfoot in Saskatchewan. Wendel pulled Bubbles to the truck and pushed him into Jesse's cab, muscling in after his friend, slamming the door with the slam he knew it would take to shut them in tight.

"Looks like you fellers have seen taller grass," Jesse James quipped. He lit a pipe from which hung a feather and passed it to Bubbles, who took a ceremonial whiff and pushed it on to Wen. Jesse drove around the block and stopped for some wine at Napikwan's, understanding the beverage might make for a simpler trip home. Bubbles smiled when Jesse returned with a sack of chiming bottles. Wendel rubbed his head. They left town and drove into the moonlit prairie knowing the road back to the Walking Box would be okay.

"Wave goodbye to the wine life, boys," Jesse said as they wheeled out of town. Bubbles stomach grumbled audibly. "That's it, Bubbles, get your gut movin'. In a few days you'll be needing some real nourishment." Jesse unscrewed a fifth of wine, took a polite sip (more to wet his cottonmouth than to get a buzz), and passed it on to Bubbles, who drank long and hard. Wendel managed away the bottle for a last gulp and tossed the empty into the box behind, nearly bonking Jesse's faithful blue cowdog in the head. Bubbles mumbled for another bottle, and nudged Jesse with an elbow.

"Enough for now," Jesse snapped, fumbling under the seat. "You need food. Here. Have some cheese and crackers. Eat some a this."

Bubbles nibbled at the cheese and crackers, and gulped from a canteen of Wolf Springs water. Jesse handed him another fifth of fizz as reward. Bubbles sipped and quieted down until he wrangled up a thought of food or sex or somesuch notion and asked, "Mabel still's cooking then, init?"

"Plates hot and high with cookshack delights waiting just for you. She's lonely for her man."

Bubbles grinned. He conducted a split life, the drinking life and the Mabel life, the bad medicine and the good. It lifted Jesse with hope to see Bubbles drift back for another spell with Mabel. It seemed there might not be so many more returns left.

"What's today?" Bubbles asked, awake with thoughts of Mabel.

"I don't know what day it is. A good day for you to stop yooking it up. What's it matter which day?"

Bubbles heaved an empty wine bottle out the window— the muffled crush of glass on rock.

"Godammit Bubbles, that glass can cut my cows' hoof."

"Ha."

"Ain't you seen the TV ad? The crying Indian."

"I'll stop littering when you give me a week to clear my head."

Jesse clacked his yellow teeth and sighed. "That's a deal." He fished out another bottle of wine and handed it to Mabel's man. "Just hand it back to me when it's empty."

"Hai-yeh," Bubbles toasted. "It's a week of R & R for me and my pal here, then. Ain't he a prince." Wendel bobbed in flawless oblivion. "We'll watch satellite TV, relax with our feet propped up on stools like whitemen, catch up on Oprah— learn how we should be thinking these days. In no time we'll be ready to ride. He'll write a little, I'll draw some."

"Withdraw, you mean," Jesse said.

42

Bubbles grunted.

"Does Wendel know about the buffalo?" Jesse asked.

"What about the buffalo?"

"You know what about the buffalo."

"No." Bubbles put a head lock on Wendel, who moaned. "HorseMan here has been oblivious to our world for a full decade I believe, a darn sight longer than me I'd say, now init Jesse James? Told me he's learned how to write poems to keep the sanity at bay."

"Insanity at bay."

"Whatever. Said he came back to us to heal. Told me his Japanese jockey taught him poetry and discipline. A path led him back here."

"Japanese jockey?"

"Oh yeah, HorseMan here is a big and famous trainer of racehorses in Washington State, it seems."

"Seems you and him had quite the time in town?"

"That's right. Quite a time in the railyards. Realbear. You probably heard."

"I heard."

"We all need to commune with the realbear now and then."

"Then more than now, I think," said Jesse.

"Wendel communed like a redman. I saw what happened. Saw the bear. He sure enough hopped freight with mama griz. It means something," Bubbles said.

"Interesting times to come is what it means," Jesse replied, his smile half-cocked. He watched Bubbles grab the skin that hung under his chin and stretch his lips over his teeth. How a man like Bubbles could drink wine straight for a month— hell, almost a year—and still think and speak straight, amazed Jesse. He figured Bubbles to be the last true Indian of America,

43

a horse medicine man holding forth stories from the ancient edge of time.

Bubbles told many a cookhouse story during Wendel's childhood a score of years ago. But after Wendel left, Rip Ripley, the ranch owner, boiled over during a telling one dinner and put a stop to it. No more stories at supper. Jesse should have intervened and done something, but he didn't. However sacred the storytelling ground, Ripley somehow had the last word on an Indian matter rightly within Jesse's jurisdiction. Rip claimed certain stories weren't fit for a Christian table. After that the cookshack eating became some parody of religious ceremony which could not be blasphemed by stories of native belief.

The dictum drove Bubbles into a bad space. It drove everyone who graced the cookhouse into a bad space. Of course the stories were told elsewhere, but without Mabel and the comfort of her food it just wasn't the same—a long ten years without cookhouse stories. Wendel missed out on the injustice, long gone to Spokane, unbelieving that eating without storytelling could ever transpire in Mabel's cookhouse. Wendel came home for the stories. Bubbles had started leaving time and again when he couldn't tell them in his woman's kitchen. To make up for the storytelling loss, Jesse started bringing home expensive art supplies for Bubbles—painting a replacement version of storying. It didn't work. Bunkhouse Chris tried to lift Bubbles' spirit as well, encouraging this art. He came and sat and watched Bubbles paint and prodded for a bunkhouse story. Just wasn't the same as over food with Mabel listening, the crew settled in with food and legend. Bubbles left the ranch last time with a picture unfinished. A palette of colors waited in the corner of the bunkhouse, beside it a half-finished canvas—a Milk

River change of season without a sky.

The prairie road roughened. Wendel rode loose-necked, his head slamming the gun rack with each badger hole, every two trucklengths another hole. The road topped a hogback ridge and the ride smoothed. Another mile and Bubbles slept, the shaman and horseman home in one fell swoop. Jesse hid the remaining wine and a pint of Jim in a section of seat he'd hollowed for such storage. He'd dole out the stash as necessary to keep the wolves at bay; his and theirs. If he had his way only Bunkhouse Chris and ranch matriarch Diana Ripley would know of their return, at least through the first day or two. Of course Mabel would understand when Jesse requested a basket of food to take out to the bunkhouse. He pictured Mabel smiling with the news of the strangers' hunger. In a week the two men could start work. Hopefully they'd help bring the ranch into a more natural flow. As he drove along, Jesse felt lifted by thoughts of renewed efficiency. But then his spirits drained as he wondered how long it would take for Rip's daughter to return and stir things up. Like every man on the Walking Box ranch, Jesse had fallen in love with Gretchen Ripley. But for him she was never to be, not like she was for Wendel Ingraham. Jesse sighed, weary of pained thoughts of love, love that never was. Horses, cows, grass, hay, Native American church services—not much else happened to Jesse anymore. Most on the ranch had had their share of love. Gretchen Ripley was long gone for now. Wendel and Bubbles had returned. Best not worry about her or anyone else who wasn't part of this prairie world, take it day by day.

A view of the entire ranch unfolded in the half moonlight. The truck eased off the long ridge. A flow of critters in the distance caught Jesse's seasoned eye. He braked the truck, slamming Wendel and Bubbles' faces into the dash. He didn't mean it—Gretchen thoughts had put him in a knee-jerk mode. The men groaned. He watched the movement across the earth, something migratory in the moonrosed distance. Cattle astray. No, not quite cattle—buffalo. Buffalo on the loose again, the tribe's growing herd of buffalo. Jesse shut off the motor to watch. The drinking men rubbed their heads and moaned through their yen.

Wendel didn't know buffalo were back. They came eight or nine years ago, not long after he'd left. In fact it was the buffalo that tipped Rip over in the forbidden storytelling regard, Bubbles' story of their grand return. Buffalo were having their way with men and fences alike. They were an unknown quantity to the ranch owner, too well known by his men and not well enough known by him. Only a few at first, a wild and dangerous few. Now a couple hundred roamed, a herd big enough to knock out fences as they pleased, to roam the reservation free as wind. Bubbles refused to fix fence knocked down by buffalo. 'Too sacred to mess with' he told Jesse James the last time he left for town. 'Fences and buffalo don't mix. Or fences and me.'

After Bubbles' departure, Jesse vowed not to send anyone from the Walking Box to chase the buffalo away again unless it was of the rider's free will, which was sometimes the case, because, indeed, buffalo were fun to chase horseback. Otherwise, if Ripley wanted buffalo off his land he could just go chase them off himself. Jesse wanted to talk with Wendel, visit with him about the buffalo, what had happened. So much to tell, and not tell. He started the truck and proceeded on, accelerating and slowing, hoping to sway Wendel awake. But the wastrel slept, the ebb and flow of the truck only taking him further into some great dream of ranching. Wendel wasn't in any condition to visit about anything. Not just yet. The wind blew warm. Warm winds made everyone happy this time of year; buffalo, horses, men. Cattle and Indians.

Jesse's headlamp swept across a group of travelling cows. The pregnant critters stopped to inspect the truck, sniffing the wind, checking for feed—cows freed by fencewalking buffalo, happy cows moving off to where they knew the grass was green and sweet. They wiped their wet noses with nimble tongues and resumed their march toward the meadow Jesse had hoped to save for late summer. "Enjoy it tonight. Come morning I'll be bringing you home," he told them, conversationally. His cows moved on, the temperate wind blowing their casual tails. Far ahead under the moon the buffalo herd moved off. The cattle followed the path the buffalo had trod, cows chasing after the secret lives of buffalo. Jesse eased his truck along the marching cows and announced, "My horsemen have returned."

He veered the pickup truck down the last draw into the ranch, his riders oblivious to buffalo and cattle. The road slickened near the bottom, snowbank melt greasing the ruts. The truck surged, yawing downhill. Jesse straightened her out, deft and efficient. Through the mud he cut the engine and rode the brake past Rip's home, squeaking to a stop at the forlorn bunkhouse. Jesse pulled a bottle from under the seat and cracked the seal, certain the snap of screwtop aluminum would awaken his passengers. But no, they slept. He opened his window to let in the Chinook. Bubbles wheezed, Wendel purred, a duet of snores. Soon Jesse himself snoozed, becalmed by the presence of his friends; wind warm, future bright.

When he awakened light spoked the eastern sky, a sun ready

to rise. He opened his door and stepped outside. The air smelled of spring. Jesse pried his people out of the truck and led them to the bunkhouse in the gray dawn. Once inside their sickness descended upon them reminding them who they were, the bunkhouse cold reminder of detox past. Jesse left them to their demons. Withdrawal commenced. Between deliriums they took turns yodeling into a yellow toilet—sunlit bathroom tremens. By noon the next day Wendel's eyes stopped swimming enough to stare at the ceiling. He tried to focus, imagining the days to come, conjuring strategies to buffer this sickness, forlorn about the daughter he'd abandoned in Spokane.

Bubbles made no such effort at dealing with suffering to come. He bore no remorse regarding unwise decisions past. He drank plenty of water and took his pain as it came, chewing on baneberry root from his horse medicine bundle to quell the trembles. Bubbles had given up the fight decades ago, succumbing to withdrawal as his people succumbed to withdraw from their ancestral way of life after the buffalo vanished.

Blackfeet Indians—or Blackfoot, as some spoke of themselves—were the last native confederacy to be conquered by the United States Army. Their tribe consisted of three nomadic groups: the Piegan, Blood, and Northern Blackfoot, collectively known as Blackfeet. Before the time of the horse the entire confederation met each summer to celebrate their buffalo culture. After the celebration, they went their separate ways to chase the various herds across their various homelands. The horse arrived, and then the gun. Both changed the culture. Manifest Destiny subsumed them, eradicating their buffalo. Nonetheless, the Blackfeet defended their homeland to the very end, and on a wedge of that homeland they remain. Subjugation, disease, and starvation followed reservation life. The Piegans remained south of the Medicine Line in Montana. The Bloods and Northern Blackfoot ended up on Canadian reservations above the 49th parallel.

Bubbles was born a Blood Blackfoot, but ended up in America where he was raised by Piegan relatives after his parents were killed in a reservation housefire. The Middle Fork of the Milk River that flowed behind the Walking Box bunkhouse flowed up into Canada and through his ancestral homeland. He slept above the water's whisk, dreaming of childhood before parental death. He rallied periodically and painted this lost culture. When want overtook, he bit the wooden handle of his paintbrush and sweated out the pain of his people.

The dead Cherokee ranch hand who had occupied the bunkhouse previous to Wendel and Bubbles' return had been on oxygen. When his Cherokee family came to take him away to die in Oklahoma, they left the green bottle, not believing in machinery to prolong life. From time to time Bubbles latched on to the Cherokee's oxygen to revive himself, the refined air a wonderful tonic. Poison flowed out of him after each stint on the O$_2$—sweats and shakes and wails filtering off a year of accumulated spleen. Oxygen. Pictures painted. Between stints on the easel, he marched outside to smudge braided sweetgrass, a pungent purifying smoke. Wendel joined the oxygen and sweetgrass ceremonies, no questions asked. After a day or two (they lost track of time) they felt better and constructed a sweat lodge next to the river—raw cowhides draped over bent willows. They heated rocks in a pinewood fire and ladled them into the center of the sweatlodge. Bubbles situated himself in his place of honor. Wendel hauled in two buckets of riverwater—hiss and steam, burn and sweat. Back outside to plunge in the cold, cold river. Back and forth, hot and cold, time and again. Renewal.

Bubbles spiraled in and out of spells of creativity. Beauty, he painted beauty—buffalo shepherded by wolves, wolverines digging up the frozen corpses of avalanched mountain goats. Horses and more horses. Grizzly galloping after mountain sheep atop the high rocks of the world. Coyotes eyeing the stragglers of winter. Stories in pictures.

Daughter separation delivered Wendel to a strange world. Bubbles urged him to write his poetry to unload his baggage. Wendel was inconsolable. The distance from his little girl pervaded every quarter of his body, no cell spared. His journal held splashes of incoherence after the first few days, scribblings of fretful thought. By day three he became acutely aware of his failings and frailties. More withdrawal. Then flowed poems, haiku the jockey Akifumi had divined in the camphorated tackrooms of Playfair Washington, Spookaloo haiku.

Thus, the two whittled time away—Wendel with postured words, Bubbles with brushes and color. Bunkhouse Chris brought them food, a secret splash of port in the soup to calm their begging synapses. He cleaned the bunkhouse for them, the two unable to manage much looking after themselves. Bunkhouse arranged the paintings and notebooks he found scattered about the bunkhouse, saved what art he could on a bookshelf, knowing someday someone in the world might want to peruse their creations.

At the end of their first week he came across Wendel's journal spilled upon the floor. Chris noticed his own name at the top of the page. The passage described Wendel's continental divide journey from the day before. Bubbles had sent him up Cut

Bank Creek to seek a vision and Wendel recorded the journey. Chris smiled his memoried smile. He read the words as if they were addressed to him. He sat at the desk and carefully took in the writing:

Bunkhouse Chris sent me on my way with his grim grin of knowing. I left with the morning star low and bright, mourning for my lost parents and missing child. The Indians say the morning star is the child of the sun and moon and I feel like that star with no sun and moon in sight.

Jesse drives me to Cut Bank Creek in Glacier National Park. The sign at the park boundary says 'Leaving Blackfeet Indian Reservation.' A bear clawed up the sign for realbear reasons. The words are broken, the wood splintered. I wonder about bears and bemoan the fact that I have no horse along as planned. The trailer had a flat tire this morning and neither Jesse nor I were willing to fix it in the cold darkness. Bubbles said, "Just as well, best visions attained without horse." He assured me bears would not bother a man like me.

Jesse drops me off at the trailhead. He will return in the afternoon to pick me up. If he is early he'll visit with the volunteer ranger with the yapping dog from Weiser, Idaho, Jesse's Métis soul singing stories of this time and that to an eager listener. Jesse James understands wandering. He knows I could hike forever, summit the divide and slip down the Arctic Drainage to St. Mary—on through Babb, north along St. Mary's River, floating toward the Arctic down the Saskatchewan, swirling into Hudson's Bay for to cross the Ocean to Iceland... Jesse's a storyteller, he knows me and counts on my return.

I begin my ascent to the top of the world, the last sacred slice of the homeland to be taken away from the Indians. The trail is flat at first, then climbs toward Triple Divide Peak along the cartwheeling Cut Bank Creek. Bubbles hopes I have a vision, a holy see, something more than railroad realbear. I hear his laugh on the wind, and I march upward.

I climb. Exertion incites dizziness, and then visions. Women lure me along and up the trail. I chase them, craving their soft touch and emotional understanding. I chase them one at a time all over the mountain. When I stop to rest I find them all sitting together before me, as if in judgment, perhaps at my funeral; wife, daughter, lovers, loves; dark skins and white. The apparitions dissolve one at a time into a thin mist. Attentive figurines fade into the image of my little girl, who comes alive. She bursts ahead fairy-like and chases a leaping weasel up a tree, from under which water flows. I follow and run to drink the springwater with her, but when I bend over her reflection is the weasel's, and mine is realbear. She is ermine white, her blacktipped tail flagging, and she scampers up the tree afraid of me. Out of the tree above flies a grouse. My girl is weaseled atop the grouse. She is flying away, weasel-she, her bird-horse winging through aspens, gliding into the dark air, then she is gone... and is gone.

I find myself staring at the ground. Windblown leaves tumble and tell me all will be well—somehow, someday. The stony mountain hangs over me—I rise and climb upward. Little birds I've never known skitter alongside. They dip and flare in crazy flight. I pull myself through an impossible labyrinth of trees and rocks. Chipmunks chatter, hidden in the myriad, then scuttle away and flash their stripes brilliantly. Near the top as foreordained, wolverine rises from behind a rock, yellow-bellied and stinky.

I ask her: Ignite
my life. Give me power to

blend with this hard world
Wolverine screeches reply. Her scream echoes, and she disappears. Delirious, I climb on…
I crest the divide
Utmost reach of three oceans
Part dog and part wolf
The wind sifts wetness over the Continental vortex, a soft and kind mist. In the new distance highborn chasms deliver melted snow. Distant waterfalls work off mountain walls, smoothing away the stone. Far off mountain goats graze the green of cirques, their hooves spring over primordial layers of sediment. I rise and walk toward Iceland. I trip and down I fall to my hands and knees. In mud I see wolf scat, smell it. I spot fist-sized footpads in the earth that lead me down the trail. I track the spoor until all dissolves and I don't know where I am…
I should know better
Than to follow this, for
The Wolf tells nothing
I rise and march back over the Vortex. I leave the Arctic Ocean spirits asleep in their couloirs. Sky above and rock below, time everywhere and nowhere. The petrified ocean tilts and yaws, holding forth a seascape of primordial relatives we share in common. Seahorses gitty-up and chase the buffalo away. Sheep come and go, mountain sheep. The glide and lift of raptors I can and cannot remember. My yellow-bellied skunkbear rises and screeches again. Her cry chases me down the mountain, her hot stink riding a cool wind. I trot. I run. Where the trail flattens I rest before walking out.

Jesse waits at the bottom. He has sing-songed the afternoon away with Mr. Weiser. We load up and motor past Bad Marriage Mountain by nightfall and ride curves of land back to the Milk

River in silent darkness.
  The moon—slow and late.
  Limestone road. In drizzling cold
  Our Bunkhouse Chris waits.
  ——

Wild stuff, Bunkhouse thought, holding dear the references to him at the beginning and at the end. He closed the journal and smiled, wondering what it might be like to be young and troubled again.

Chapter 5

JOURNEYMEN

Bubbles and Wendel left the bunkhouse at dawn in a cold rain and walked to the cookshack for their first breakfast. Resident ranchhands are always happy to have their fold bolstered by fresh help, especially of this caliber. The winterworn crew welcomed the two strangers back. Greetings worked up and down the table and tapered to a natter of nibbling down the meal at hand. Mabel pranced out of her kitchen, eyes atwinkle. She gave Wendel a big, big smile and rubbed by Bubbles holding high a plate of pancakes all hot and steamy. She set them before him beside a ship of chokecherry syrup and a bowl of spooning cream. The men tucked into Mabel's cakes with insatiate abandon, sustenance for the long day ahead. Along with this specialty, she served up scrambled eggs and bacon, orange juice and a nutty coffee. She poured a tall glass of foamy cold milk for all those who wished one, chilled through the night, cream-topped and fresh from Chris's Jersey milkcow.

Rip Ripley made his entrance. He was a large square-headed man who wore his Stetson pulled down over his square forehead. Dressed like some reincarnate Virginian, vest and silkscarf tie, he removed his cowboy hat with a certain arrogant motion and placed it high on the hatrack space reserved for him. His bared head revealed a shock of red hair that had faded with age, becoming translucent, red only in certain glints of light these days, a lot less red than Wendel had ever remembered. His boots knocked loud across the cookhouse floor, the rowels of his spurs talking business. "Hi, hello. How is everyone?" Jesse raised and circled his index finger, signaling that everyone was okay—in other words; everyone present as expected. Wendel and Bubbles' nodded their respects to the owner of the outfit. "Good to see you two back where you belong," Rip said to them. "God knows we need the help."

The cowhands ate fastidiously, breakfast becoming a version of work in Rip Ripley's presence. Spurs on his feet, something was up. Rip not horseback for a month and suddenly he shows up at this breakfast ready to ride? Bubbles flashed a ha-HA look Wendel's way—spurs, some serious chivalry to contend with and only the first day back on the job.

A curvilinear radio beamed classic country music from a shelf high in Mabel's kitchen. Agriculture news bridged the warbling Hank Snow to the croons of Ernest Tubb. Heavenly pancakes smothered in chokecherry syrup topped with fresh Jersey cream. Magpies yakked outside, waiting for their share of the feast. Second helpings of bacon sizzled and smoked through the aroma of freshbrew coffee. Cattle futures up and the price of corn down. Wet weather ahead and the Tennessee Troubadour sang. Rip patted his belly and smiled. He dolloped sweet cream atop his syrupy hotcakes, a market report that made him happy.

The men ate and thought about Rip's spurs and what the big idea is wearing them into the cookshack today, but Rip fed his men well and they couldn't say much about his spurs with their mouths full. The cookshack allowed the master of the Walking Box the privilege of getting close with his employees one might say, an occasion to express his views of the world, however distasteful they might be to the men. It did the potato-famined Irishman Rip Ripley proud to see healthy appetites filled, the pleasure of his food doing the filling, the potatoes and beef raised right here on his own land. No workman of Rip's could ever say he skimped in the cookshack. Rip's men were well fed. They knew how to eat, and eat well, and man oh man could some of them ride, because Rip didn't skimp on horseflesh either. Rip was right proud of these two things, his well-fed men atop well-bred horses—for what more is there? The radio quacked on, Mabel hummed and hovered about, taking good care of her eaters. They ate their fill and slowly, one by one, sat back to relax.

Mabel was a College of Great Falls educated chef, a bachelor of arts in home economics, a full-blooded Indian woman who added her native touch to every dish, berries and roots and love. Pemmican for long rides ahead. Cuisine galore erupted from Mabel's kitchen, native and otherwise. Rip and Diana furnished the best ingredients for Mabel to nourish the Walking Box crew. Food got an honest day's work out of honest horsemen. For those who feared they didn't get enough breakfast there were cinnamon rolls for dessert. No one went hungry on this outfit, not like some of the less fortunate in town, not like the starvation winter of 1883 that decimated the reservation Blackfeet. Diana Ripley and Mabel Old Coyote made sure of that.

"Anyone want the last pancake?" Wendel asked, before dishing it up.

"Go right ahead," Jesse offered, glad to see healthy hunger sated, appetite the bellwether of hired-hand promise.

"Toothpicks please," said Badtooth Gene.

"Thanks, Mabel," Rob the mechanic offered, slipping away to grease the Walking Box world, slipping away to have a little swig of the raisin-jack he'd brewed below the bunkhouse, a swig to grease himself to soothe mechanical friction of the Walking Box day to come.

"Right fine breakfast, Mabel," Bubbles remarked, winded from enjoying his first square in months.

The two younger men, American Indians from Babb, cleared the table and sang their accolades to Mabel. Others sat with their coffee cupped in their hands to await the day's instruction. The feedwagon operator departed to feed his cows in waiting. Badtooth Gene thumbed Copenhagen out of a trademarked tin and fingered the tobacco into his shank-toothed mouth.

Jesse spoke: "Wendy, why don't you wrangle the colts Badtooth brought in. Saddle up those green four-year-olds. Take your time and break 'em solid like you do."

"My sort of work," Wendel said, smiling Rip's way.

"Halter those yearlings, too, if you get a chance," Rip put in. After a look from Jesse James and a pause he said, "Mainly get those four-year olds colts broke to trail cattle. We'll be moving herd to the mountains afore we know it." The boss smacked his lips and brought his teeth together with a clack, satisfied to get in his two bits. No one said anything for a minute. Thoughts about breaking the colts floated through Wendel's head. Mabel sudsed dishes in the background, the clink of plates underwater. She'd shut the radio off to hear Jesse assign the work. Jesse shifted his eyes Bubbles' way. "Won't you calve out the rest o' them heifers, Bub? 'Tooth here 'll be helping ya."

"Seems I'll be helping 'Tooth," Bubbles said, smiling his

pumpkin-faced smile. His nimble tongue tossed a toothpick around his happy mouth.

Jesse sat back, relieved Bubbles had recovered so well, a strongwilled brother. His mere presence had already lifted a great load from the rest of the men. Somehow Bubbles had a way with time, he made it pass all the much quicker. Jesse fingered the wooden match he'd been picking his teeth with and ripped it along the underside of his Levi thigh. Inflamed sulphur brightened his face with brief light. He produced a thick handrolled cigarette out of his shirtpocket and brought the woody flame close, lighting the cig in ceremonial fashion. The men filed out, burps and clunky boots. More thanks to the cook. "See you at lunch, Napi willin'," Mabel said to them all.

Rip remained at the table treating himself to jellied toast. He bit and chewed deliberately, eyeing Jesse's smoke, trying hard to ignore the misdemeanor scent. Once rabid about weed, he'd mellowed over the years after realizing pot replaced the foreman's jones for alcohol to beneficial affect—made him a much more efficient strawboss, stable and calmer. Crushed chokecherry and tobacco incompletely covered the spleef aroma. The fug rose to the cookhouse ceiling and slowly drifted to Mabel's kitchen fan. She paid it no mind. Outside the rain had eased, and the sky suddenly cleared. The sun worked cymbals off the flowing river. Paired waterfowl maneuvered out of the sky and splashed into the flow out the window before them.

"The collapse of intimacy with a woman is a lonely road, especially when one feels at fault, you know," Rip said to Jesse. "Seems like Wendel is feeling at fault," he added. Rip spoke as if he understood the verities of love, but still, not quite sure,

59

he asked his foreman, "What do you think? Why'd Wendel return?"

Jesse shook his head and took another drag. "Women happen," he said, "and then kids. The woman happiness vaporizes, life becomes hard and heavy. Drink sneaks in there and shit happens. Split happens. Drift follows," Jesse explained, "he drifted back to the only place he could drift."

Rip stopped chewing his toast. He had experienced similar youthful wanderlust, as had most of the Walking Box others. Smitten men were never alone on this outfit. The price of marriage was nothing new to this spread, more the hub of it. Here men sought shelter from connubiality, the Walking Box a refuge for the scorned and forlorn. Mabel offered needed nutritional sustenance to all types of wedlocked and unwedlocked men, men despairing of love, and even life. Mabel restored them, the Walking Box much more than a cow outfit, a space into which Bubbles and Wendel had returned for a certain sustenance unavailable anywhere else in the world. Like the others, they had returned to survive, Mabel's cookhouse becoming a hinge of renewed existence, where they told old stories when Rip wasn't around, and planned to someday tell more stories when he was, when the time was right. They worked around stories old and new. A lot of talk about days gone by, legends of horses and buffalo, legends before horses, before buffalo, all to help understand where they'd arrived, from where they'd come. Work and eat and tell and listen, the lovely sleep that comes after a hard day in the saddle, the dreams inspired by stories… migrations and peregrinations, life lived within and without, life lived past and future, life lived.

Days went by as days go by on a ranch, swift and hard. Birdsong woke them as spring edged its warmth into the grasslands, birdsong becoming a daily aria, water birds and prairie birds returned from somewhere faraway to dine on the bounty of the great Rocky Mountain Front. Mammals big and small awakened from incredible hibernations. Coyotes and wolves welcomed them all.

Bubbles visited the horsebarn between his heifer watches to gentle the yearling colts. He haltered them with savvy, no roping. He taught them trust—faith in the world and trust in their bipedal keepers. Bubbles Ground Owl helped them accept captivity, taught them the expectations of mankind. In return, Wendy, as they called him now (and always had, except for Bubbles' occasional HorseMan), relieved Bubbles' from his heifer nightwatch at three o'clock every morning. This allowed Bubbles some time with Mabel, healing time, sleep-with-a-woman love his afternoon nap could not accommodate.

Wendel did time atop each of the four-year-old colts, a lot of time. That's what it seemed to take with horses. Time, time and patience. In time he rode each horse out of the riverbottom to roam the Walking Box rangelands. Work blended into life, but the wind seemed difficult to contend with, and he had a daughter who lived far, far away. Too far away.

Chapter 6

STUDMAN

Ripley bred the horses Wendel broke to ride. He topped Texas Quarter Horse speed with Kentucky thoroughbred blood. The rancher's current stud was a son of Secretariat out of a Native Dancer mare—distance class, the cream genes. Rip picked up the blueblood for $15,000 in Phoenix; the colt's name: Proletariat—a notion beyond Rip. He became aware of the iron-colored stallion at a cowboy golf tournament over a decade back. As he bent over to tee-up the first drive of the day, a trainer from Turf Paradise mentioned a 'hell of a deal at the track for anyone in need of a broodsire, prettiest slate gray this side of Kentucky.' After a round sliced with contemplation, Rip left without adding up his score to inspect the horseflesh.

He couldn't resist. Proletariat was a most noble steed standing a full seventeen hands, a grandiloquent stallion. Never mind the inferior check desmitis and deep digital bow unveiled by the doctor pulled in to vet the horse. The diagnoses glided over Rip's head like serendipitous magpies. Rip's eye measured the overall animal, and he was not one to be influenced by overwrought veterinarians. Discreet physical infirmities played second fiddle to the horse's generous size and matchless color. And oh what a hip. The trainer assured Rip it was the horse's ability to run so fast that tweaked the injured tendon, the injury that in fact ended Proletariat's career on the track.

Everything made good sense to Rip. He wrote a check on the cattle-trading account, bought a horse trailer and had a hitch installed on his Lincoln Continental and towed his prize all the way back to the Walking Box, arriving with a smile big as Arizona.

Rip delineated the bloodlines of his great gray horse to all Walking Box guests, horsewise and otherwise. The hired men tired of his pedigree soliloquy long ago. They'd suffered through meal after meal listening to Rip's bloodline horseshit, all the while yearning for Bubbles' random stories. Nonetheless, Rip had his captive audience. He boasted genetic manipulation as the key to prosperity in this god-smitten country. Rip believed that cattle and horses needed fine-tuned genes to flourish, genes fine tuned by men like him. Great benefits were to be had from stamping the ranch's get with the finest blood around. Bubbles Ground Owl told Old Man stories after Rip left, stories about parents trying to make their children marry certain others. It was no secret to Indians that dictated mating meddled with that which was sacred.

Through the decades Bubbles experienced plenty of Rip's genetic shortfalls: calves gestated too big to be born, or when delivered, too weak to stand and suckle. Foals birthed too bent-legged and weak-hearted to rise and suck, too thin-skinned to survive the hard, wet cold of a spring squall—too stove to run from a wolf. Bubbles preferred natural selection. Nature had cared well for his ancestors' sea of buffalo. Rip's attempts to create a cattle more efficient—to improve upon Old Man's buffalo—were absurd in Bubbles' eyes. How the man, any man, overlooked the pre-existing perfection of Great Plains bison was beyond the horse medicine man. The only thing to ever come along that approached perfection before the whiteman intervened upon America was the horse.

Bubbles finished calving the heifers in April, about the time Wendel had the crossbred colts cattlewise and rope-savvy. They'd gentled nicely, horses connecting man to the land. Mid-May brought on the first real solar heat, and Bubbles mingled the virgin bulls with the virgin heifers, slowly he mingled them. The horsemen eased the cows with their calves to the spring pastures. Over the next month Wendel, Bubbles, Badtooth Gene, and transient other horsemen escorted the cattle out of the Middle Fork swales and over the Hudson's Bay Divide, pushing them down into the St. Mary River drainage—the Badlands—a sea of cattle ushered to a sea of grass by American Indians atop Wendel's cowbroke ponies. Each week the crew pushed another herd, one thousand animals each trip, five hundred cows with their five hundred calves, each journey energized by the introduction of twenty rambunctious bulls willing and ready to breed, to seed Rip's cows.

The horsemen shaped the cattle into a serpentine procession, stringing their passage over the oceanic divide. Bull fights, a breeding, the cattle and men and horses loving their world, cows and calves strung along for miles marching to summer grass, bulls unstringing them. Every so many miles the herd gathered at a waterhole, a lake or spring creek, where they drank heartily and grazed and laid down to rest. The men dismounted to rest alongside their cattle, eating the lunches Mabel had crafted for them. Days long in the saddle, days long and happy in the saddle. They followed the cattle up the Old North Trail. Bubbles told stories of men coming down the selfsame trail as legendary seas of buffalo darkened the landscape, ancient migrations of men and minds—stories of a time before written words, stories to clarify the present:

64

In early times this land held no people, or so those who study people tell us. And then they came. Fifteen thousand years ago they came, some say forty thousand years ago, or even fifty; imagine ten-thousand-years ago, imagine fifty-thousand years past: men, women, and children descending into a world uninhabited by their kind—journeying for the untold reasons folk journey. By land bridge and sea, ice-walking they came. Others sailed and rowed, migrants crossing great seas, navigating great rivers to breach great mountain passes. Animals and men and land mixing, colliding. Some families alone, most together. Clans and brothers. Mothers and daughters, mothers and sons. Fathers, fathers alone. People afoot, people coming together, travelling down the cordillera between ice sheets, tossing down rivers through great plains; buffalo and wolves greeting them, extinctions; mastodons and sabertooth tigers and three-toed horses. Men lured across the great mind of the world by the great herds of grazers, grazers shepherded by carnivores—birds above, fish below, world soul surrounding them. Earth homes, mud homes. Animal-hide homes. Caves. A constant hunt for food. Migrations south to the southern continent seeking kinder winters; a climate in which to cultivate, to make a home in one place forever. To become civilized, to rise and to fall.

Siberia, Polynesia, Australia, and China threw their humanity at this New World, all the world nomadic, all men afflicted with the hope for freedom. Civilizations divided and conquered— men fleeing to do and to believe. Men moving through the world, women and children with them, children born along the way. Some returning to bring others to their newfound world, a more bountiful world with the freedom to enjoy the bounty. Exiles, fugitives, and adventurers—dreamers chasing dreams. Dauntless travellers, endless journeys, men seeding societies to come; worlds to be. Down from Asia. Across the middle of the world from China. An occasional lightskin skimming over the top from Scandinavia, more than occasional—Leifur the Lucky, and those before. Polynesian boatloads from the southern hemisphere. All color and shape of mankind flushing the nature of North America, bringing knowledge and hope and language to new geographies. Dog days.

And then the horse returned to swirl the New World, the buffalo hunted to near extinction. And now cattle trailed to grass...

Paths trod and retrod, paths followed, a path followed now by Bubbles and his horsemen, horsemen swallowed into the last bloom of America; ranchhands herding the grazers, journeying the unending journey men journey, the last corner of Indian homeland pushed to sustaining cattle as the great grazers of the last great grassland.

One fine spring day the final drove hoofed and lowed over Hudson's divide into a southwesterly wind. Chief Mountain ranged over the futility of the late calvers and half-crippled stragglers. Three decades ago the mountain had cracked. A huge mass of limestone fell off and shattered to scree. "The mountain Falls Apart like the world falls apart," Bubbles declared the year Wendel was born.

Jesse James waited on a knoll sitting on a horse as red as he. He counted the last of the herd into summer pasture and wrote down the number in his little book, cows and calves pushed into the green swales of St. Mary's River—purest drainage of the continent, purest water in this world, Indian water flowing north. Glacial alluvium bent light through the flowing river, St. Mary a turquoise serpent.

Wendel and Bubbles stepped off their horses and loosened their cinchas. They turned the horses loose in some deep grass to graze the bounty.

"You fellows are getting pretty comfortable with them young horses, now ain't ye, letting 'em run free?" Jesse asked in his happy-go-lucky way.

"When were we ever not comfortable with our horses?" Wendel replied. The grateful animals picked up their heads, as if awaiting Jesse's reply. But there was no reply, just smiles from all three men. The steeds dropped their heads back down to graze—varip, varip, varip.

The view into Canada was immense, mountains giving way to foothills. "Like looking across Montana used to be," Bubbles said. A crisp wind cleared the earth's haze and the view reddened Wendel's blood. The horses held their reins to the side and sidepassed into lusher growth. Bubbles and Wendel strolled along behind, leaving Jesse to continue his counting. The Canadian Rockies swam in the solstice heat—distorted and elevated.

"This is all nice and fine, Bubbles," Wendel said. "But I've been too long away from my daughter."

Bubbles stuck out his chin and rolled down his lower lip in reply. They caught up their horses, cinched and mounted. Their horses ambled through the grazing cattle, urging them down the last grade of the journey. Calves bucked and danced, instinctively knowing the season of bliss that awaited them. Their mothers wrapped tongues around the abundant grass and rolled it into their mouths in lingual rhythms tempered by time. Bubbles and Wendel pushed them on, cows grazing on the move, their udders round with milk, tongues snaking bunch after bunch of grass.

Badtooth Gene followed behind with the drag. His brave laggards dribbled down the mountain assisted by gravity. Unable to keep up with the others to the bottom, they bedded down and ended their travels for the day, a few grazing as they lay. Stars and moon would press them to the river by night, where horse-belly-high grass awaited their deft tongues.

Sweeps of aspen hid the living things of the badland plains. Grizzlies and cougars and wolves sniffed about somewhere hidden. They waited patiently for the men to leave and the cattle to settle in. Jesse looked over Gene's stragglers and shook his head. Predators would take the weakest, and soon. Rip blamed vanished calves on thieves, implicating Indian ranchers that neighbored the tribal leases. But Bubbles knew better. He'd witnessed predation plenty, bears feeding on cattle and elk, anything within their grasp. Hungry mama griz, casual cow. Out of a thicket the griz slams into the beef—teeth gnashing, claws ripping; snapping the neck—quick, forceful; nearly humane. Sound and fury—whoosh and dead and dinner time. Some of the older cows were savvy to griz. Calves hadn't a clue. When the cattle arrived the griz moved in from the medicine grounds, the peaks and valleys of Glacier Park. Tourists chased them out onto the plains with their cameras and bells and bear spray.

Despite this mystical predation, the men left their cattle to fend for themselves and headed home, riding back over the St. Mary/Milk River divide to the Walking Box. When they approached the homeranch horsebarn in the plum dusk they noticed a strange car parked at Rip's house. Closer they saw the Iowa plates. Gretchen Ripley had returned. They untacked their horses and brushed them down. Not much was said as they walked to the bunkhouse and readied themselves for Mabel's dinner.

Wendel missed his daughter. The return of Gretchen weighed upon Wendel; a heavy, unexplainable sadness. Mabel took charge when Wendel walked into the cookshack. He often came early to empty the trash and sweep the porch. The two stood alone in the kitchen. The long table already set, the floor swept. "They'll be a boy here to see you at breakfast tomorrow morning."

"A boy?" Wendel asked. A boy? he thought.

"Gretchen has a boy along with her, her son Padrick."

"Oh," Wendel said, glad she'd married and had a child. A great thing, that. He had run off and done the same, except he'd returned without his child.

"Wendel, look at me and listen," Mabel Old Coyote said, grabbing his shoulder. "I understand you may not know this, but I believe you are the boy's dad."

Dad. The word struck Wendel. A ten-year-old son he didn't know he had? Wendel sat down at his place on the end of the table. The other ranchhands filtered in, privy to his news. They ate quietly and without appetite, as if to share Wendel's altered soul, all ranch souls one in the quagmire of love. Twice during dinner Mabel eased behind Wendel to rub his shoulder muscles. He thanked her, and everyone else, even managed a quaint smile as he slipped out the door. Breathless and queasy, he hiked up Cream Creek to Good Medicine Flat to witness the sun fall behind Chief Mountain. Wendel's own father gone, disappeared, and now a son arrives. Luck. Plain and blessed simple. How lucky could a man be? —Thirty-three years young, father to a Blackfeet son and a Spokane daughter.

Twilight overtook the amethyst sky. Wendel collected his breath. He closed his eyes and prayed to the sun. He prayed to the Virgin Mary and Napi and Buddha and he prayed to the wind. The sun wheeled a headdress over Chief Mountain as she fell behind the backbone of the world. First the earth and then the sky darkened, mountains holding an eerie afterglow. Wendel waited for full darkness, but it did not come. Would not come. Blood running like horses through his heart, his blood running through a Blackfoot son. He laid down upon the grass and watched stars fill the sky.

Wendel awakened prostrate under the Milky Way. A swan with perfect wings flew above him. Grass pricked his cheeks. He rose out of the plains in the night and walked through bunchgrass down the draw to the bunkhouse where he undressed and crawled into his bunkhouse bed. Children in his dreams running through native grasslands, yes, a great expanse of grass and children running, his children.

Dream on, Wendel, dream.

And he slept and dreamt of grass and children.

Chapter 7

GRASSMAN

Men with children who aspire to tending the cattle and horses of the world contemplate grass. All prosper when the resource is secure. The best grass is native grass. Blackfoot country nurtures the finest grass on the continent, the same grass buffalo sought millennia ago, grass anchoring the great abundance of the earth then as now. Rip's wife Diana, a well-connected member of the Blackfeet Tribe, used her Carlisle education and tribal connections to secure the grasslands needed for the Walking Box cattle, abundant grass that allowed Rip's ranch to prosper. If Wendel Ingraham wasn't heir to this secure world of grass, he now had a son who was. He didn't know where this would take his ranching dream... into The Great Perhaps with everything else, he supposed.

With Trish fatherless in Spokane he swirled into worlds he could not contain—great grasslands of horses, uncatchable horses untamed. Grass ungrazed.

"Paddy, this is your father," Diana said, facing Wendel to his child before breakfast; a strapping boy; smiling and shy. The son couldn't manage any more words than the father, scarcely able to look Dad in the eye. Wendel dropped his hat to his side and ran his fingers through his blond hair. At first, no substantial reality connected him with his darkhaired boy; but then a strange consciousness overwhelmed him, all this happening sometime somewhere before—a father leaving seeming something like a son returned—blood disjoined by land and time rejoined by land and time. Ten years later for Wendel, a lifetime later for his son. Wendel tried to speak, to utter the words he'd rehearsed in the labyrinth of night. He opened his mouth, instead of words a sigh emerged. He reached out and grabbed his son's fine-boned hand, and then his shoulder. Paddy reached out to his father, grabbing Wendel by the wrist. The two stood, awkwardly connected, and looked one another in the eye.

"Why don't you two run down to the barn and fool with the horses?" Diana said, breaking the silence.

"Sounds good, Grandma," Paddy said, his eyes finally leaving his dad's.

"Show him those colts you're gentling up, Wendel, and watch that son of yours," she said. "He's done some riding and roping." Wendel nodded okay. The two stepped out of Diana's home and strolled down to the barn, wordless. The horses watched them come down the hill and they knew the father and son who moved toward them, comfortable with their moving toward them. The horses met dad and son in the arena and Wendel caught the two boldest colts. Paddy oated and brushed them down while Wendel moved the others out to a grassy paddock. They saddled up and rode down the riverbottom before rising into burgeoning grasslands, father and son riding side by side, sitting their horses like centaurs, horses becoming them. Ambling hoofbeats glossed over their bewilderment. On top along a great ridge they trotted across open ground in rhythm with the world at last.

Chapter 8

OTHER MEN

Paddy was short for Padrick. Wendel hadn't a clue to the name's origin. The cookhouse drift mentioned an Irish bloke, Gretchen's someone after Wendel departed ten years back, a significant other long gone to Iowa, an Irish bloke Rip had handpicked for his daughter.

It was rough going for Wendel trying to connect with Gretchen about their son. He didn't understand how she could have NOT told him. Irishness in the way, he supposed, rather than American Indianness. An Indian would have told a man about a son. Wendel wondered out loud if he indeed was the father. Diana assured him he was. Anyone seeing the father and son together knew it. Their resemblance was remarkable, more than remarkable. The boy, despite having his mother's chocolate skin and black hair, was a physical Wendel. They sat horses like twins; the same sosie touch, identical legs and long-fingered hands, like-minded horsemen.

They rode. The son calmed Wendel, leveling his world. Maybe somewhere in his psyche he himself had known of his son. Maybe that's why he returned. He remembered well enough the lovemaking that brought Padrick about. Maybe Gretchen had tried in her way to tell him. Somewhere he held a memory of a son, always thinking it just a wish, some dream perhaps. Maybe it was *his* father's memory, an allusion or reflection of that memory, a shadowing.

"So Dad," Paddy asked, trotting up to his dad after lagging behind to watch a badger and coyote team up to dig out gophers, "how'd you gather this pasture when you were a kid?"

Wendel unfolded a hand from his reins and gestured. "Same as you must have gathered it son."

"Tell me, I'll see if you're right."

"Well, we used to push up that ravine from the bottom and come across the top with 'em. That was before Rip bladed a road up that bluff."

"Was your dad riding with you back then?"

"Oh yeah, from time to time we rode this country together. Yes. He gathered every pasture on this place one time or another."

"And then he left?" Paddy asked.

"He did. Split up with my mom. Love trouble, I guess. Not unlike your mother's and my troubles in a sense. Of course, I suppose its always that sort of trouble."

"Why is that? Why are dads always the ones leaving?"

"I've put a lot of thought into that, sure enough it's a good question."

"So why'd your dad leave?"

"Didn't say. Had another life to live somewhere else, I reckon. Didn't get along with mom."

"Where's she now?"

"Seattle, last I talked to her."

"And your dad?"

"Don't know."

"You ever wonder?"

"Sure I wonder, I wonder every day. I've heard talk, but no

74

one can say for sure. Didn't you wonder where I was?"

"Sure I did. Ever since the day I realized you had to exist I wondered all the time. Any kid would."

"So then, when did your mom tell you about me?"

"I'm not sure if she ever did tell me, outright anyways."

Wendel left it at that. Not really anywhere else to go with such dark questions. If Wendel thought he was deprived in time's passage unknowing of his son's existence, it didn't hold a candle to Paddy not being clear on his father's existence. No memory of that reassuring entity, that model of manhood, of future manhood. Poor Paddy, no photo, no memory of a Father's touch. Nothing at all, paternity bottled and secret. Changed now, thank goodness, all changed. Despite their prolonged separation, Paddy seemed fine.

"What were the names of the horses the men owned when you were a kid, Dad?"

"Horses they rode, you mean?"

"Horses you rode."

"You are right, though, about owned," he said. "Whoever rides a horse owns him, in the horse's head at least, and that's what matters, and maybe it's not so much ownership as partnership. One thing about this outfit is that we each possessed our string of riding horses. Rip made us feel that way, at least. The horses we rode belonged to us, but the deal was the horses couldn't come with you if you left. They were ranch horses and at the ranch they stayed. You might leave and when you returned your old horses were still here, but they might belong to someone else by then, you see. And that was never good. Happened to me a couple of times through high school. Horses can't read words, but they can sure read a man. And it's not about ownership anyway. Horses don't understand ownership. They don't care, and neither should we."

"What were some of those horses names? What were your horses' names?" Paddy asked. His father's horse stepped out a brisk walk, an amble. Paddy had fallen behind and trotted up alongside his dad to reiterate the question, shouting over their footfalls. A father's horse always seems to walk faster than a son's and that was another thing Paddy wanted to know about, gleaning Wendel's father-experience to bolster his own.

"Well, I had Becky Burr, as honest a horse as one could ever ride," Wendel answered. "A fine mare, one of the rare few females allowed as a riding horse on the outfit. She knew more about cattle than any five men, that's why Rip allowed her in the riding string. Most of the rest were geldings."

"Like who?"

"Stumble Bum was a real goer. Strongwilled. I remember him well. Took him awhile to come into harmony with his legs. Then there was a sorrel colt named Jiminy B Quick who was a sharp son of a gun, a real sweet horse, sweet and agile. Kind. Apache was another fine cowhorse, a great one to rope calves off. Put you right on 'em, stick with every dodge they made."

"When would you say a horse reaches his prime, Dad?"

"Five or six," Wendel answered without hesitation. "Once in a while a younger horse will find the zone before that. After five or six, most become quite accomplished at the cow work expected of them. Most are good 'til they're fifteen or so, depending on leg infirmities they acquire through time."

"Who was the fastest horse you ever rode at the Walking Box?"

"Redbone outran every horse on this outfit."

"Redbone," Paddy said, trying out the name, a good sounding name.

"Redbone. Yeah, an outcross. Rip hated the fact he'd come over from the Gall outfit as a long yearling, a catch colt Mister Gall returned after finally getting the cayuse weaned off of one of his grade mares. Gall insisted the colt was sired by Rip's prize stud, which seemed obvious enough. But Rip disliked the idea of what he considered a mismating. He thanked Gall, who suggested gelding him right away so as not pass on any bad blood from the North Fork of the Milk. Because Gall suggested it, Rip waited a year to geld the leggy thing, waited 'til he was two. I think that made all the difference. If you leave the hormones in them while they're growing it thickens the bone. Redbone. Some name eh? Bubbles named him. He knew good bone when he saw it. And you know, bone is red, the inside of it is, anyway. Prettiest red in the world, marrow."

"Bubbles named the horses back then?" Paddy asked, enamored by his father's telling. Wendel looked to the sky smiling, cogitating. Paddy waited for an answer, clarification of the past. "Well? Did he?"

"Yup. Bubbles. He'll be naming horses forever, he's the horse medicine man."

"What's that mean, horse medicine man?"

"It means Bubbles was bestowed the horse power handed down by his ancestors."

"Power?"

"The power to make horses run, or not run. To heal. Powers to make the sick better and the weak strong."

"I wonder who named Bubbles?" Paddy asked.

Wendel laughed. "His sister. I guess he drooled as a toddler, mouth sores from a vitamin deficiency, some sort of scurvy… blowing bubbles through the soothing drool all the time."

"What is it about his horse medicine stuff that's so special?

He seems pretty regular to me."

"You'll have to ask him yourself. He might someday have to pass the power on to you."

"Why not you?"

"I'm not in that line. I'm not an Indian. But you are."

They rode the prairie silence. Paddy reconstructed a younger father perched upon his shiny Redbone, steed and rider gallivanting across the prairie strides ahead of struggling horses, Bubbles working his magic so Redbone would win. Someday, Paddy figured he too would ride the fastest horse.

Father and son rode together most every day, a blessed way to reconstruct time lost. In bed at night Paddy wondered how their lives would go from here on out. He contemplated their futures, his dad's future, the talk of his mysterious halfsister in Spokane. He wished the girl, whoever she was, happiness and health, humming the Indian prayers Grandma Diana taught him to sing. He prayed for his mother, to keep her travels at bay. He slept and dreamt his ranch boy dreams, blood pulsing a renewed vigor through his heart. He awakened into a dream each day, life with a real father.

Wendel dreamt likewise—a son, a son! Poems appeared in his journal, verse more jubilant than the bunkhouse haiku, poems of the land ...

Continental Drift

Milking Glaciers Crack and Boom
Flow
Recede
Continental Glaciers

Continental Drift
Glaciers Carving Mountains, carrying grist to Foothill Prairie
Foothills of time
Glaciers Calving Icebergs into cirque lakes, millennia released
Glaciers Moving Moraine
Grinding rock to Silt
Silt to be carried beyond mountains to secure foothill Bunchgrass
    Stone to plains to plants. Water all the way.

Sun hot. Glaciers Melting. Ice Age over. A wolf howls for
    salmon.

Echoes crack out of mountains shattering the green hum of
    spring.
Avalanche! The Avalanches of Glacier County,
Guttural Resonance rolling out of the front—
Earthen inertia shouting for freedom, loosened, escaping.
Hear. Look. See!
Limestone dusts the sunlight.
Violent rollout of noise, canyon to foothill to beyond.
Cross fired purls soften as they
Diffuse the pulverized sealife, sealife to stone to
Silt drifting, water and wind taking it east
To be caught by the grasses of time, endless spooling of grass
    and time.
Sea dust seeking repose, finding it, letting the grazers take it
    from here, cattle now,
Buffalo gone.

From the ancient Indian settlement on the bluff over the
    South Fork the Avalanches can be heard clearest.

Sundering geology, the cleaving of earth from time...
Mountains to Plains, an earth subsumed by
The Quiet thrum of entropic Spring.
A good day for evolution.

A good day for fatherhood.

Chapter 9

WOMAN

Gretchen's life ticked counterclockwise losing her son to his father. She worked the kitchen each morning, impatiently helping Mabel cook and clean, huffing about. She left to the big house when the men stamped in to eat, returning to martyr herself at the long table after they left —peeling potatoes, dicing veggies, kneading breads, pinning pie crusts. Mabel appreciated the help, but threatened to boot her out and didn't mean maybe if she didn't cheer up. Boss's daughter or otherwise, she did not allow anyone to envenom her nourishing atmosphere, not for long. "Why don't you go clean their bunkhouse? It'll get you out of your dissatisfied self for a few minutes. Do you some good."

"I don't clean up after men like that."

"I'm not asking you to clean up after men, I'm asking you to go clean up after yourself."

Gretchen took Mabel's advice. She started cleaning the bunkhouse when Paddy and Wendel left on overnight rides into the Arctic sweep of the ranch. Curiosity more than therapy made her do it. There was little to discover other than dirty socks—no hints of love, poems unfound. Wendel didn't know what to say when they stumbled into one another as she left his bunkhouse one unexpected afternoon after he had returned from a long ride. Chickadees hopped through the river brush pecking at seeds and insect eggs unseen. The two parents stood and looked at one another wedged together under the bunkhouse threshhold. Magpies hopped and squawed in the driveway. Ravens cawed from the bluff above. Birds, birds everywhere.

"Gretch," he managed.

"Well. Hello, Wendy," she said, her voice stiff, unpracticed.

"Where's Paddy off to?" he asked.

"Shopping with Grandma Di."

"Shopping?"

"Clothes," she said, not quite looking at him.

"Clothes?"

"School clothes."

"Where's he going to school?" Wendel asked.

"I'm not sure. We might move to town for the school year."

"Don't do that," he said.

She bristled.

" —Please, don't," he pleaded.

Gretchen huffed past Wendel and strode to the cookhouse. A visit with Mabel whirled the cookhouse air. After dinner Mabel heard Wendel's side. She offered her wisdom to both.

The next day, hoping to soften the storm that had become his life, Wendel informed Diana and Gretchen he was also father to a daughter… and yes, husband to a wife—a Spokane Indian. Diana swallowed and squinted her eyes her certain way. Gretchen left the house and sped off in her car.

Diana stared out the window of her home that overlooked the Walking Box. Wendel was father to her grandson and now also father to a Spokane Indian daughter, a tribe too far away and salmon dependent to be enemies of her Blackfeet. She caught her breath and held her tongue, subduing tribal emotions. Neither had much more to say. Wendel left and fell back into his horses. Diana digested Wendel's situation over the next days, recriminating herself for not having told him earlier about his son.

Wendel had informed Paddy of his family much earlier, on one of their first rides it was. Wendel had not told Paddy to tell no one, Paddy just knew to keep his secret half-sister to himself. Wendel hadn't expected his son to tell anyone, and was honored the boy had not. Trust bonded them. Father and son shared most everything about their lives. They rode day after day, moving cattle, breaking colts. The ranch propped them up. June burned on, then came a Fourth of July rain. Breeding season ended when the bunchgrass went to seed. The wind blew unseasonably hard in August. Wendel and Paddy rode their horses through the entire Walking Box herd. They sifted the bulls out and brought them home.

"Why do we bring home the bulls early? Why can't we wait and bring them with the cows in the fall, Dad?" Wendel let the word 'Dad' ring in his ears. He did not answer, just follwing along after the bulls. "Why, Dad?" Paddy persisited.

"Their work is done. Remember that old vet that used to come up this way, ol' Doc Ray?"

"I think he's slowed up," Paddy said, "but I know who you mean, the king of cow doctors, they say."

"That's right. Old doc Ray, he's the one taught me about herd fertility, said to always get the bulls out after two months breeding time, best thing a ranch cowboy can do—prevents diseases from gaining momentum in the herd, separates the mothers from the cowboys. Keeps the herd healthy, disease free, a good thing."

"How so?"

"Any cow not yet settled with calf after two months is liable to be diseased, venereally you know. Best get the bulls out before they try to breed those few barren cows and infect themselves."

"Barren?"

"Barren means bred but not pregnant. Infected cows don't conceive when they're bred. They don't take and they keep cycling. The bulls, having settled the healthy, chase after these unbred cows, exposing themselves to venereal diseases some of them may carry, savvy?"

"I guess," said Paddy, learning more than he wanted to know about breeding disease.

"Taking the bulls out early keeps the calving season shortened up, too, you know," Wendel added. "You know how things fall apart when calving drags on and on. It's best to keep the calving interval short, six, eight weeks max. Bringing the bulls home keeps it tight like that. It's a big thing in maintaining ranch sanity, keeping the birthing season short. Less disease build up, less wear and tear on the men tending the heifers and delivering the calves. The bulls always come out this time of year on the good ranches. Bringing the bulls home after sixty days with the cows is the most important thing a feller can do for a ranch. Don't you forget it."

Paddy smirked and nodded. "Let's bring 'em on home then, Dad."

"Home we go. They've bred the best and it's time to get out of here."

"Sort of like you bred my mom and got out of here?"

"That's one way to put it, I suppose," Wendel said, taken aback.

"That's how you ended up fathering me?"

"Turned out so," Wendel said. He stopped his horse and looked at his son, who stopped as well. "Confound it all," he added, clenching his jaw.

"You didn't know," Paddy said, or asked. Wendel couldn't tell if it was a question or an answer—an excuse, it was an excuse, Paddy was excusing his father for not being around all those growing years.

"I didn't know, son," Wendel said. "Think what you may, but I just didn't know."

"That's what Bubbles said."

"Bubbles? What about Diana?"

"No, she didn't say much. Just Bubbles."

"Had I known, I'd've stayed, stayed and been here for you."

"I know that, Dad."

"You do? But you never had a chance to talk about my exit with your mom?"

"No. That'd be your job, now wouldn't it, Dad?"

"I suppose it would be."

"Not much for us to do but just make up the lost time. If Mom leaves for Iowa again, I'll stay on here."

"Iowa?"

"That's where she goes, Dad. Iowa."

Wendel winced at the thought of Paddy leaving. A sideache stitched his flank, a stabbing at his kidney.

"Talk to her about it, while you have the chance," Paddy said.

"I'll try."

"She could up and leave at anytime."

"You think she might?

"Maybe."

"Soon?"

"I don't know, but I'm getting tired of Mom and Grandma fighting about it all the time."

"Fighting about what?"

"You and me."

"What about you and me?" Wendel asked.

"*Everything* about you and me."

"I'll do what I can."

"Do what you can?" Paddy said, his tone again between question and suggestion.

"I don't know. Your mom's hard to reason with sometimes, a lot of the times, actually, for me at least."

"Well, I can't even begin to reason with her about Iowa, either. If she wants to leave, she up and leaves. She travels back and forth a lot. Not much I can say, her no-backtalk rule, you know, no back-talk allowed. Something she got from Grandpa Rip. His rule."

"Everything's backtalk."

"She doesn't allow backtalk. No arguing with Mom."

They trailed the bulls home saying little more, their minds swirling.

Paddy started school but stayed at the ranch. He commuted on a schoolbus with four other kids, thirty-six miles east to Del Bonita each morning. The white schoolhouse sat on a knoll, school windows looking to the big empty north of Canada and over the rimrock east of high-plains Montana. The Sweetgrass Hills titted the far plains, visible only occasionally—sometimes full, sometimes flat and empty, dependant upon the atmospheric curve of the world. The highway north led to a redbrick Canadian border checkpoint protected by a shelterbelt of hardy trees. After a day in school spent with a vivacious schoolteacher and ten others, Paddy rode thirty-six miles back home listening to Canadian AM radio. He arrived around suppertime at the cookshack.

He often recited his day's learning to the Walking Box men and Mabel's kitchen crew. The men asked him questions about what he had learned, occasionally throwing in with their knowledge of the world as they knew it. They became most interested when Paddy talked about the non-schooling part of school, the gossip gleaned from the other kids, reports on the families and farms and ranches and hired men to the east. Nothing like the rumors of how things transpired on other outfits to keep a crew alive, talk to keep them from the dour thoughts of their own failings.

On weekends Paddy rode with these men, moving cattle horseback, rounding-up. The great thing about cowboying as a profession is that it has little to do with size or age, the youngest smallest man can be the best cowboy, and Paddy was this. He gathered the furthest cows and brought them home for the winter—gratifying work for which he was duly honored. Energy is a cowboy essential, and with youth comes energy. Paddy and the men brought the cows home, cows and calves lowing in the holding pasture by night, grazing the bottomland after a long summer in the prairie wilderness. Their tails swatted the last feeble flies of fall, ears rocking to the motion of grazing, or cudding, a cow's ears always rolling, always listening. The herd relished the hayground grass, grazing that last lush greenness as if their lives would go on forever should they only get enough.

The cattle trucks began their descent on the Walking Box—Peterbilts and White Freightliners driven by Nebraska cornhuskers, big boys come to pick up the Walking Box bounty. Come to wheel the beef east. The yearlings shipped out first, some weighing over a thousand pounds, their life on the range ended, steers and spayed heifers, luckier than most to have been held over for a second summer. After the yearlings, Wendel and Paddy worked the last pairs home. Bubbles processed the livestock through his intricate flow of corrals, sorting and sifting, weighing up, shipping out—cattle understanding their lot almost as well as the horses understood their men. By October a cold whiteness sunk its teeth into the land. Blizzards came cold and heavy. Walking Box—vortex of the world—weather erasing time: the last of the calves shipped out in November. The finest heifers were kept back as future bloodstock, Rip doing the picking and choosing.

All the mothers were pregnancy tested by Doc Ray, Jr.— the non-pregnant backmarked for shipment to the great grassland in the sky, hauled away to never return. The pregnant cows in good flesh stayed on another winter. They had another birth to look forward to come spring, another green summer, their lives shaped by grass and horsemen, by winter and backfat. The weaned mothers paced the reservation fences, looking for their offspring to relieve them, udders swollen and swinging with pain. They trotted and mooed, frantic in their child-loss. Their offspring in Nebraska by now, eating corn. After three days they abandoned their longing and took to eating heartily, ravenously—eating for the next calf growing inside each and every one of them. They settled into the fall grass, tonguing it in, munching it down, cudding it up; green bottom grass, high-country fescue. Brushy coulées yielding the last protein of summer.

With the fall work finished Wendel hoped to break away

to visit Trish in Spokane. Willow's last correspondence suggested he could spend some father time with his daughter. He hoped to spend a couple of weeks. Attempting to arrange this time, he called Willow and discovered a disturbing uncertainty: Willow had only planned on him visiting his daughter for a couple of hours. She expected him to show up from 500 hundred miles away to have lunch with his daughter.

The Walking Box days thinned. Long nights, blizzards and blowing cold. Thanksgiving snow drifted the coulées and stayed, hard snow. Bubbles and Wendel fed hay onto this whiteness, hay and cattle contrasting the white world. Coyotes gathered on the edges of their activity. Wendel never left the ranch to see his daughter. He couldn't bring himself to leave with the thought he'd only get to see her for an hour or two.

Bubbles hung on with Mabel, a cookshack life. Paddy attended school and Gretchen sulked.

Chapter 10

WOLFMAN

It took until the end of January for the days to noticeably lengthen. A struggling sun heartened into the world a little earlier each morn, rising a bit higher from points further south as it made its New Year's journey down the Glacier Park Rockies. By February atmospheric turbulence spun up lenticular clouds that cocooned the ivory mountains—wind clouds forecasting big wind to come, this particular wind-cloud wind seldom warm. In March the days brightened until one day a Pacific ensconced their world. The system swirled in with colossal snow and rain. Then followed the wind, the world adrift, followed by more wind, and then finally a warm wind that cleared the grasslands of snow, a Chinook. The gravid cows left the feedgrounds and hiked up the ridges to graze the exposed grass. Grass and snow, snow and wind. Longer days, shorter nights. Cold returned, and with it ice. Cattle require fresh water daily to ruminate and survive. They cannot survive on snow alone as a fluid source like horses can. They cannot live on ice. Sometimes the whole county became ice. Frozen water was the reason the buffalo left this country in the winter in times past.

Each day Wendel and Bubbles saddled up to ride upriver and open the ice. On a certain bend of the river under which the water was known to be deep and wide they dismounted to chop through and furrow the liquid out for the cows to drink, and drink heartily. The herd gathered about them, water dependent, looing gently, swallowing their cuds in preparation to drink long and cold. Wendel chopped. The sun shone hard and reflective. Bubbles dented the ice with a crowbar. The cows waited, aspiring to the aroma of water. They waved their noses in the crisp air and licked their lips. Milk River, milk of the earth—ice guarding the alluvial liquid.

When Wendel finally penetrated the ice and air reached the milky water, the river sucked the atmosphere into her flow. She croaked and buckled along her petrified length, a glottal wrenching. Water erupted from the crevice and flowed freely over the ice. Closer the cattle came, the men molding a trough in the ice. They kicked shards of chipped ice around the edges to provide traction for the cloven hooves. The cows pushed in to drink. The men milled backed through the cows and watched them drink. No day passed without fresh water for the cows. Cattle love water, they love to drink. Men love freeing water from the earth so cattle can drink.

That day as the cows slurped in their fill, Bubbles spotted a wolf—a blowsy dog silhouetted on the ridge. Bubbles signaled Wendel with his crow bar, a subtle wolfward tilting. By the time Wendel spotted her the yellow creature had started down the slope toward them. The cows backed away sucking their lower teeth, their chins drooly with drink. They mooed worriedly. Islanding together, they moved up the slope away from the hiss of the wondrous river. The she-wolf trotted to the water hole and lapped—her long tongue yo-yoing rhythmic, tossing water into her mouth. Her fur, lustrous and flaxen, parted and dancing in the breeze. The low sun shadowed her long and ready legs. Fine-boned and big-pawed she drank. Wolf.

The cows milled uphill, back-stepping, waiting for wolf to move off the way she came so they could return to drink their fill. She finished lapping and trotted back up the hill, as the cows knew she would. She stopped at the top to look back, before disappearing into the whiteness, the sky white as the plains, wolf gone.

"Good sign there HorseMan. Better get yourself a good drink of that milkwater." Bubbles gestured to the water hole. Leery but thirsty, the cows crept back. Wolf in their nostrils, some snorted and pawed. "Sign of fulfillment if you go kneel down to the world and have yourself a drink of her water. Follow her path, know your direction."

Wendel sighed. He didn't feel much direction in his life without contact with his daughter. He kneeled to drink. Bubbles raised his hands and held the cows back until he finished.

"Know yourself, trust the world," he said. "Trust the wolf. She talks to you with water."

"And not you?"

"I'm too old for the wolf to bother with me, HorseMan. Much too old."

"How old?"

"I don't know."

"Never too old for wolf talk, come on now. How old are you?"

"My mom forgot the year I was born."

"What about your birthday, when's that?"

"No birthday."

"She forgot that, too, the day?"

"Days were different then, a different time. Days when their number didn't matter."

"Spring, summer? Some native moon, come on, what season you were born?"

"I tell you, it's all unknown. Mom died before she could tell anyone those things."

"She must have told someone."

"Whomever she might have told is dead too, then," Bubbles said, matter-of-factly.

"I'm sorry."

"She was gone like water, my mother."

"Then what?" Wendel asked, an eye squinted shut.

"Then I went with my uncle, an original horse medicine man."

They watched carefully for wolf in the days that followed, but saw little of her. Every day, after they left their water mining, she came to drink the cow's nectar—next-day tracks rare and ephemeral but not beyond Bubbles' weathered eye. Neither Wendel nor Bubbles revealed her presence for fear the GallStone airplane would sound the skies and gun her down. When the river thawed, all sign of wolf disappeared.

Gretchen began to friendly up with Wendel 'for Paddy's sake'—all of a sudden sweet as ever. Parents and son began spending time together watching Rip's collection of western videos—Paddy dozing between Mom and Dad in a wish-come-true childhood. Cowboys and Indians chased one another over the great screen of television, a coziness shadowed in western drama. The search for a lost gold mine, the great dream of acquiring a spread of one's own—the price one pays. Talk. Touch. A remote life suddenly sheltered. Paddy slept hard there lying between his mom and dad. For the parents came recollection of love. And then an awkward dizzy return to it—a recapitulation of time back then, when Paddy was conceived. A realization of that past—a past creating a son; the eleven lost years. Each night at the end of the movie Paddy and Wendel hiked back down to the bunkhouse, where Paddy had started staying.

Chapter 11

LADY'S MAN

Time reawakens love. Ranch isolation ignites passion, or re-ignites it. One winter day Wendel's shirt inexplicably bore the telltale black of the shop floor. "Which rig had a flat?" Bubbles asked, never knowing HorseMan to change a flat, ever. A week later calving-shed straw clung to the underside of his sleeves, calving not yet underway; straw concomitantly adhered to Gretchen's scarf. The next day: mussed hair both, a likewise patina of hay-truck chaff, fairy dust sprinkled over the two of them. Bubbles understood the tireblack, and now Mabel was in with the telltale chaff. With Indians observation is key. There are no secrets.

The equinox approached as March whistled by, days catching up to the nights, days lengthening beyond the nights. Soon there was light everywhere, earlier and longer. The snow blew off the range. One Chinook afternoon Diana spotted her daughter and Wendel in a not-quite-hidden swale of distant riverbottom. She watched them approach one another, stalking together from different directions, their love taking nearly an hour to devour. The river flowed high in its banks.

Chapter 12

RANCHMAN

Rip Ripley ignored the rejuvenated love—or whatever it had become at this stage of human ritual. He considered Wendel might land-scam a love for his daughter, his land, but he knew better, or he thought he did. Nonetheless, the rancher pondered weddings and inheritance. He considered transfers of wealth, transfers of land. Oh, the forlorn rags of growing old. It bothered Rip that Wendel came to know him and his ranch so well. Rip despised getting old. Thinking about succession made him feel death. He was not ready to give up his ranch. Others had died by his age, yes, but not Rip. Time dulled his joints and brittled his bones, and he felt it. Still, he was not ready to give anything up. Changes in ownership would be at his discretion, not Wendel's, or his daughter's, or even his wife's, the true owner of the land, if it indeed it could be owned by anyone at all. Climate owned the land in this country, and always would—Mother Nature; the supreme ruler of grass and cattle, atmospheric conditions that made Rip's mornings stiff and slow, cowboy stiffness a unique arthritis, a relentless ache in the spine and shoulders, a throbbing in the knuckles, noise in the knees.

Rip's timeworn carcass had been dragged over the breadth

of this range, yes it had. Cattle had trampled every measure of him. Cattle and buffalo. The fringe herd of buffalo nearly exterminating him one day eight years ago. That was the day Wendel's Dad saved Rip's life, sacrificing his own, the day Willard Ingraham departed the Walking Box for the last time. Not bucked off a horse and hitting his head on a rock like they told Wendel's mother (who never informed Wendel, like she said she had and would), but gored to death, a buffalo horn in the thorax after he rode his horse between an enraged buffalo and his employer, taking the bash meant for Ripley. The bull bison had tossed Rip's horse out from under him leaving Rip defenseless on foot, Wendel's dad swept in and the bull took down his horse and him as well. An untold story.

Doom happens, Rip thought. Extermination and expiration were not his fault. Death filled life with tragedy, and sometimes death was best left alone. He knew by now that Wendel hadn't heard about his father's demise. Or that he remained in some strange trance of denial. Everyone on the ranch knew. No one could bring themselves to tell Wendel the truth his mother had failed to deliver.

Rip shirked a responsibility that by a measure of any man would be his. But hadn't Rip endured enough tragedy of life and death? Hadn't he earned the right, earned it with his muscle and bone, to own cattle and land and not be bothered with death? Muscle and bone were what it took in this country, muscle and bone and land and cattle. Every square inch of his hide had connected with hoof or horn. Rip did his time on this side of the world. His will to rule the land prevailed over any obstacles the world had yet born upon him. He would leave death alone as long as he could. Wendel was better off without it as well, no?

Rip went to bed early and woke early. In the morning dark he sat in his chair overlooking the ranchyards. He waited for the cookshack light to come on and he waited for the sun to rise. Each morning he watched Mabel's silhouette dance about her kitchen. She waltzed to the freezer on the porch, two-stepped to the washroom behind. Rip sat and watched and waited and thought, not smoking or chewing anymore, not even drinking coffee these days, but green tea, doctor's orders, sitting and waiting and thinking, sipping, sometimes a yawn, his legs propped before him on an empty bookshelf, socks of the finest Merino wool. He would stand and do his exercises, stretching and looking out his window, then down to the floor on a rug on his back, doing the yoga routine a Bozeman lady had taught him. One day a mouse ran out to watch him. He laid on his back and watched the mouse, the mouse feeling safe with Rip on his back, the mouse knowing there would be no quick movements from that position. Once Rip had tried to shoot the mouse with his .22 rifle, but missed. He stood and gestured to the gun cabinet. The mouse darted away and Rip thought about making one of the barn cats a house cat, but he didn't allow cats in the house. He would get the mousetrap with the plastic that looked like Swiss cheese, specially impregnated with a smell, best mouse trap ever invented, no fiddling with peanut butter.

The next morning he stood in his window, he could see his reflection in the window, skin sagging about his pug nose, the wrinkles in his forehead furrowed. He watched his men marching through the dawn, coming to eat as to work, hitching from the bunkhouses to the cookshack in the wolf light, morning alpenglow reflected back over their valley from mountains west. He watched them arrive, and through the

98

window could see them sitting, he envisioned their elbows on the table, their cowboy fingers spooning sugar and pouring cream into their coffee, cream from the new cow Chris milked, a friendly range cow who'd lost her calf. He strapped on his spurs as he watched his men, taking time to adjust them carefully, tuning them, finding the right strap length for the boots he wore. He stepped outside and took a deep breath before walking down the hill to the cookshack, smiling, listening to the rowels roll on the shanks of his spurs, feeling the rowels roll.

"How're them heifers lookin', Bubbles?" Jesse asked as Rip stepped inside a cookshack filled with food and laughter.

"Calves everywhere," Bubbles replied. "Don't you be worrying yourself about them heifers. They're mine to worry about, mine alone." Breakfast plates sang under big appetites, softening to a tinkling as Rip sat down.

"Storm's a coming," he said, dishing his plate with Mabel's vittles. "Supposed to hit tomorrow. Maybe tonight. Smelled it in the air walking down the hill." Rip knew the weather patterns, had learned weather the true north way. He understood what sundogs meant. He knew about low barometric pressure sucking moisture over the Rockies, about blizzards rolling across the plains from the east. He knew wind and he knew cold. Alberta Clippers. Eastblown whiteouts. His face showed it, his joints felt it. If nothing else, the crew believed in Rip's weather reports. As they ate a wetness filled the air, a blowing mist, water in a state between rain and snow.

The men finished eating and left to bed down the newborn calves with extra straw. Wendel and Badtooth Gene and Paddy brought in the cows and heifers that looked close to calving. The Heart Butte boys, Eli and Monty Red Bear, sniffed out all the half-frozen newborns and their wind-whipped mothers and eased them to the snowshed behind the barn. Diana and Gretchen nurtured the weak back to life; suckling them, warming them, rubbing them, feeding their mothers big helpings of oats to nourish their weakened babies. Bunkhouse Chris milked his cow three times a day. He whipped it together with a nice mixture of replacement milk and fed the orphans. The old coot wouldn't be left out, doing his part as he had for half a century of calving madness.

Above it all, Rip paced about his house, his perch over his world, unable to rest his weary bones. He fretted as he watched his herd multiply, the men and cattle moving like ants through carefully designed corrals. They mothered the confused and weakened newborns, milked out cantankerous swingbags. Big trailers of hay crawled out of the bottoms, tractored out of the stacks and to the cattle, motored up the coulées and out along the ridges, luring the healthy pairs up out of the bottomlands to clean country above. Gophers bounced across melting snowbanks, freed from winter, amazed at passage of cattle—sun hot off a soft snow. Spring unraveled in rhythms, calves bucking and racing deftly. Mothers eating, tonguing it in, a head-sway motion, poetic. Warm days came to pass, vegetation springing out of the earth, a rich green anxious to grow. Birds above, crossing and connecting the whole wide world. Meadow flowers exploded, a bursting green: snow-charged mountains beyond.

The cattle grazed, freed of men and everything about them, one eye weathered on their new calf, the other surveying forage. They ate the grass and nursed their young and laid down on their sternums, coming to cud—ruminating away. A mystery about it, their casual meditation—the subtlety of grass, chewing the grass, rechewing it, grass to meat and milk. They fed their calves—grazing, cudding, ruminating. Cattle loving the grass as buffalo must have. In two months' time Rip's herd nearly doubled, spring complete—men and women wore down and out.

"How's that daughter in Spokane?" Bubbles asked, seeing Wendel's opaque eyes.

"Haven't heard."

"Better find out."

"You think so?"

"If you want her to be right with the world when she's older."

"How so?"

"Like I know, medicine man so."

Chapter 13

LINEMAN

The next day lightning struck Wendel as he trailed the last stray cows over Milk River Ridge—a white bolt of lightning coming out of a prairie thunderhead hot and electric. When the lightning didn't kill him or his horse, *barely even burned them*, he realized his duty in the world: Get back to his daughter. It wasn't the wolf at work, or the bear, it was the everpowerful Thunderbird.

Gretchen saw the capsized look in Wendel's face when he rode into the ranch afterwards; empty, lightning empty. "What's wrong, Wen?" she asked as he rode by, the same empty look in the horse's eye.

"You don't want to know."

"I do want to know. Tell me," she bid, skipping beside the galvanized horse.

The horse ignored her, carrying Wendel on to the barn.

She ran after Wendel, his horse a fast walker. She came alongside and placed her hand on his horseback thigh, a pleading look in her eyes. She tried to speak something, but was out of breath, and then Wendel beat her to it: "I just realized I don't love you."

"Don't *love me*?" She stopped and braced her hands on her hips. Her face knotted up; her eyes, her lips, her nostrils; her every feature knotted. "After all what's happened this spring you tell me you don't love me?" she sobbed. The horse walked on. She caught up again, winded. "I thought we were going to work everything out."

"So'd I until a bolt of lightning struck me." He stopped his horse and tilted his chin sideways with his hand to show her the side of his face where the lightning had singed him, as if its voltaic aftermath might be apparent to her.

"A bolt of lightning. You'd be graveyard dead if a bolt of lightning struck you."

"That last bolt before this one didn't kill me, now did it, Gretchen?" Wendel's horse was unhappy about stopping. He bobbed his chin artfully, gradually working slack into Wendel's reins, inching… then lurching, forward. Wendel turned back to Gretchen who stood miffed.

"What last bolt?" she implored.

"That bolt that hit me when your mama told me I'd had a son for ten years that I didn't know about. That bolt of lightning." He re-enacted the hit from the sky, collapsing astride his saddle. His horse spooked and stepped sideways and carried him off to the barn.

Gretchen's face came unknotted. She dropped her shoulders, dropped her head, hit by the same lightning.

Wendel lifted himself up from the saddle horn as his horse ambled barnward. "I'm sorry, Gretchen. We're over." He stopped the horse and stepped off and walked back to her. His horse trotted to the barn without him. It was a long stretch across the ranchyard. She stood and waited for him to walk to her. He grabbed her shoulders, unleashing sobs deep within her chest. "I can't come to terms with you not telling me I had son. All those years of not knowing won't let me go on with you."

"I couldn't tell you."

Gretchen saw Wendel's lightning. She wept openly, sucking and wailing.

"I'm sure you had plenty of reasons, Gretchen. I'm sure you had plenty of people telling you not to tell me, but I still can't forgive you. It was a bad thing for Paddy. You, his mother."

"You had that woman in Whitefish," she cried. "That was as mean as it gets, having her while I was pregnant," she sobbed. "How could you do that? How could I tell you with her?"

"I'm not talking about other women, Gretchen." Then Wendel realized she'd meant Nancy, back in high school, when he'd wintered in Whitefish with the ski team. "Wait a minute. I never had her. Nancy? Not then."

"Not then, what's that mean? Now? You have her now?"

"She was a ski teammate with a covey of boyfriends, none of 'em me. It was your folks idea for me to go race in Whitefish. Getting me away from you was what it was." He realized he hadn't been breathing and found himself winded and shaking.

"What're we talking about then?" Gretchen blurted.

"It's not about her. Not then," he gasped.

"What's this *then* stuff? What are *you* talking about?"

"I'm talking about Paddy's life already lived. It was a horrid thing to *not tell him*. You've scarred him for the rest of his life and hurt yourself along the way. You're still hurting, and so is he. A child, it's too much for a child not to understand father. Hell, it's too much to not have a dad around, to not know where Dad is when he might be needed, to not know if he's even alive."

"You don't know where *your* dad is, do you Wendel Ingraham?"

"We're not talking about my dad." Wendel felt the aftermath of lightning, he felt the voltage collecting between his shoulders, electricity spilling down his spine.

"He's dead, Wendel. Your dad's dead, dead and gone forever. They wouldn't let me tell you that, either."

Out Wendel's feet the lightning sparked. The current hit his toes and dove into the ground, a halo of vapor rose around his ankles. Wendel looked to Chief Mountain. He rocked back on his heels, his legs giving way. Down he went, following the lightning into the ground. Now he'd heard what he'd always expected to hear. Death was the best reason of all for a father not getting in touch, a much better reason than not caring. He didn't need to know when or how his dad died, not right now. He feared it might be his alcohol, but it didn't really matter. In the past, not knowing when or how, he didn't really have to believe the death he'd always sensed since his father went quiet. He could just go on dreaming about his dad like he had all along, hoping he'd show up someday if only to say 'Hi, hello. How are you doing these days, son?'

"I've got to go, Gretchen. I'm going to Spokane to see my daughter. The truck is waiting." Wendel stood and limped to the barn after his horse. Rip and Jesse had the cattle truck readied for Wendel to go fetch bulls in Spokane, to patch up the affairs of his other fatherhood. He unsaddled and brushed down his horse, tingling all over. He finished his horse duty and stepped out of the barn and walked past Gretchen, who stood stranded in the middle of the barnyard of her parent's great ranch.

Wendel headed straight to the semi and climbed into the

105

cab to start the diesel engine. Smoke brimmed out of the stacks and dirtied the air. It puffed thick and black, sinking in around the buildings and corrals, swirling past the solitary Gretchen. Wendel jumped out of the truck and ran past her to the bunkhouse to grab his bag. Gretchen turned and watched him run and looked back to the smoking truck before walking to Mabel's cookshack. The engine hammered away, smoke losing its color.

Wendel climbed in with his bag and drove off. Uncertainty pulled the rig uphill, uncertainty and Wendel's vague memory of double-clutching. His anxious desire to be gone resulted in the semi lurching up the hill. He persevered like he'd always persevered and climbed the outfit up the road out of the Middle Fork of the Milk River, its empty aluminum trailer rattling. Synchrony overtook chaos once he reached the top. Wendel began to get a feel for the gears and gently throttled the truck over flatter going, where the engine cooled to a growl. Bubbles' ancient world spooled out before him. Bad Marriage Mountain stood split in half, a kink in the spine of time, a cleaved mountain—together below: apart above. The neighboring peaks cowered below Bad Marriage, the sons and daughters of such angst, the knowing and the unknowing, star-crossed children of troubled parents. Bigger mountains jutted down the front, children of happier mountains, solid mountains with solid foundations in time. The setting sun lit a wind on fire from the back of the world, twilight falling to owl light, and the sea of grass mingled into darkness.

Chapter 14

HIWAYMAN

Down the road Wendel found himself between red and white, between father and son, between children. He drove believing—half-believing, half-unbelieving—conveyance salving his half-doubts. Motion lifted his spirit, motion to penetrate the mountains to penetrate truth. Escape. Return. Which? A waiting daughter. A waiting son. *A dead father.*

Wendel caught his breath. He thought of his mission to acquire bulls for the breeding season. He relished the movement of the truck, the ramble of the empty trailer behind. He tapped the money clip in his shirt pocket, a year's pay in cash banded to his expired Washington State driver's license. He considered the work ahead, the bulls he would purchase for Rip, the long haul back. And then the wickerwork of fatherhood suffocated him—a daughter to see, a daughter to father, *a father to mourn.* He shot along Highway 2 into the mountains, the tunnels and trestles of Glacier ahead. Realbear hid in the trees waiting patiently to rummage train-spilled corn, to hop sidetracked freight.

An obelisk marked the Continental Divide, as plain an obelisk as there is denoting Marias Pass. Virgin forest above. Virgin forest below. Nightshades of forest. Forest whitened by some unidentified light, the Milky Way, or is it an unrisen moon? The road spiraled downward through the deep curves of mountains, over canting bridges—a river far, far below. Beyond Essex the camber of travel straightened into Nyack Flat. Wendel cracked his window as he breached Montana's own hillbilly heaven. Westside air seeped into the cab, heavy air, windless and thick. Houselights and homelights appeared here and there, the woodburners of West Glacier insomniac as woodburners anywhere. The hamlets whipped by; Martin City, Coram, Stoner's Inn. He shot over the South Fork at Hungry Horse and motored toward Badrock Canyon where the Flathead River carved the ancient bedrock. Westward ho and the huckleberry villages thickened. Midnight streets, cabins with plywood windows—an intermittent civilization. Then around a curve in the road a moon risen. Clouds clearing, stars searing, truck rolling. He reached Nan's Whitefish— opportunity come… and past. Soft lips of memory. Whitefish Nancy. The semi engine hammered, father death quelling Wendel's desire to visit Nancy. His head swam dark and deep and the truck rolled by the road to her bungalow. Perhaps he would stop to visit Nancy on his return.

His thoughts shifted with the gears, droning deeper into darkness. How would Spokane present itself after a year gone? He tried to prepare himself for unfulfilled expectations to places revisited. Why did it seem whenever he returned to his past residences all the things he wished to be the same changed, and all the things he wanted to be different lingered? He hoped he might accept whatever he found, a hope wanting to find something to validate his precipitate departure a year ago. What change would he find? He sensed something foreign, something strange. Fear grabbed his gut when he thought of Willow. Wendel did not like confrontations with his wife with fatherhood at stake. He looked askance to the forest and asked realbear for help.

The bottomless sensation passed. 'Remember reliable things,' Bubbles' voice echoed, 'Forget the unreliable.' He thought of reliable. What did that mean; reliable? There would be the same racecourse. That could not change. There would be his friends, Bo Triplett and Paul Mitcheltree, friends entwined by horseracing. Those two would welcome him, openly and without judgment. This reliability Wendel knew, and it must be what Bubbles voice meant.

The unreliability would be Willow, his wife and his judge. If not her so much, his daughter, twice grown by now. The travel slowed and calmed. Wendel eased through the a.m. whisper of Kalispell, mecca of out-of-state wealth. Subdivisions, lights, gridlock. Wendel drove through and beyond the city and floated by the numerous Flathead Lake ranchettes—cabins in the wood. Condos. Communities planned and unplanned. Gated. Lakeside homes, gargantuan and secure and empty. He reached Big Arm and took the road up and off the lake. Westgoing, he breached the open boonie of homeless prairie, hale country—Montana nothingness. Constellations lit his way to Niarada and Hot Springs. In time the Clark's Fork of the Columbia greeted him. Above the river Old Man weather flurried. The splatting rain of Pacific wetness met him at Interstate 90, transmogrifying travel into a version of skiing. Onward. Freeway transit through unsettled sleet. Upward. Lookout Pass into Idaho, the turnpike spiraling down into the Sunshine Valley of silver-mining death. Upward again, Wendel shifted his rig over Fourth of July Pass, gateway to the Land of Lakes. Coeur d'Alene lit the night, her valley of sprawl reaching all the way to Spokane. Transit intensified each westward mile, trucks and vans brawling off and on the freeway ramps, ramps crazed with Inland Empire commerce.

Wendel detoured off the freeway seeking solace. Sun inched up behind him. Stars dwindled ahead. City lights swamped by a funk of bronzetone, distant skyscrapers blurred in a veil of aluminum smog—civilization contained by a maze of concrete. An overpass crossed the railroad tracks. He stopped to take in the tainted morning light. An endless line of freight clunked under him, each car an empty day of his Spokane past.

Wendel drove on to the lowing midtown stockyards and parked his cattle truck. The stoppage of diesel yammer delivered a welcome hush. He jumped down to the ground and stretched—the cool edge of night lost to the bustling heat of a metropolis. He walked a railyard mile to the racetrack, dizzied by fumes of creosote. The sun limbered him along. The cramps of travel loosened by the time he reached the backside gate. He showed the dozing security guard his expired trainer's license and took the pony path to his stable. He landed on the moth-eaten couch in the tackroom and flopped down to sleep. It had been a long haul. His weary bones sunk into the St. Vincent de Paul cushions. Stillness, distorted memories, the liniment edge of tackroom dust. The last time he slept here, over a year ago, he'd just been booted out of his home.

Within minutes life became surreal. Dreams shapeshifted him into horse, into wolf, or was it dog? Wendel was running, running, running down halls of remembrance, resurrected remembrance. Sleep and the scent of horse delivered him into a previous existence.

Chapter 15

MARATHON MAN

Wendel awoke from his catnap to the harrow of a freight train whistle. He had slept deeply but knew not for how long. He tried to determine if the whistle had any bearing in reality. And if so, which reality? Was it a product of sleep? Bubbles considered dreams the ultimate reality. He detected ambulance sirens in a thin distance; they seemed real enough. Perhaps he had heard the warning sound of a tractor in reverse loading straw from the stables to deliver to the mushroom farm. He sat up and listened more intently. Train whistles indeed, their curvature of sound indisputable. He stepped outside and strolled down the shedrow, slipping in and out of the stalls of horses he recognized. Their people had not yet arrived. It was still early—relatively so—around seven he reckoned from an orange sun.

His big horse, Dharma Bum, nickered remembrance. Nice. Others, the youngsters and newcomers, sniffed and snorted at him suspiciously until his ease about the shedrow relaxed them. He touched the horses he knew, kneading their necks, feeling their legs, stroking their backs; noting each blemish as if it were a woman's beauty mark. Suddenly trainer again, he felt hearts pulse and watched lungs breathe. He rapped their hooves with his knuckles, palpated joints to check for inflammation. He liked the feedback horses afforded him, a trust he sought in men and women. After finishing the examination of these old friends, he sat on a bale of hay to absorb morning sun.

The equine presence drew him into a reverie of former times, his mind wandering back to the fluid life. Horses made life move, their nature a living liquid. He wondered how he'd lucked into here years ago, or if it had been luck at all. What was it drew him here? What drew Willow to this same place, this world in which they met? What drew them together? Was it mutual escape from prairie loneliness, from Reservation isolation—different reservations, different lonelinesses? Perhaps their mutual search for safety planted them together.

Wendel winced at his sodden remembrance of the last months in Spokane, drunk in this selfsame shedrow. The shame of abandoning his daughter knotted his gut. Ranch life became a shadow, like this life had when he reached the Walking Box, one life shadowing the other. He swam in shadows, shedrow shadows, mountain shadows. He stood and paced, this time stopping to check each horse's teeth. He started with Dharma Bum. After some tactile reassurance, he deftly pulled the horse's tongue out the side of its mouth and felt each and every tooth. Dharma obliged the horseman. Wendel learned from Bubbles that if a horse resented what he did, he was doing it wrong. Simple enough. He learned to do things the horse's way. Bubbles taught Wendel that the problems men had with horses had little to do with the horse. It now seemed that wisdom might apply to women as well, in his case at least, wisdom Bubbles hadn't mentioned.

Wendel corrected the dental defects, smoothing the sharp points with his dental files he found rusting in the tack room. Unlike most species, horses' teeth grow nearly all their life, and that allows horses to be aged by their dentition. In a natural existence their teeth are smoothed from endlessly foraging the grasses of the plain. When stabling hinders this continuous chewing, problems arise. Teeth overgrow. Artificial diets don't wear teeth like the silicon grasses of native plains do. Teeth grow abnormally sharp in stable situations. Points irritate the tongue and cut the cheeks, cause for great pain, mouth pain. Horses won't run with pain, not tooth-driven pain, not against a bit. Paul Mitcheltree, Wendel's former assistant and now head trainer, had been lax on teeth as well as feet since Wendel departed. Wendel floated their teeth—floating, a nice word describing the finesse required to move a file along all four arcades of a horse's cheek teeth. Floating—the mental state the procedure takes the horse into if done skillfully. The filing floated Wendel as well the horse, floated him into a past. He reflected on circumstances that landed him here; the pursuance of horses into a city, a search for fulfillment in a concrete world.

It was unusual that no one had yet showed up to feed. The horses became restless—kicking and squealing, talking to Wendel. He fed them, much to their contentment. In Wendel's time trainers showed up two hours before sunrise to feed their charges, never two hours after, two hours and counting. His first year as trainer resulted in notable success, a stakes win and an allowance victory. Then came the big score, the Inland Empire Futurity, a wire to wire win, a $17,000 windfall by Dharma Bum. Success bred success. By the next year Wendel saddled winners with regularity, one jubilant win after the other. Horses, people, and money. What a mix. His stable grew by leaps and bounds; winners, claimers—soon it was stakes horses. Public training became full time employment. He quit his yardman job at the stockyards and became a permanent fixture at the track, captain of his own ship at last.

Money surged, money ebbed, drained away only to reappear tenfold out of thin air. Money turned the horseracing world, or overturned it. Gambling interspersed poverty with riches, a financial rollercoaster that strained his marriage. Willow never recovered from the $17,000 futurity check. Money lost its glitter—money in the bank, money vanished.

Training took its toll. Wendel spent day and night establishing his reputation with horse owners, day and night year after year. He knew how to get honest run out of honest horses. He understood the man saddling the winners would always have horses to train, and with that he had more horses than he could sometimes handle. A five-year run. And then it crashed. In the span of a year the fickle world about him lost interest in horse racing. Other gambling imperiously surfaced to take its place: Indian reservation casinos, dog racing, live poker, video poker, Black Jack, and lotteries galore; everything legal but craps. But all forms of gambling gravitate to a crapshoot, a universal trajectory that didn't spare Playfair. Overnight the Russian olive trees that looped the track—those wonderfully thorny Russian olives—overgrew, strangling the racecourse.

And now this emptiness. Wendel gazed about the backside—a cocoon from which the butterfly had long since flown. Across the way stalls wept for horseflesh. Disjointed doors outnumbered the jointed, some splintered and strewn half a shedrow away. Planters empty of flowers, flowers that once draped winners' necks. Five years before flowers grew everywhere, florid memories floral no more. A gust of wind slammed a hinged door shut. An empty resonance echoed, the stall empty like so many others, emptied by races running no more. Back in the glory days it took great effort to secure stalls for Wendel's string of runners. He remembered greasing endless wheels to keep those stall numbers secure—applications, proof of meritorious runners, money under the table, money over the table, money everywhere during the days when every stall on the grounds held a horse, stables emanating life, the smell and sound of horseracing—a world of intense competition.

Thoughts of the Marathon Series rushed into Wendel, classic races that became recklessly popular in his heyday—four celebrated long-distance races each meet, each race a month apart, each race longer. One and a half miles to begin the meet, a three mile finale by the end of the season—horses pounding five times past the grandstand, the one true horserace of the year. Horseplayers came in droves to bet the Marathon Series. The closest thing to a cinch was betting the Ingraham trained entry. Seasoned horseplayers dubbed Wendel 'Marathon Man.' His talent became route races. He developed his ability to dose common horses with endurance, horses he rubbed sound and worked fit. Wendel taught his horses to run, and then he taught them patience; when to run. Control. Pace the horse and go the distance.

Toward the end the marathon races belonged to Wendel Ingraham. He won the finale three of the last four years it ran. Between marathons Wendel chimed in with claiming and allowance victories. A stakes win every so often made life delicious. Evening racing packed the stands, summertime eves, a delicious time to race horses. The pulverized twilight of Spokane electrified the sport. Gambling. Sleepers and winners. Losers and ringers. The glory went on, a good half-decade of run. Snoozers. Fixers. Hoppers. Shockers. Gaffers. Blockers. Stiffs. Whiffs. Miffs. Near misses and marathons. Wendel

Ingraham loved every minute.

Then racing died, Wendel's dreamwork foiled. Life lost meaning, soured. Wendel faded with Playfair, faded into the cold dream of horses running across the shadows of higher and higher skyscrapers. Concrete won over, smothering this last slice of urban wilderness, but not before a last stand. America experienced one last run at the bucolic life, bucolic life in the middle of a city. In a dwindling natural world, the hope for great horse destiny began here. Columbia Basin Indians— extinct of salmon runs—spawned dreams of renewal at Playfair. Montana's mountain men chanced their last dollars at striking winner's circle gold. Ranchers from Eastern Oregon survived bankruptcy and drought to experience one final triumph. Whoever they were, whatever breed of horseman, they brought horses and they brought hope, hope that horses could revive a manifest heart. The last gold rush in America gathered to a bullring in the middle of Spokane, Washington—a place stitched and cross-stitched by the last American Illusion, the horse.

Glory holes of this rare kind are a long time coming. A long history precedes such a thing. When Wendel arrived from Montana years back he knew to consort with old folks to learn the rules of the game. He chose his mentors well. Bo Triplett, a Vietnam veteran carrying a full ravage of war—a war a quarter century past—was his primary teacher. Shell shock led him to the peacetime pleasure of rubbing legs for a living. Playfair became his therapy, a space where animals healed people, the horseracing a secondary condition, a necessary evil. Triplett coupled to his horses, metaphysically and physically he communed with them. This connection attracted Wendel. He watched Bo handle his charges daily, head to tail handle them, withers to hoof; necks, spines, bellies, sensuous ears, silky noses, every measure of each horse handled daily. To his knees he connected with their legs, always the legs, praying before the legs, worshiping their legs—rubbing their legs, fragile keys to racing success.

Playfair Racecourse was a bullring, a tight-cornered 5/8 mile track, much tighter turns than the one-mile tracks on the coast. Such sharp racing invoked extra strain on a horse's limbs. Trip's hands became the glue that held cornering speed together. The movement of a horse's legs—a biomechanical poetry—responded to his intimate maintenance of synchrony. Bo knew the rhyme and meter of every horse; Bo the poet, horses his verse. He engaged in continuous communication with them, a tactile language, a discourse in touch, lyrical fingers of conveyance. Wendel watched and Wendel learned.

Bo fused with his horses. He listened to them. He studied their every antic and nuance. He penetrated each joint of every animal, knew every joint's peculiar motion. He practiced a horse religion not much different than Bubbles'. Bo heard horse confession and absolved horse pain. He spent every hour of every day with his horses. He slept with them, ate with them, pissed with them. He conquered their every weakness and mastered their every strength. His horses knew him well, they loved him—relied on him. Ran for him.

He and his wife, Alice, lived in the tack room at the end of their shedrow, their home no better or worse than their horses', no fancy apartment needed for a life after war. Alice worked at the backside café. She baked the tastiest cinnamon rolls this side of Seattle, rolls best eaten an hour before daylight, gooey-hot rolls, squares of butter melting into white frosting—fare quicker than bacon and eggs, quicker to lift one into the day.

117

Each morning Alice readied her husband to train horses. He slurried down her cinnamon rolls with industrial coffee while his horses ate their own carbohydrate loads of breakfast grains and sugars.

The year Wendel arrived and began helping Triplett, Bo won the Playfair Mile with a marginally bred horse owned by the Greasy Grass Clan of the Spokane Indian Nation, a horse aptly named Chief Spokane. Triplett livened the horse to his powerful name, made him a horse for the bullring course. He secured the Indian Nation the richest win of the year: Chief Spokane, spirit of the reservation, coaxed into replacing vanished salmon one fine September day. This magic elevated Triplett to legendary status with Indians. He never mentioned to anyone but Wendel that he was one himself, his great grandmother a Kootenai from the finger lakes of Glacier Park, a mountain tribe of fishing Indians.

Winning the Playfair Mile was an incredible accomplishment given the horse's marginal breeding. Chief Spokane was burdened by a local pedigree, the Kentucky class generations back. Triplett activated run hidden in the horse's ancestry and in doing so activated Indian pride. Triplett gave Chief Spokane heart, the heart to win. Wendel recollected the day. Chief Spokane strode gallantly to the paddock, calm under Triplett's hand, oblivious to the grandstand chaos. Quite a day for the Spokane Nation.

Chief broke well. Easing behind clamoring horses, dropping into the rail from the eight hole. At the first turn he settled behind the early speed, some of the speed drifting wide. He bulled his head and held to the rail, tight around the sharp curve of the small track, holding his head to the inside and squinting his eyes to keep the dirt clods from doing damage.

Aldo delaFlor, Triplett's jockey, saved the horse in this early going as the unfamiliar hook of the 5/8 turn took the spunk out of the bluebloods from Seattle. The jock had Chief sailing comfortably the first time past the grandstands. delaFlor waited, patience the key, flexing his game mount along. The coastal speed drifted even wider on the clubhouse turn, Chief still sucked onto the rail. Down the backside he moved inside the blowing favorites.

Out of the third and final turn the Chief let loose with All of Kentucky. His ears pricked at the eighth pole when Aldo delaFlor clucked. Chief caught his top gear and passed the leaders like freight passing a bum. Aldo hand rode his runner to the finish. Victory, sweet victory, a two-length victory drawing away. The Indian Nation exploded as Chief crossed the line. Animal power lifted the tribe to an exalted glory, a salmon harvest revisited.

Witness to this performance, Wendel acquired the bug to win the big race, and to win it all. Triplett taught by example. It was during this time that Wendel met Willow, a Spokane Indian. The two fell together under the spell of Triplett's training. In horses they found a shared sanctity, sanctity beyond their respective heritages. The next year Wendel had a trainer's license, a stable of his own, and a wife. A year later he had a daughter.

Bo continued to teach Wendel the hocus-pocus of leg care, the formulation of leg paints, the application of sweats, massage techniques and more. Both leg and head therapist, Bo had a formula for every infirmity, a solution to curtail every bad habit, a method to ease every lame step. He taught Wendel the art of observation—observe the entire horse, visually inspect every tendon, ligament, and bone. Watch every step the horse takes, let nothing by. Note every misstep, understand why they made the misstep, investigate, discover the root of the problem causing the lameness. Triplett showed Wendel how to correct the bad moves and augment the good. He demonstrated the importance of knowing each horse's mind—know your horse, but most importantly, know yourself. He explained horses possess a split mind; half wild, half domestic. Learn to split your mind in order to communicate with them. Balance your mind in theirs if you want to win races. Establish trust. Wendel came into himself training horses. The sweet feel of winning seduced him, erasing his past, beckoning his future.

By ten o'clock his pacing began to aggravate the horses. Some of them pinned their ears and lunged at him as he strolled by their stall doors. They treasured the peace and quiet to which they'd become accustomed. On some passes by he would moan aloud. Other thoughts wiped a silly smile across his weary face—a recollection of a win or gamble done right. Memory both haunted and amused him. Another train whistle scattered off the empty grandstand. The year of ranching had not quite cleared the Playfair life.

Wendel played the arguments through his head one more time. Horseracing was at its end, right? He'd made the right move going to the ranch, no? He was exhausted from driving all night and fretting all morning—the broken-family pain taking its toll. He winced at the thought of confronting his wife, of being confronted by her. Fear sent him back into the dark safety of the tackroom. He latched the door, stuffed some leg wraps in a feedbag for a pillow, and flopped down his memory-worn mind. He tried to focus on the possibility of a happy day with his daughter. Five minutes passed into nothingness, and then into dreams... humpback salmon leaped their way up Spokane Falls, their bodies dissolving in the mist of a fictive return.

Chapter 16

LEGMAN

Doctor Richard Higgenbotham pulled at the tackroom handle. Jammed? Locked? The pert-dressed man rattled the door thinking it odd to be locked from within. Mitcheltree's tackroom was never locked. Not that it was wise to leave it unlocked, that was just how the trainer operated. Paul Mitcheltree wasn't one to secure material things. He'd been Wendel's right hand man for years, and now he ran the stable. As head trainer it was his prerogative to leave doors unlocked.

Doc stood at the door staring at Mitch's name crudely carved across the transom—Mitcheltree. Quite a handle, Doctor Higgenbotham thought. A name like that must have a past. What in the world was a Mitcheltree? No matter, the question at hand was who'd locked himself inside Mitcheltree's tackroom. Doc sensed the presence... he thought he heard a certain snoring within. No—couldn't be him, just couldn't be Ingraham. Painless Higgenbotham tilted back his 10X Stetson cowboy hat and grabbed his chin to think the situation over. He cogitated in this same manner when diagnosing lameness in horses, a certain upward tilt of the high-styled Stetson, a certain fingering of the chin. Who other than Wendel Ingraham could have returned? No one. It had to be him. He'd intuited something significant would happen today when he awoke senselessly late. He knew the Marathon Man Ingraham as the runner he was, a horseman destined to return, to never quit certain things.

The doctor saw that the horses had been fed and knew then that it must be Wendel in the tackroom. He dragged a bale of hay into the sun and sat down. The veterinarian was a tall lanky man, his face wrinkled by time done inside a horse, the surgical time that eventually wears all horsedoctors down. It's not the needle that takes the doctor in the end, but the scalpel. His breathing shallowed as he contemplated the consequences of Wendel's return. There was more than veterinary medicine at stake this morning. Higgenbotham collected himself and tried to slow his breathing. He became acutely aware of the disarray within. A magpie dropped out of the sky and hopped before him, squawking, explaining something the good doctor would never understand.

Wendel will be happy to hear about all the winning his big horse did since he left, Dick Higgenbotham told himself, trying to divert the more important matter at hand. He remembered what Wendel told him the day he hired him on as stable vet. 'Speak to no one about my horses' legs and you'll do my vetwork forever.' Wendel stressed confidentiality, a trustworthiness Doc had upheld in all matters veterinary. Doc tapped his chin and licked his chapped lips, wondering if the Marathon Man still drank? He sniffed at the door, no hint of alcohol. Oh, how he missed that aroma, the liquorious texture of air that allowed him that first space with Willow.

The last information Higgenbotham had heard regarding Wendel's travels came from an exercise girl that arrived a month or so after Wendel split, well over a year ago now—a certain Nan, as Doc recalled, the one who swooped in and hustled morning gallops like she'd been exercising at Longacres all season. But she hadn't been as far as anyone knew. She came out of nowhere, which is an odd place for exercise girls to appear from at Playfair. Triplett took her on for a full week, happy to be legging up such a beautiful thing. She could gallop a horse all right, and connectingly. Of course Triplett wouldn't have had it any other way, good-looker or not. After he got comfortable with her ability she admitted to be looking for one Wendel Ingraham—claimed she needed him to train some big horses, some Kentucky stuff. Triplett chuckled and took a drag of his cigarette. 'Don't hold your breath on that one,' he advised. When Wendel didn't materialize, and no one offered to fork over any info that might materialize him, she thanked Bo Triplett and left Playfair, but not before running smack into Willow.

When Willow heard the woman's request for her estranged husband's services she wasn't too happy. Of course the ever-present Doctor Dick was front and center to comfort Willow at the time. He recalled his not-so-noble intentions and the breathing he'd meticulously restored shallowed. Something in his chest tightened as he sat on the bale of hay in the morning Playfair sun. Sweat popped through his aftershave, scenting the air with Old Spice. He stood and walked to the tackroom door and stared at Mitcheltree's engraved name on the threshold before him, tall a man as he was.

"Wendel? That you in there? Wendel Ingraham I say..." Knock, knock, rap rap.

Nothing.

He kicked the bottom of the door with his boot. "It's your old pal Doc Higgy. Answer if you're in there." The racket worked its way into Wendel's dream. Higgenbotham put his ear to the door. Soundless. "What's wrong. You okay in there or what?" Higgenbotham headed out of the Mitcheltree shedrow. He strode to the racetrack and looked at the empty grandstand. He returned and bickered with the handle some more, trying to convince himself that the door somehow accidentally locked itself and no one was in there. As he stood there, his tic started in. First his cheek began to twitch, and then an eyelid. He made a move away from the door, heading to his truck for some medication. A bumping inside the room stopped him in his tracks. Doc stopped and wiped his watery eyes before turning around. The door opened—a wiry arm reached some water from Dharma Bum's waterpail and splashed it in his face. An electric heater sung galvanically from within. Warmth and the odor of used leather spilled out the door, but no hint of whiskey.

Doc stepped forward for a better look—Marathon Man Ingraham indeed.

"What's this? You'll start a fire," he said sidestepping past Wendel, who did not seem to notice. "How you been?" Doc asked, his voice muffled within the room as he rubbled through a mess of tack to unplug the electric heater. A spark flashed and the orange helixes of the heater faded to a slate gray. Doc stumbled back into the shedrow. "'Bout time you showed up. Where you been so long?"

Wendel looked at him but did not answer.

"You were a fool to leave," Doc managed. "Could have had it all if you'd stuck around."

Wendel gave him the eye.

"I'm telling ya, you could've gone big time by now, Wendel. There's the horse. He did it all." He nodded toward Dharma.

Big time, Wendel thought—Longacres, Tanforan, Del

Mar—that big time? And Doctor Dick still peddling his wares here in Bushville? Ha. He hadn't expected the stable vet to be the one welcoming him back to his old shedrow, hadn't thought two seconds about Higgenbotham since he'd left. Maybe he should have. Doc asked Wendel some weather questions, but Wendel had nothing to discuss with the man about weather. Where the hell was Mitch? He was the one supposed to be running this stable, not the veterinarian here.

Doc Higgy gave Wendel his usual vetting. He assessed the former trainer's weight and color, analyzed his demeanor and carriage, comparing today's features with those clearly remembered from a year ago. Everything looked a damn sight better, he had to admit. Wipe off the sleep and Wendel looked vital as he ever had, a man fit to ride. If anything, the missing year had thickened his bones. "You sure look healthy," Doc said, in summary. "Looks like you've been hard at it."

Wendel ducked into the big horse's stall and rubbed Dharma Bum's hip. The horse looked back to him, approving the knead, curling his upper lip. Wendel inhaled the strawy aroma, ignoring Doc's prattle. The man's nerviness unstrung the horse and Wendel, his voice unsettling.

"Back to visit your daughter are you?"

Wendel kept massaging Dharma's whorlbone.

"She's quite a cutie."

Wendel felt himself begin to tingle.

"How's the horse look to you?" Doc asked. "Case you didn't know, he's been running down everything in sight, winning races in Seattle and Portland. Big races."

Wendel felt like cuffing the lanky man. But lightning, or some memory of lightning paralyzed him, and he remained standing in the stall.

"Great runner there, ol' Bum. Yes siree."

Runner. Bum. The words rang Wendel's ears. Doc had watched Dharma Bum ignite Wendel's career. He'd vetted the horse the morning he won the Spokane Futurity, good medicine and oh what a futurity run, Doc Dick shadow to it all—shadow still. Before Wendel departed Playfair he had signed Dharma Bum over to his daughter. He recalled personally giving the papers to Doc Higgy to deliver to his disenchanted wife, Doc happy to accommodate the favor. The possibilities became clearer to Wendel, a logic rising out of this memory.

"Things haven't gone so well here lately though, as you can see. Bum's the last stakes horse stabled at Playfair. All the other big runners have left," he continued. "Yup, everybody with runners is shipping out, most going to the new track in Seattle where Dharma ran big last summer. Emerald Downs, you know. That new track on the coast." Doc was full of information, determined Wendel get the picture of how things stood with the horse. Wendel knew Emerald Downs well enough, a converted wetland, red tin barns, synthetic shelter from the coastal monsoons. Longacres, the good-old-days Seattle track was his preference—a spacious expanse with roomy stalls and peaceful treeshade, Saratoga-like. It shut down a few years earlier, shadowing Playfair's demise.

Doc babbled on, filling in more details. "Bum kept right on running after you left, a real champ." Wendel wasn't surprised. "We trained here and vanned to the coast for the big races. He won the New Track Mile under a full inch of rain." Bum liked mud, the deeper the better, his cupped feet, feet molded by Wendel over the years. "Pocketed a huge purse on that one, Grade II action. Whoo," Doc said.

No wonder there were no searches for Wendel or legal requests for money, Dharma had been faithfully financing his absence. Some horse. Some vet. Doc related more news—good and bad—something suspicious hid under it all, something ugly. "Won two more big ones after that; the Space Needle Handicap and the Mukilteo Mile. Then we shipped down to Portland with him to run second in the Columbia Handicap. More mud. Another second in Seattle early this spring. He needs this rest. We're thinking bigger, now. East, maybe. Detroit, Cleveland."

Doc moved to personal details. Daughter Trish was a well kept child because of this horse Wendel bred and raised and formerly owned and trained. Despite Wendel's last request, Dharma Bum was apparently put in Willow's name rather than his daughter's. "He's become a golden goose," Doc explained, everyone waiting for another big race, another big payoff. "There's talk of California." Oh Christ, Wendel thought, not California. Horses run so hard and it all ends with a bad step on those hard tracks. At least the money was going to a good cause; Trish taken care of, the wife well-heeled, Mitcheltree getting his 10% and a hefty monthly training fee. Doctor Dick getting his cut in hop and block and Wendel wondered what else. Dharma Bum had provided well in his absence, the horse rising to the task, securing the dream after Wendel fled the loop. Such is racing luck.

"Your wife said it was good luck you named the horse Dharma; good luck for her and Trish with you gone."

"Pretty good luck for yourself as well, eh Doc?" Wendel said, whiffing a rat.

Higgenbotham sucked the air through his lips. "Yeah. I s'pose so."

"My daughter, has she been happy?" Wendel asked, not yet fully resigned to the unimaginable replacement that stood before him.

"Happy as a filly out to pasture. A sight to see."

"And the wife, I suppose she's a sight as well?"

"Willow?"

"That's right, Doc. My wife, Willow."

Doc slowed down his talk, spaces fell between his words. "Pretty as ever," he said, paling. "I better get back and clean the stalls."

"You better do that," Wendel said. He took a deep breath through his nostrils. Blooming lilacs softened the smack of hackneyed metropolitan air.

A horse whinnied.

Chapter 17

GENTLEMAN

Wendel ditched the gibbering Doc and found himself sandwiched in the jilted payphone booth at the backside entrance. The past buzzed in his ears, an amplified dial tone. He felt dizzy. The trip, the sweaty sleep, Doc's curious behavior—a renewal of worry. Wendel needed salt, sugar, and fluids, and wouldn't a sup of whiskey taste good.

The narrow booth propped him upright, eye level with all the scribbled numbers. He wiped the receiver on his shirt and dialed up his old Spokane number. Memory pushed the buttons, an automatic finger. A cyber beep followed by a recorded message—'The number you have dialed has been changed. The new number is 586-6666. Please note this in your telephone directory.'

Doc sauntered past. What now? The man seemed glued to Wendel's return. This phonebooth appearance nailed it down for Wendel—Doc and... Doc and Willow? No. Never.

'Once again the new number is 586-6666.' With a smooth number full of sixes Willow had started up a travel agency, Bum having amassed her an adequate starter fortune. She'd always wanted a business to call her own, an identity, a life. Now it sounded as if she had one. Wendel understood it was a substitute for something else, something Wendel could not fulfill, did not fulfill. More than a travel agency, she had wanted a husband who related, someone who paid unending attention to her. Something—despite sincere effort—Wendel could not accomplish.

He dialed the new number.

Willow's line purred in his ear.

"Hello, Ace Travel, Willow speaking. Where might I send you today?"

The word Ace mesmerized him, her peculiar way of hissing the letter C. Wendel struggled to say something, anything, anxious to identify himself and talk to her, his wife. "Hello," she said, as if the call might be a dead ringer.

"Yes, Willow."

"Wendel? Is that you, Wendel?"

"It's me."

"Where in the world are you?"

"In town."

"Wendel Ingraham, returned?"

"That's right. Doc Higgy met me at the stable. Quite a welcome."

"What can we at Ace Travel do for you?"

Wendel gritted his teeth. "Maybe an outing with Trish."

"You've come to see her, then?"

"I have, yes. I've come to be with my daughter."

"She hardly knows you, Wendel." He felt himself losing his grip on the situation. "If it wasn't for me she wouldn't even know she had a father."

"I came here to try and remedy that, Willow." Wendel slumped in the booth, attempting to muffle any pain that might be leaking from his throat. The phone caught him halfway down, hooking him like a fish. He pushed himself

131

upward. "Perhaps I could take her to supper." Silence on the line. "Supper, you know, a meal together or something," he added. He could hear Willow breathe.

"Well," she said, after a pause, "that might work. She does ask about you." Silence again. "I finish up here at six. Why don't you," she began to say the words slowly, as if she wrote as she spoke, "pick her up at seven, 1488 South 20th, the South Hill, straight above Playfair. 1488 South 20th? You got that? Have her back home by nine, her bedtime."

"Fine."

"She likes that new pizza place by the Fireside—there's kids' stuff, a playhouse and slide." Her instructions sounded rehearsed.

"Still calling all the shots are you, Willow, down to every last detail?"

"Oh, cut the crap, Wendel. Other than Trish, we're history."

"And some history it was."

"Some historian, you."

They stopped their old game, caught up by it—a few wordless seconds listening to one another's heartbeats. "History, yes, everyone has a history. Fine. But let's be nice. For Trish's sake," he asked, "just be nice."

"You be nice, too. None of that subtle shit you're so famous for."

"What subtle shit?"

"You know what I mean, Wendel. You may think you don't connive, but you do, and I'm not putting up with it, ever again."

"Okay, whatever." Wendel felt delirious at the prospect of seeing Trish. 1488 South 20th. He wanted this conversation over. He looked out of the booth. Higgy wandered about pretending to need the phone next, listening even, the prick. Wendel gave Doc Higgy the eye as Willow spoke, opening the booth door and waving the receiver toward him to assist his attempt to overhear. "We'll talk tomorrow," Willow declared. "Lunch at the cafe across the street from your old cardroom, the only decent place in town they sell Jim Beam."

"I think it's time to say goodbye, Willow. Your place. 6:30."

"Our place. Seven. Goodbye." Clunk.

Our place? The clunk bracketed a sudden silence. Our place—possessive plural. Wendel slowly gathered it together, 'our place' he said to himself, looking at Higgenbotham and his contrite little smile. Painless Higgenbotham my eye. Wendel felt himself delaminate. He dropped the phone. Dick Higgenbotham DVM. The phone twirled, upside-down. Buzzing. Buzzing until a computer voice erupted, "If you would like to make another call, please hang up and dial again." Wendel retrieved the phone and hung it up. Doc had turned and was walking away. Wendel stepped out of the booth.

"Did you need the phone, Doc?" he yelled. Doc turned around, his face pale. "She's all yours." Wendel gestured at the booth, the fury of cuckold realization fully upon him. His mouth felt dry. His back ached. He couldn't really feel his hands as he rubbed them together. Until now he hadn't thought of his wife's life so much as he had his daughter's. Suddenly Willow felt like no wife at all. Doc loomed as her new man, welcome as the plague. Something inside of Wendel died.

"No, Wendel, don't need the phone. I need you to come take a feel of Bum's back." Higgenbotham shuffled about avoiding eye contact with Wendel.

Bum's back. Right. The doctor needs the trainer to take a look at the horse's back. Wendel felt stupid and sick. A drink,

133

he definitely needed a drink. The horsedoctor's been fucking my wife! Wendel collected himself best he could. "So you've finally moved up in the world, eh doctor? The South Hill? Who mows your lawn? My wife?" He reined in a desire to sucker punch the weasel dick, despite the man being nearly a half foot taller than him. For the first time Wendel felt the burden of dissolution, painful stuff with another man in the saddle. He found himself in the middle of a river he couldn't swim. Too winded to swim, he could hardly breath.

The late-arriving trainers crept to their stables. Everyone waved at Wendel until they saw Doc meekly standing in the shadows beside him. Their faces expressed Wendel's just-figured story plain and simple. Someone's boffing someone else's wife, and the someone else just figured it out. Wendel now knew what the whole world had known for a year. With this knowledge settling in, his rage diminished. Wendel experienced an odd relief, a burden lifted—Willow suddenly Doctor Dick's responsibility, not his, but not so the daughter. Nonetheless, Wendel could hardly fathom the realization that the vet, his trusted horsedoctor, was screwing his wife. Traffic stirred the spittle and scum collected in the big pothole of dirty water near the track entrance. Wendel stared at the agitated water. The next vehicle hit the hole head-on and splashed his pants.

"She told you about me?" Doc asked, watching Wendel's clenched fist like a hawk.

"In her way." Wendel recalled how Doc had always adored Willow. This all made perfect sense. Doc didn't drink, maybe an occasional touch from his black bag to keep the racetrack madness at bay. Doc was waiting there for Willow the day Wendel split, a better man than he, a better man for her. Wendel remembered how much time the two had been spending together before he left, Willow always there to hold the horses when Docky came to vet them. What the hell, Wendel thought, it was better to have Doc hanging around little Trish than some stranger he didn't even know.

However Wendel squared the situation, it hurt like hell. Doc didn't say a word, the sorry low-life bastard. He stood there waiting to receive the punch that never flew. Wendel turned back to the barn, words becoming impossible. He tried to walk tall, but the cuckold weight slumped him. Maybe he still loved Willow. He felt helpless, betrayed. If you can't do anything about something, he told himself, you have to grin and bear it. He tried, but all this was hardly bearable. Everyone had his own cross to bear, and now Doc bore Willow's, and not Wendel. The man really didn't have a bad bone in his body. Wendel regretted the notion of clocking him. Trish was who mattered most. Maybe someday Wendel could relate to Doc about Trish, maybe Doc would someday help with his daughter.

From a safe distance Doc sheepishly followed Wendel back to the stable. At the shedrow Doc stilted about, eyes distant, feet scuffling. Wendel paced around not knowing what to do with his body, let alone his mind. Mitcheltree arrived amidst the angst, and began busying himself with the horses. He could see Wendel's predicament, the desperation to repossess a child while confronting the someone who had taken his place as father. Mitch saw the trapped-animal look in Wendel's eyes. Mitch's displaced parenthood and husbandhood weren't that far removed. He didn't envy the scene. He waited in the company of his horses, reluctant to throw in. Involvement in this mess was not his forté. Doc had moved on, attending to the few horses across the way. Wendel paced up and down the

135

shedrow agitating the horses and wearing deeper the groove he'd started that morning. Mitch brought out Dharma Bum for his daily massage.

Doc came back over when he saw the red horse cross-tied in the shedrow. Mitcheltree shook some drops of liniment into his hand from a small blue bottle and started massaging the horse's back behind his withers. Wormwood penetrated the air, a relaxing aroma that seemed to draw Doc closer. The horse pinned his ears as the tall man approached, as if to share Wendel's displeasure with the needler. Wendel couldn't keep to any one spot. He walked around the horse, eyeing each angle of every leg. Doc backed off to let Wendel take his look. Wendel circled to the front end, hands to hips, looking. He nodded at the front feet, pointing out overgrown hoof—a sign of faulty husbandry. No hoof, no horse. No woman, no cry.

The horse's feet needed attention. Wendel grabbed the shoeing tools and pulled the left front shoe and trimmed the foot. "I think you should leave him barefoot awhile," he told Mitch. The trainer nodded in agreement. Doc's expression seemed to indicate he thought Wendel was making a mistake leaving the horse barefoot, but the two horsemen knew better. Wendel moved to a hind foot, and then on around. Mitch held the horse as Doc handed Wendel hoof knives and nippers as requested. The three men and the horse briefly faded into the rasping and smoothing of hooves. Doc felt relief, watching Wendel's attentions shift from woman to horse. Mitch was glad a fistfight hadn't erupted. "We're a little behind with the hoofcare, I guess," Doc said, for lack of anything less obvious to say. "—a shortage of shoers, you know."

"No shortage of men in waiting, though, eh, Doc?" Wendel

quipped, sweat dripping off his nose.

"Just trim the feet, Wendel," Mitch interceded. "Docky was on to Willow before your train ever left town. One of those things. Everyone knew it. If you'd been half lucid you'd a seen it coming yourself." Mitch rubbed Bum's neck as he talked, calmingly. "Let's clear out the bullshit right now. We got a runner here and we need to keep him fit—somehow, somewhere. Rest is all fine and dandy, but we don't want him softening up. He's the best horse we got left. If he stops running our stable is finished. You two knock off your woman shit. It's not like this is some big fucking surprise."

Doc sulked, silent.

Wendel pared out the last frog, the right front, his knuckles white.

"It's a pretty simple story, between you two," Mitcheltree proffered. "An old story. The triangle thing." —whoosh-wish, hoosh-wish, whoosh-wish, hoosh-wish went Wendel's rasp over Dharma Bum's hoof. It was not the simple story to Wendel that it was to Mitcheltree. Mitch didn't mince words. The sermon he sang was not the one he wanted to hear. Nonetheless, it brought him to his senses in the Willow regard. Wendel set the fourth foot to the ground, and stood up to take some deep breaths. Mitcheltree put Dharma back in his stall and stepped into the tack room and clinked through the box of camphorous leg liniments and breathing compounds. He found what he was looking for and tossed Wendel a dust-stuck bottle. It seemed to float through the air, arcing through the shedrow in a slow twirl until Wendel's hand snatched it out of flight. He held the bottle to the sun to determine what might be inside. He opened and smelled. It was whiskey and not liniment. Without partaking, Marathon Man rescrewed the

137

lid and tossed the bottle back across the shedrow. Mitch, reminded of a horse called Fly Whiskey Fly, caught it and tossed the bottle back into the footlocker.

"So who owns Dharma Bum these days?" Wendel asked, "I left him to my daughter when I left. Is he still hers?"

"Sure," said Doc. "Dharma is hers, Trish's for sure. A few technicalities with the paperwork, her being a minor and all, but the horse is hers all right. Sure enough yes he is. Don't you worry about that."

"Let's just refer to him as *our* horse for now, Doc," Mitch said. "We're thinking Saratoga, Wendel—that dream world Saratoga, the trees and all the glory you always told us all about." Mitch laid out his plan to get the horse up to snuff in order to become eligible for the Travers. Wendel became lost in the idea. Mitch broke a bale of hay and distributed flakes down the shedrow as he explained the strategy.

"You have the races figured to get there, then, all the stepping stones?" Wendel asked, after an interlude of contemplation.

"Yeah, well, we're working on it."

"He's in Willow's name?"

"I don't know who owns the horse officially, Wendel, but I do know Willow's been signing the checks. She calls the shots. Seems I work for her these days."

So Saratoga had rubbed off on Willow. She *had* realized Wendel's secret aspirations, one of them anyway. "The Travers, that's some plan," Wendel said.

"Your idea and you know it," Mitch said.

Saratoga seemed reachable ever since Dharma Bum won the Playfair Mile last summer, breaking the track record. Turbulator, the previous record holder, had gone from the Playfair Mile to the Travers and run a third in the signature race of the classic Saratoga meet. Quite a show. A little known fact Wendel shared with Mitch long ago. Wendel remembered telling Mitch if Dharma ever won the Playfair Mile they would go east with the runner. But Wendel hadn't won the Playfair Mile with Dharma Bum, Mitcheltree had after Wendel departed; Mitcheltree, Wendel's wife, and the stable vet: R. W. Higgenbotham DVM. The only official participation accorded Wendel Ingraham was as breeder of Dharma Bum. Breeder, there it was, Mitch pointing out Wendel's name on the *Racing Form* clipping stapled next to the door of Dharma's stall from his Playfair Mile win—

Dharma Bum Montana bred
Trainer: Paul Mitcheltree
Owner: Willow MoonChild Ingraham
Breeder: Wendel Ingraham

"Too bad they don't mention the vet, eh Docky?" Wendel said.

"Get over it, Wendel," Mitch snapped. "We all know you set Dharma up to run and win that Mile, okay. If you wanna stay in on the horse's journey, wise up. I ain't putting up with any shit between you and Docky. Drop it. We're talking horse here, not wife or daughter or anything else."

"We're talking all of that, now aren't we Doc?" Wendel countered.

Mitcheltree retrieved the whiskey and took a sip, coughed, and passed the bottle to Doc, who refused to partake. Wendel snatched the bottle and feigned a drink before spilling its contents onto the shedrow. He felt tired and hungry. He needed food, sugar. Coffee maybe. Something. Horseracing was suddenly too much, whiskey spilled too hastily. He felt empty and displaced. Mitcheltree hurt to see Wendel feel it. He told Doc to finish the chores and dragged Wendel off the backside, away from his wife's man.

They slipped out a hole in the fence into the parking lot. Mitcheltree fired up his pick-up, the engine snapping to a loud life. The chassis sagged under an overhead camper, Mitch's home sweet home. They drove to the Mayfair Café. An inner-city qualm greeted Wendel as they ducked into the back door and took their usual booth in the back near the lounge. Wendel brushed straw off his pantlegs and sat down. He looked across the table at Mitcheltree. He wore the same stained straw hat and was missing the same front tooth, a perpetual three-day beard, a gaunt, skinny man. Mitch lit a cigarette and blew smoke across the table. "Cough up what's bothering ya fella. Get it out, right here an' now."

Wendel didn't feel like coughing anything up. Between the horses and Doctor Dick, he'd gotten everything out of his system that he needed to back at the stable. Mitch's L&M cigarette curled blue smoke into the smell of deep-fried chicken. Mitch went over the racehorse year past for Wendel, just as Docky had—the wins and places and shows, in that order, and now the empty dates. The cig hung at the edge of Mitch's mouth, jumping as he talked, a trapeze act of words and smoke. The fumes burned Wendel's tired eyes. Itinerant odors channeled by their booth like street people, each whiff a note of some murky Spokane past.

"What ever happened to Ingraham the poet?" Mitch asked, smiling. "That Japanese stuff Akifumi taught you always cheered everyone up. When horses wouldn't run and times were tough, I remember you arriving before sunrise reciting nature poems you'd dreamt up the night before, versing from your heart." Wendel's recitations had lifted the moods of Playfair past, something about his soft cadence soothed horses and people alike. Mitch knew poetry could cheer Wendel up. He kicked at him under the table. Wendel gripped the outside edge of the table and pulled himself upright, still unwilling to say much. "Anything I can do for you, Wendel?" Mitch asked, snuffing out the cigarette. "Anything you need?"

"Reassurance you'll get on a little better with the horses. I want someone there in the morning before sunrise. The horses expect you there, need you there then. Whether there's racing or not, you still gotta be there first thing. Stalled animals hate to wait. It darkens their heart."

Mitch tapped the pack of cigarettes hanging in his shirt pocket making sure the next smoke was there. A silence lingered between the two men. Mitch didn't like criticism, especially when he knew it was valid. He pushed the pack of smokes out of his pocket, rolling the package down his arm to his waiting palm to poke up a cig. He nabbed it with his other hand, rolled the cigarette through his fingers in a slight of magic, and tossed it up to his yokel lips, catching the cigarette in his mouth. "Your daughter will cheer you up. Think of her seeing her pa." Mitch lit the cigarette with a flip and zip of his gold pocketworn lighter.

A smile settled on Wendel's road-weary face when he thought of Trish. The crinkles around his eyes went slack.

"What'll you sweeties have?" the waitress interrupted, pouring them coffee before she'd fully stopped walking. Wendel's cup had a remnant of lipstick below the rim. Coffee swirled over the rim, melting it.

"Steak sandwich, well-done, mashed potatoes, white gravy,

tomato juice, white bread." Mitch recited.

"Same for me. Steak rare, if you please."

The waitress grabbed Wendel's hand and squeezed it gently. "Good to see you, stranger. Good to see you made it back to see me."

"Good to see you again, too, Rachel. Thought you'd be working the Ridpath by now." Little beads of kitchen sweat glistened the brow below her bangs.

"Not me. I'm no dancer."

"You love it here, don't you?" Wendel asked.

"It's my life, sweetheart. I better love it."

Rachel slid silverware out of her apron onto the table and fled back to the kitchen, her hips shifting, nice hips. Wendel yearned for a life as simple as hers. Hers probably was not any simpler than his life though, not in this town, not in this café. The back of the place harbored a piano lounge.

"You should start eating your meat rare, Mitch," Wendel advised. "It'll counteract the poison in those L&Ms." Wendel didn't smoke or chew anymore. Chris and Bubbles had weaned him of that habit as well. Sunflower seeds and sweatbaths.

Chain-smoking in the Mayfair waiting for grub. What a life, what a horseman's life, Wendel thought. Metro horses, bullring horseplayers. Gambling. Wendel toothed the ice out of his water. He'd soon be with his daughter, he figured, and he needed fluids and nourishment to rise to the task. The food arrived, Rachel smiling, smiling and sweating. Hips. Salt and pepper. Mayonnaise.

"Anything else?" she asked, sliding her palms down her apron over her quads. "No?" Wendel watched her pump back to the kitchen. Mitch ate in his practiced rhythm, bite after bite. Dollops of mayonnaise, spits of Tabasco, volcanoes of ketchup.

More water. Pepper. Buttered bread, gravied bread. The food renewed Wendel's strength, first square in over a day. He finished and relaxed, nourished at last. Mitcheltree burped and smoked. Talk and chuckle echoed from the lounge, a hoot now and then. Rachel pranced back and forth, some of the hooting at her. Mitch settled their tab and left her a five-dollar tip. He drove Wendel back to the track, led him to the tack room and threw him a down pillow smelling of camphor and horse sweat. The horses ate quietly, munching their midday hay. Wendel stretched on the musty couch, laid his head back into the feathers, and slept.

Dreams took him to Saratoga Springs.

Horseracing dreams.

Chapter 18

NEWMAN

Dharma Bum rolled in the next stall. A hoof hit the tackroom wall splitting Wendel's dream. A gallant run to the finish ended when a crack overlaid the glory. Just as his dream horse surged into the front-running pack—snap—the haunting sound of shattering bone gashed the race, a broken leg cutting short an accelerated stretch run. Nightmare. A horse down, two others down behind. Jockeys fly. Wendel cannot tell which horses go down, if one of them is his horse or not. A collective gasp uttered from the grandstand. The cypress and oak image of the Saratoga Springs backside splashes into redness, redness pierced by shards of angry bone… Wendel sat up, dizzy and deluded. He smacked his lips, licking his teeth to clear the film of tackroom grit. The bitter taste of nightmare needed a thorough tonguing. His fantasy of Saratoga hadn't included broken legs. Dharma Bum's wake-up knock cut short Saratoga, broken legs breaking a broken dream. Wendel suddenly longed for the grassy reaches of Montana. He'd come to treasure that safe space. He lifted his arms above his head and stretched his stiff back.

He grabbed his toothbrush and knapsack and headed for the showers. On his way he stopped to drink from a shedrow faucet. The processed water nettled his taste buds. The crack of the snapped leg peddled his heart. He rinsed his mouth, gargled, and spit before gulping some hefty drinks to flush his system. The chlorinated nudge of Spokane municipal water wakened him fully. He entered the backside latrine and paused in the room's stink. Stagnant water charged dank air. Toadstool slime marbled up the wooden walls. Light worked through a hole near the floor illuminating the disgust. He considered that perhaps a shower here wouldn't make him feel any better, not to mention smell any better. Nonetheless he turned on the specific shower he remembered to have the best pressure. Hot water spurted out in a solid stream. The room steamed as water played across the cold floor scattering straw and horseshit. He had to fish out all sorts of horse hockey out of the drain to get it flowing. He propped open the door for ventilation like so many times before. The rush of new air diluted the stench. He tested the temperature with his knuckles, turned up the hot and stepped under. Pounding water limbered his back and relaxed his mind. If it was the same water heater from last year he'd get ten minutes of heat.

He pained for his little girl. What's a feller to do for two and a half hours with a six-year-old daughter he hasn't seen in over a year? Maybe Triplett could guide him out of absentee fatherhood. He knew most things about track life. Would fatherhood be part of his repertoire? Probably. Wendel's head raced. How would things go with Willow and Doc? Triplett could help. Wendel soaped off and stood in the water until the heat faded. He felt good after the shower, the cold feeling of impending divorce temporarily quelled.

His desire to set things straight boiled down to sustaining a relationship with his daughter. He rummaged out crumpled clothes from his bag and hung them in the steamy room to soften the wrinkles. He wanted to look good for his little girl. He jumped into his road jeans and wandered toward Triplett's barn. The afternoon horse crowd moped about finishing chores for the day. Wendel avoided everyone he could, dipped into Triplett's shedrow and slid into the dimlit tack room. Triplett was neither surprised nor impressed with Wendel's return, only happy to see his smile.

"Wendel my man, welcome back. Montana's treated you well, it seems. You look good."

"You too, Bo. Good to see ya." But Bo didn't look good.

"It's winters that keeps you young, ranching winters. I can tell you've been ranching, you lucky bastard. And me stuck in a tackroom in a city. No races to boot. Hot damn it's good to see you. Tell me about your new life!" Triplett sat on his bed which served as couch by day. As he talked he snapped his suspenders, fingering them up and down his paunch. Triplett was truly interested in Wendel's well being.

Triplett fumbled around as Wendel's eyes adjusted to the dim light. He located and lit a filterless Pall Mall and inhaled an incredible drag of smoke. He stood and folded a little kitchen off the wall, lit a flame on the portable propane burner to reboil cold coffee, puffed and exhaled. He laid out sandwich makings from an icebox. While Bo prepared the fixings, Wendel looked around the room. What a place to live, such a hemmed-in existence compared to the Walking Box. Triplett's smoke inundated the seedy decor. Wendel wished for air, for open space. He fled to his childhood. A small room déjà vued somewhere, a room like this. Triplett's easy presence allowed him to explore this remembrance. Too often during the past year he had felt afraid to look back. Here he could search freely. Here

146

Bo shared life with him like a father might, and in Bo a father he sought.

Wendel thought of his own dad, his real dad. He'd taught Wendel as best he could when he had the chance. Turned out over time they would share a lot of life experience. Neither had done well in family affairs. Wendel figured his dad taught him as best he could in *what little time they'd had*. His words of wisdom were few, but Wendel remembered 'Look people in the eye when you talk to them, more importantly when you listen. Spend more time listening than talking.' He clearly remembered his father reiterating the virtues of listening, 'When things heat up remember to listen son. I've been around and know you'll get farthest by listening to people. Keep quiet and listen. Some spontaneous thoughts are not fit to be uttered. Be careful with your words.' Wendel thought of this and looked into the grotto of darkness beneath Bo's hat brim. Rheumy eyes swam in a wizened wetness. Clinging tears radiated a glaze that penetrated the room's darkness, a sparkle to Bo's eyes. Wendel knew better than to speak. He didn't have to say a thing, not here. He was lost in thought and Triplett knew it, incited it. They sat in contemplative silence—their minds tended by horse movements; hoof stomps, nickers and neighs—music to them, equine music quieting the clatter of their lives.

"So tell me what's up," Bo finally said after the silence had served its purpose.

"Montana, Bo. I've been horsin' around Montana under that Chinook arch we always used to talk about." Wendel whittled at his fingernails with his pocketknife.

"Back with wind, then? That clean country?"

"That's right, Blackfeet rez, Glacier County. The place

of my raising."

"No Chinooks here in Spokane. A wet cold all last winter. Racing's gone. It won't be back. Not like before." He lit another cigarette. "You made it out just in time."

Wendel squinted to see the expression in Bo's deep face, but years of post-war emotionlessness masked any meaningful gesture. "I like ranching Bo. I do."

"Well you should. It's the last true life, Wendel. Mark my word. For a feller like you ranching's the thing. Yes siree bob." Bo tipped his hat back. A sudden smile wiped the slate of war off his face. He looked Wendel in the eye, and Wendel looked him in the eye back, listening. "Forget this track life. If you have a ranch, best you ranch it. Me and Alice, we'd be out of here if we'd anyplace decent to go, especially if it was a ranch. But we don't got no ranch, nothing close to it. We're stuck here making the best of what's left of Playfair horseracing, which ain't much. No siree bob." Bo took another drag, the stertor of ill-health apparent. For one seemingly at peace with the world and so outgoing toward others, Wendel found it disturbing Bo smoked incessantly. Said he'd started cigs in the war, and until the war left smoking would stay. "Want a cinnamon roll for dessert? Alice baked 'em fresh this morning." He hacked out an extended cough. Living in a barn of brotherly horses hadn't dissuaded the habit. Smoke. Smoke and fire. Triplett knew how horses hated fire, but that didn't stop Triplett. Wendel winced at the fragility of the horses and men of Playfair.

"Thanks, but no, I just ate with Mitch. Mayfair grits. I'm headed to see my daughter."

"Great! You lucky son of a bitch. Wish I was young and lucky as you. Whole life ahead. A beautiful little girl and a ranch to bring her home to some day. What more could you ask for?"

"For that to happen. To bring her home to the ranch." Wendel didn't feel young.

"Someday, Wendel, someday. Be patient. Women things take an awful while to sift out. They have trouble letting go a things."

"The ranch isn't mine."

"So what. If you work a ranch it's as good as yours. These horses ain't mine, but they sure as hell think they're mine. Sure as hell, I'm theirs. That's what matters. If you work a ranch you own that ranch, the animal's own you plain and simple, and that's what you want. It's the whereabouts of your mind what counts, the ownership of your mind and heart. Know who you are. Own yourself and own any ranch you want."

Bo illuminated certain perspectives for Wendel. When Chief Spokane finished fourth in the Playfair Mile the year after he won it—half the Spokane Indian Nation treasury down the drain—Wendel was waiting at the stable to cool out the losing horse. Bo led the horse back smiling, god damn happy his runner had survived the brutal race. He knew winning the big race could only come once in a lifetime for a horse of his caliber. It was too much to expect Chief Spokane to win two in a row against vengeful competition hauled over from Seattle. They weren't going to let a common horse steal a win again. Class ran the Chief down that day, but in Trip's mind his horse was still a winner. 'Well at least it weren't the Kentucky Derby,' he said. 'He may not o' been the fastest horse out there, today, but he sure as hell was the happiest, I made sure o' that.' He laughed and waited for the Indians to show him their empty pockets. Triplett had them feeling good about running fourth by the time they left.

"You seen Willow, lately?" Wendel asked.

Trip smiled.

"There's plenty women in the world, Wendel. Don't fret over their scornings. I've seen Willow, you know I've seen Willow. Plenty. And speaking of scorned women, shortly after you skedaddled this beauty showed up looking for you. Introduced herself. Said you'd told her about me. A fine woman."

"Who you talking about?"

"Galloped horses for me for a good week. Got all my horses fit for the end of the meet. The little woman rode better 'n you. A beaming smile, a happy heart. A treat to have around. A real dandy, you know. Maybe she's your one. That Nan, what a peach!"

"Nan?" Wendel thought. "You mean Nancy."

"Told me Nan. Wanted to know where you were. Said she had some horses for you to train, some rich-blooded critters her folks claimed back east. I told her you were off chasing down your ranch roots. It's where I figured you was at. She milked me about you for all I was worth. Then she crossed paths with Willow. Went on her way when the sparks started flying."

"Sparks?"

"Yeah. Even Doc Higgy jumped into the fray."

"Higgy? Then what?"

"You can guess what, Wendel, but there's no guessing now. The man's had your wife bridled since you hit the road. I knew for sure when he came lanking around nosing into the Nan deal. Shit, I had to run his snoopy ass out of my stable.

He was making my horses nervous."

Wendel tried to piece together the twisted news, Nancy trying to track him down here.

"All this crap don't matter none, Wendel. Get up there and see your Trish, every time I seen her I told her all about her Daddy. She hears all about you everytime she's here. A great girl, mucks the stalls, waters and feeds, grooms all our horses. You'll always be a winner in her eyes. I've told her all about you being a winner, I tell her all the time."

Wendel was grateful Trip related him in a positive light to his daughter.

Bo continued. "Her little blue eyes glimmer at your name. Alice watches her for Willow a couple times a week. We made sure she'd never forget Daddy. See the smudge marks on the win picture with you and Bummer? Every time she visits us she wants to touch her daddy. I hung the picture up for her after you left."

Wendel had given Triplett a win picture from the Spokane Futurity—a photo fulfilling the destiny to keep his daughter connected to him. Wendel gave Triplett a handshake and a hug. Bo gave him his keys to his stock truck to go get his daughter. Wendel left feeling confident. All that was needed to completely vaporize the Spokane fog was to see his daughter. He wanted to be clean for her. He needed to rid himself of the cigarette stink from Triplett's tackroom. The sad clothes that waited in the shower clung to their wrinkles. He snapped them taut as he could and changed. He stepped outside and scrambled the four stories up the camera tower to take one last look at the track, accepting he most likely would never saddle a horse at Playfair again, finally comfortable with the notion.

The view from the tower revealed the hazy crawl of the city, the crazy haul of commerce that Spokane had become. Racetrack at rest, a greenspace in a sea of industry. No place for horse or horseman for long, no place for Wendel Ingraham. Crows squawked, plentiful in the grassy infield. Wendel took a last look, the Playfair grandstand yawning over the homestretch, empty. To the north flowed the inner-city Spokane River. Wendel could make out the cardboard homes of the bums hidden in the willows along the torpid flow. Below, Triplett lazed in his chair; disheveled, smoking, an old man dreaming of an old youth, always dreaming of something, dreaming of horses.

Fatherhood awaited Wendel Ingraham. He laddered down the tower and slipped out that same old hole in the fence to the parking lot.

Chapter 19

MILKMAN

Triplett's stock truck groused up the South Hill smudging the tonsured lawns of affluence with a patina of blue exhaust. The rig moaned, the streets steep. Wendel caught a lower gear, his noise abrading the peaceful neighborhoods of Playfair horseplayers who once bet on the horses he trained. At the top of the hill waited Willow and Doc's spiffy residence. The festooned driveway barely accommodated his rig. He cut the heaving motor, the timing off, the engine sputtering sacrilegiously until he dropped the clutch to end the quaking. He stepped out and approached the door—a thick door, hand-crafted wood, leaded glass. The thought struck him that he hadn't brought a gift. He'd always gotten in trouble from Willow for not bringing home gifts. Was he supposed to bring his daughter a gift for this, their reunion? He'd sent her Indian handicrafts from the Walking Box for Christmas, a starquilt Mabel Old Coyote stitched especially for the Trish she'd heard so much about. No gift today. Next time he would bring his daughter a gift.

He picked up and dropped the doorknocker, one clunk, a gilded horseshoe. Wendel waited for his daughter to appear. Willow half-opened the door to greet him, canting an eyebrow, sniffing the air about him. Doctor Higgenbotham sulked by behind, ice-clinking drink in hand. Wendel caught glimpses of shag carpet and horse art, Trish nowhere in sight.

"Where is she?" he asked. He wanted his daughter now, front and center. He needed her balance in this precipitous state he found himself.

"In her bedroom," Willow said. "Been looking out the window for you all day, ever since I told her you were coming for her. I've never seen a girl so excited."

Wendel bit his tongue. Willow turned to her Doctor Higgenbotham who stood towering behind her. "Richard, could you please bring Trish downstairs?" She held a sheaf of papers in her hand. As Doctor Dick pedaled upstairs she presented them to her husband. "Wendel, I want you to sign these before you leave with her." She narrowed her eyes and snugged her lips together.

Wendel sucked air through his teeth. He grabbed his long blond hair into a ponytail, Custer like. "Can't we take care of this stuff tomorrow?" His heart drubbed. He could feel the blood hammering through his chest and he didn't like the sensation one bit.

Willow squinted her determined eyes. She didn't look as Spokane as she used to look, her hair didn't as seem as rich a black, her skin as brown. She stepped back and with a swing of her torso curtly shouldered the door shut in his face—a heavy door, a complicated latching. Shut. Déjà vu, a nastiness she couldn't seem to help. He breathed deeply and slowly, the brass horseshoe kicking him in the face. For Trish's sake he'd try to forgive this nastiness, to understand and forgive. Attribute it to culture or upbringing, attribute it to himself.

The door reopened. Trish squeezed through her mother's legs, smiling, knowing—his little girl. "Daddy," she chirped, her voice a delightful music. Wendel brightened. Infused with euphoria, he knelt and swept his girl to him. In his arms she felt warm, warm and alive, so real, his daughter finally real again.

The world blurred.

The imperious voice above him faded.

"Hoolahan, hoolahan daddy, hoolahan!" Trish wanted a hoolahan, a vivid remnant of her father memory, a trick she had almost outgrown in his absence. They waltzed onto the lawn. Wendel put her strong little body before him and faced her away. She squealed with delight. He clasped his hands behind her upper arms and swung her between his legs—one, two, three, flipping her up, up and over and onto his shoulders, a 360 arm trapeze. Trish giggled with continuous glee. "More, more," she cried. He rolled her off his shoulders, 360° to the ground. She jumped and spun about to face him, her dress flaring, fatherly delight, innocence. Doc and Willow watched astonished by the girl's affinity for her dad. They backed into the shelter of their redbrick house waving limp-wristed goodbyes.

Wendel skipped his daughter across the lawn to the truck and scooted her aboard. He jumped in and twisted the key, the old stock truck a great excitement for a young girl. The motor rolled, a willing mesh of metal. Trish sat high, strapped in the passenger seat. They backed out of the driveway, the motion of fatherhood thrilling Ingraham, daughterhood enchanting Trish, their feelings grand. Wendel took her to a fine dining establishment, candlelights and flaming food. Trish was enchanted, prawns and rice and iced tea. Peas you ate in the shell. Waiters floated the food to them, one course after another. Piano music, Trish off to the piano between courses enchanted by the play. Back to her Dad to talk horses. One thing was clear to Trish. She understood Wendel's connection with horses, horse excitement her best memories of him. She knew when and where Bum had been winning big, she knew all the details. They talked and ate and listened to the grand piano. A crossroad world, a world they'd known otherwise, a debut father-daughter world.

By 9:30 Willow's fragile mind had began thinking kidnap, her salmon blood rising. About then Wendel and Trish returned. Trish hugged Dad goodbye and murmured, "Tomorrow Daddy, tomorrow again." Wendel hugged her tight, her arms slipping away, mother pulling, her little hands dragging over his shoulders. As he backed out of the driveway Willow wailed something at him, something that sounded like his name at the end of a blithered discourse. Though he couldn't understand the words, her nerves spilled into his. He stopped the truck and tried to roll down his window. It wouldn't come down so he opened the door to hear her out. By the time he put his hand to his ear she'd begun to speak clearly.

"I'll meet you at the Fireside in the morning. Ten o'clock." She waved the folder of legal papers, her offer of dissolution.

"Ten," Wendel answered, relieved they had communicated. He slammed the door, and angled back out of the driveway to descend the South Hill, motoring through the freeway poverty over I-90. He parked at the track and flopped in the tackroom. Seven hours sleep; daughter dreams. Woke around five, fed the horses and waited for Spokane's aluminum sun to rise. At six he walked to Triplett's to take coffee.

"Breakfast?" Triplett asked.

"Sure."

Bo unstrapped his kitchen from the wall. He pulled a toaster

156

oven from under his bed to broil lean rings of Canadian bacon. He scrambled eggs on some sort of Bunsen burner affair he used to distill liniments and breathing remedies, eggs from the chickens that kept Chief Spokane company, shedrow eggs, small and brown with sunbright yokes. They ate in silence, content with silence, silence coddled with horse noise they so enjoyed. Trip knew each noise, what each horse was up to from its noise—how everyone felt, how they would run if races were running. After his meal, Wendel slipped out of Triplett's smoke to clean the stalls. Triplett tidied up the breakfast doings and followed. An exercise boy waited on a straw bale in the warming sun. When Trip asked him to hop to he turned and complained of an injured back muscle. "Better get your little ass back to bed then," Triplett said, matter-of-factly. Blinded by the morning sun, he was not even quite sure which rider it was. "Wouldn't want anyone galloping with a sore back," he added. The little exercise rider limped away, properly humiliated. Bo nodded Wendel to the saddled and waiting thoroughbred. Wendel grabbed the reins and lifted his chin. Bo legged him up and pointed the colt to the track.

Wendel felt good in the irons. He galloped Bo's entire shedrow, an eager bunch who hadn't seen enough track lately. At 10:30 he realized Willow had been waiting for him at the Fireside Café since 10:00. He jumped off the last runner in a flying dismount and hurried off. "Willow's waiting," he said as Triplett shook his head. He gunned Bo's truck through the railyard hinterland and caught Willow just as she walked out of the cafe. "Sorry, ma'am."

"You fucker, Wendel. You've made me wait all my life. No more of this crap, this is it." She marched by in a tiff.

"I was galloping Trip's horses. Sorry. The sun's different in

157

Montana. You're an hour off here."

"Right. Doesn't take much to set you akilter. I forgot."

"C'mon. Let's go back inside."

Willow's eyes bounced, coffee-angered, memory-enraged—all the cleaning and cooking she'd done for the prick—the laundry, the handmaiding, the waiting and praying. She stormed back inside the café, her stride determined and reckless, this the last encounter, the last she'll ever have to have deal with the son of a bitch. She sat down, snorted, and pulled out the paperwork.

Wendel browsed the papers. "So you're sure?" he asked.

"Sure about what?"

"The divorce."

"Couldn't be surer."

"I'm not signing anything unless I'm certain Trish stays in my life."

"See her whenever you want. Within reason."

"*Within reason*? When were you or I ever 'within reason'?"

"I'm a reasonable woman, at least I was until you changed."

"I'm all for change, Willow, change for the better. Isn't that what we're supposed to be doing here? I'll be living in Montana. I'd like her for the rest of the spring and all of the summer. Is that reasonable?"

"What about school?"

"Kindergarten, is it?"

"Kindergarten is very important, you know."

"We'll continue in Browning, then. How's that?"

"Not on that reservation. I don't want her going to school there."

"*That* reservation? You still have problems with the Blackfeet don't you, some fancy dance lover from the Rocky Boy Pow

158

Wow ruined your perception of the Blackfeet Nation?"

"No," she lied.

"Look, it's been a year. I want her now, this spring and all summer. School time she'll be back with you ready for first grade."

"I suppose that's reasonable. Reasonable enough, provided you sign off on the rest of the custody stuff here." She folded her arms in front of her, high on her breasts. "Now, about the horse…" she began, with more emotion than when speaking of Trish's visitation with her father, perhaps that issue more settled in her mind than the horse. *The horse.*

The horse. Wendel did not answer.

"Do you want Dharma Bum, Wendel?"

"I gave the horse to Trish. He's hers."

"We've all talked it over. We keep last years winnings and the horse is yours."

" *'We've all'* talked it over?"

"Richard and I and our attorney."

Wendel clenched his jaw.

"It'll be best," she added.

"So you're signing my daughter's horse Bum back to me?"

"That's right. We keep last years winnings. You get the horse."

"What's the catch?" Wendel asked.

The Bum earned $322,000 for Willow, a sweet sum. She didn't want to part with a dime of it. "No catch. We keep the winnings. The horse is yours. Everyone's even."

"Even?" Wendel asked.

"Moneywise, I mean."

"Even-steven."

"Forever?"

159

"Forever."

(For better or worse, forever and ever. In sickness and in health, forever and ever.

Forever.)

(Connected by Trish forever.)

Wendel signed the papers, reading and understanding them, surprised at how reasonable and simple the legalese sounded, a tribal lawyer representing Willow, an Indian who understood fatherhood reasonably well. Wendel would be with his daughter each summer and get the big horse. Not another dime. Maybe there was more than the $322,000, something he didn't know about. Nonetheless, he signed off.

A new beginning, a clean slate, a good-bye handshake, Willow's hand pleasant, moneyed and pleasant. Before letting go he brought her knuckles to his lips and ever so gently kissed the skin on the back of her hand. She let it happen and then jerked her fingers away with a cute sort of disgust. She shuffled the legal papers together, flustered, unable to stack them evenly, difficulty fitting them in her briefcase. Briefcase, a Spokane Indian carting around a briefcase, divorce from a whiteman script. Mission accomplished, Willow strode outside. If there would have been dust in the café, Wendel would have been left in it. Instead he was left in a swirl of bacon smoke. Wendel watched Willow skip through the parking lot, Spokane skyscrapers stacked up behind her.

Doc pulled up with Trish as if by some predetermined communication. Wendel's daughter stepped out of the Lincoln Continental of her own accord, dragging a miniature suitcase, a bag of rubberized horses and cattle, a smile as big as Montana. Wendel exited the café, the smell of bacon with him. Willow ducked to Doc's window, gesturing and nodding, shoveling the paperwork inside the car to him, hugging him, whispering words not meant for Wendel, divorce a done deal.

Trish understood the score, her parents splitting, she going to live with Daddy for awhile, little girl stuff she'd discussed with neighborhood girls in the same boat, others to be visiting their fathers elsewhere for the summer, divorce stuff, routine in its sorry way. For some. At six years it wasn't so much troublesome as inconvenient, mostly friends left behind. Trish looked forward to the trip with Wendel, her father. She anticipated the excitement—other girls' storied excitement of fathers soon to be hers, the much-fabled trip into Dad's world.

They loaded up, but Bo's stock truck would not start. Would the adventure never begin? They sat in the truck looking at one another, disappointed but smiling, calm that whatever happened together would be okay. Doctor Dick wrapped up business with Willow and drove over. He agreed to give them a lift to the stockyards, the trek together softening some of the weirdness between Wendel and the veterinarian. Trish sat forward, stretching her seatbelt to the edge of her seat, anxious, piling out over Wendel when they arrived, lugging her cargo out of the back seat. Doc shook Wendel's hand and left without a word to Trish.

She wandered to the stockyard cattle oblivious to Doc's departure, or seemingly so. Old cows, yarded and lowing, cows soon to be dead and knowing it. Looking at them, she felt their despair, the end ahead. Wendel joined her. Together they watched the bony cows. Manure stench of spring. Bleached hay in the feeders, foxtailed. Some pens without water, others without feed, concrete-standing cows, the end of the line, slaughter after here—the side of ranching Wendel hadn't seen in awhile, the side needed seeing. He saw it now—his daughter witness to the foodchain they'd become.

"Has anyone been teaching you about heaven?" Wendel asked his daughter.

"In Sunday school they talk about heaven all the time."

"Sunday school?"

"Doc's church has a Sunday school. I go there."

"So did they tell you how you end up there, in Heaven?"

"Well, there's a man there, his name's God and he decides if you've been bad or good. If you've been good enough you go to heaven."

"He judges you, then?"

"Judges?"

"Like you said, decides?"

"Yeah."

"What about in Wellpinit? What do the Indians say about their heaven?"

"Faraway hills, I think. People waiting. I'm not sure."

"Well in the Blackfoot heaven the cows decide who gets to go to heaven. The cows and horses and buffalo. All the animals we encounter in our lives sit in judgment at the gates of Indian heaven."

"I like that, Dad. We'll be going to heaven, you and I."

"We'll try."

They walked back to the truck, kicking gravel ahead of them, thinking about animals and heaven—what it's like inside a cow's head, what it's like in heaven. Daddy boosted Trish into the semi. Big truck, little girl. They geared across town to the bull sale thinking about the animals up there watching down on them deciding who to let into heaven.

The bull sale, heaven on earth for the bulls, bulls fat and sassy, bedded and shampooed. Wendel selected twenty-four long-loined thick-haired good-footed Herefords with Trish's help and approval, Triplett's Tesio spirit of genetic selection. He wrote a check on Ripley's cattle account, loaded the bulls up, gently loaded them, and motored away saving the caboose space in the back of the semi-trailer for Dharma Bum.

Wendel drove smooth as he could, slow and deliberate so as to not toss the cowboys around, to ease the young bulls into travel. He toted the bulls back to the racetrack, Trish crawling about the piggy-back sleeping compartment arranging her toy herd in an imaginative array, the space a perfect make-believe ranch, mountains and valleys overlooking a screenplay of travel.

They backed to the loading dock and stepped out in a Playfair swirl of dust. Wendel hiked Trish over to Triplett's shedrow to offer their farewells wondering if it might not be their last, a cigarette dancing in Trip's mouth as he rubbed a horse. The only time the legman took it out was to cough, addictive stuff for wartorn horsemen, tobacco. What to say? "So long," Wendel said.

"Keep your feet in the stirrups," Triplett advised.

Trish waved goodbye, smiling.

"Told you so, told you he'd come for ya," Bo told Trish as she strode off beside her tall-walking Daddy.

"Told you so, back," Trish replied, wrinkling her told-you-so nose.

Triplett dropped back down to leg rubbing, kneeling under the horse he'd been rubbing on, cigarette puffing. Peaceful work. His hands glue.

Trish and Wen trotted back to find Mitcheltree easing Bum up the loading ramp familiarizing the horse with the semi-trailer compartment, easing him in to the caboose, "Easy runner, you're just going home for awhile, back to where ye was born." The young bulls bellowed about in the anterior compartments, milling and coughing, disturbed at the calamity their lives had suddenly become. Dharma wondered about the sudden calamity, as well. Mitch scooted a tackbox of racing tackle inside Bum's stall. "You should come along with us, Mitch," Wendel said. "Real horseracing on the rez."

"No," he said. "Got a stable of no-horseracing-here runners to care for, 'First thing each morning,' just like ye said. Yup."

"First thing," Wendel said. "You know they like you there early, Mitch, you gotta know it. The crack of dawn is their time of day. Be there then. It's a big part of making horses want to run for you, part of knowing them. For horses, each day comes with the sunrise, the visualization of a nebulous world. Be there as their first vision and with them you shall succeed."

Mitch smiled, having heard this Zen before.

"Be the first thing they see each morning, feed them well and they will run for you. The crack of dawn is the time to get the buzz going, the racehorsing buzz, you and your horses, the world yours together in the wolf light, and only in the wolf light. It's the only time of day mankind hasn't screwed up. Often that first light is the best light you'll get if you learn light like horses know light."

"We're hoping for some racing dates this fall," Mitch interrupted. "When that happens we can maybe get all that buzzing you're talking about going again. Not much to wake up to these days. If it don't turn around maybe I will show up your way. Say Marias Fair time, win that Oilfield Handicap in Shelby."

"Gopher Downs," Wendel said. "Original bush, Shelby, Montana. If Playfair's King of Bush, Gopher is prince, the

164

Prince of Bush. Gopher Downs, Prairie Lizard Flat." Indeed Shelby Montana could be considered the birthplace of bush. Site of the Jack Dempsey-Tommy Gibbons heavyweight title fight in the early 20th century, Shelby has been a HiLine gambling town through and through ever since. Horses, men, cards, wildcat oil wells, in Shelby they gamble on everything. Wendel and Mitcheltree weren't done visiting. They had to retell the time a bucking horse broke out of its bucking chute at Shelby, this when saddle bronc riding and other rough stock events took place between races, the racetrack part of the arena. The bucker reared and somehow opened the latch on his gate, bucking onto the racecourse oblivious to the racehorses forging down the homestretch—awful wreck, horses and jocks down everywhere. Gopher Downs. Legendary bush. Bad wreck. Whoo. "They run the rodeo at night now, I think," Wendel added.

"Take care of that horse," Mitch said, seeing Trish's impatience. She had heard quite enough of the past and wanted to get on with the present. "Keep him fit and he could win that Oilfield Handicap."

"Running around those Rocky Mountain foothills will keep him plenty leggy. Mountain pasture, limestone grass," Wendel said.

"So where exactly is it you'll be holing up?"

"Remember old man Ripley's Walking Box Ranch?"

"Walking Box Ripley? Yeah, I remember his ranch. He had a horse by that same name, Walking Box, if I remember right, a handicap horse, a miler."

"You remember right. Walking Box was *the* most famous Oilfield Handicapper, I'd say. Three-time winner. Yes sir, Rip's a prideful man about that, and he's raised some runners since, but nothing like the Walk. He'll want to test Dharma's speed with his latest blood once he catches wind of his arrival. As far as staying at the ranch, I suspect my days there might be limited with my daughter along. I found a son there, you know," Wendel said.

Mitch watched Wendel and waited, saying nothing.

"Rip's daughter is the mother."

"Yeah," Mitch responded, lightening the gravity, "Old Walking Box Rip—lots of land and just the horses to cover it with, fast. He's a bloodhound for bloodhorses and you know it."

Wendel nodded, taking one last gaze at the celebrated grandstands… a grandstand once bursting, his runner nosing a win out of the last marathon race of his last full season, the crowd frenzied, a $1600 claimer early in the season coming from a half a lap back to win the richest claiming allowance of the meet, last October day of the meet, right here, three years ago. He didn't like giving that up.

"Remember that grassland swale, Mitch, smoothest natural racecourse on the continent?"

"You know I remember."

"Below there was the pasture we nabbed Bum off his mother from. Remember her, that long-winded Intentionally mare?" Wendel asked.

"Remember? Intentionally is my favorite broodmare sire of all time. Remember Bum's younger brother out of her?"

"A nice runner, alright."

"I think the Two Medicine grass has something to do with it. Gives 'em bone and wind," Mitch said. "The racecourse up there is made for bloodhorses if you ask me."

"Quite a course. Yes, it is."

166

"A mile and a half, they say, right?"

"Maybe two miles, no one knows the real distance. It needn't be known," Wendel said.

"That sort of racecourse running might leg the Bum up right fine. Ready him for Saratoga."

"Wouldn't it though."

"Much money ever change hands up Two Medicine way?" Mitch asked.

"We don't bet with money up there so much as we bet with horses and land," Wendel said matter-of-factly.

"Horses and land, is it?"

"Among other things."

"What about women?"

"Some there feel gambled with. You could say that," Wendel said.

"But is it true they sometimes wager land on a horse race, something forever for something fast?"

"It's happened. Journey Red Plume win himself a little ranch on the South Fork of the Two Medicine. Win a chunk of river land with the half-sister of that chestnut who win a couple races here at Playfair for him… four or five years back, I believe. Win a ranch with that little buffalo-bred cayuse."

"How'd that go again?" Mitch asked, knowing Wendel loved telling the story.

"Some contractor bought up this old ranching outfit with thoughts of subdividing the splendor, Glacier Park next door and all. Development money launched over the divide from Kalispell. Some buildings went up, a nice barn, Journey hammering for wages, riding his finest mare to work from his cabin on the South Fork each day. The contractor got to eyeing the pony. Next thing he was shooting his mouth off about how fast his thoroughbreds ran. One day Journey got into a which-horse-is-faster dialogue with the millionaire, race talk, you know. Journey so riled the contractor that the fool agreed to bet his entire place that his blueblood could beat Journey's cayuse. All Journey had to put on the line was a year working for the man, who figured the race to be cinched his way. Made the bet in front of his entire crew so he couldn't back down. Best two out of three, Two Medicine Swale. Journey jumped at the chance. Bigshot's horse won the first race, but Journey's mare, one of those ancestral prairie runners, win the next two. Win that beautiful storybook ranch in the shadow of those Summit pyramids, river meanderin' down the middle, high pasture, lush bottomland, forest. Imagine, an Indian winning land from a whiteman. On the rez. True story. True as grass. I drove by the place on the way here, just the other side of Marias Pass. Sweet place. Horserace Hills I think he renamed the outfit. Journey Mad Plume, ancestral horseman."

"There you go off to that rez, Wendel. Go win us ranch, a ranch with ol' Bum, one o' them grassranches you was always putting into them poems."

Wendel had a weakness for dreaming about a ranch life, the dream of acquiring a ranch and living off the land with his son and daughter. Trish had reignited this giddiness in him, energizing him to head into the dream.

"You think you can do both things up there, race horses and ranch?"

"Rip seems to do both, somehow."

"Yeah, with that beautiful open racecourse right there who wouldn't. Sounds like your type of racing, Marathon Man, turf and all. Maybe Dharma's a turf horse and we don't know it."

"I know it, he's turf, turf all along, Mitch. We just haven't made it to the turf level with him yet. Reservation turf wasn't what we originally had in mind." Wendel gazed into the semi at his horse's feet.

"Turf is all over those feet," said Mitch. "Look at those perfect walls, that perfect angle. Perfection you perfected. The horse doesn't hardly need shoes." Mitch and Wendel peered in at the shiny black feet. Underneath they knew the sharply angled bars, the flexible soles, the deep-sulced frogs. Strong-willed feet, cuppy and flex. Shoeless.

"Sounds like you'd prefer I leave him here with you," Wendel said.

"There's no turf racing in this Northwest scene. Turf becomes bog in these parts. East is the best direction for this horse my man. Head east with him. Big turf back east."

"Native turf on the rez," Wendel said.

"You got that right. Sweetgrass turf."

Doc and Willow wheeled into view, a long Lincoln Continental kicking up backside dust. "Better get your horse moving before someone changes their mind," Mitch advised.

The two horsemen watched the shiny black car roll their way before veering away, its dust cloud drifting into them. Dharma Bum pawed at the white straw in the caboose. He nickered and weaved, spinning a loop in the aluminum compartment. Wendel burred to him, communicating, calming him. Dharma accepted the reassurance and stood awaiting his drayage. "Let's go, Dad," Trish said, eager to split. "Let's get out of here." A few more words with Mitch and Wendel carried Trish into the fatherworld she'd heard so much about, everygirl's dreamworld, fatherland.

Mitch watched them depart, the truck rumbling away. The

bulls mooed softly, settling in to the movement. Dharma looked back through a small window in the aluminum trailer at Mitch. The horse provoked memories from summers past—win, place, show. Money on the nose to win! Followed by feigning a lameness, a few outs off form before sending him back full speed, money on the trigger. Failsafe jockeys, good odds, money unlikely to come home again anytime soon with Wendel *and* Bum departed. What a time. Wednesday and Friday evening racing, Playfair pulsing the city, summer twilight, droves of people trying their summer luck, the frontside tight with horseplayers. Halogen…helio…halo, night lights making the track a shrine, the horses illuminated, the silks bright. It all diminished into the distance, history fading into time.

Wendel captained his delighted daughter and their anxious passengers through the suburban gridlock, ferrying up the Spokane Valley. They kept out an eye for the river they knew was there, but it meandered between factories and subdivisions and couldn't be seen. By the time they merged onto the freeway the bulls had relaxed. Dharma Bum munched his hay. They motored into the breast of the continent, east.

"Dad."

No answer.

"Dad," she shouted.

"What is it, Honey?"

"Can I git a dog."

"A dog?"

"You know, Dad. A dog."

"That might be nice." He looked over to his daughter. He smiled and winked.

She was serious about a dog.

Chapter 20

HIWAYMAN

Homeward bound, Wendel and Trish took in every nuance of roadgoing. The countryside began to open up, spooling by, the diesel yammer backgrounding their speechlessness. Smiles, sign language. Daddy looked at her and winked, thinking a dog might be a good idea. Fingers on the wheel, eyes, eyes on the road. Trish practiced winking, one eye at a time, the right eye, same winking eye as her father's. She started pointing things out with her nose, her happy, leaping nose—anything and everything—a tree, a train, a cloud, another cattle truck, roadside animals. "Look," she squealed, queen of the road. Daddy acknowledging the whatever, building on it, looking for something to point out himself—togetherness zooming— life theirs, unwedged. Body language. Indian talk. Words. Giggling for any reason. Laughing for no reason. Glimmer eyes. His, hers. Roadgoing communion, communication beyond language. Blood. Conscious contact. Sense of belonging. Worldly silence. Mile after mile Wendel trained the diesel down the freeway.

This candescent focus eventually allowed their ears to hear one another's words more clearly, their central nervous systems learning to sift out the sounds around their voices. "What's that, Daddy?" Daddy explained the whatever, soon realizing his daughter thought he knew all of the world. They visited, freely and easily, each knowing when to talk and when to listen. Wendel delighted in his daughter's vocabulary, her intellect. Trish became enchanted with her father's wisdom. She thrilled at the movement of his lips, the sound of his voice, his truck maneuverings. She adored his head nods and hand gestures, all the switching and shifting, the gearing homeward, a home she'd never seen. Passage. Time and space. Their separation soothed. Time apart dissolving. Lake country. Clarified water. Coeur d'Alene. Spiltmilk clouds, intermittent brightness. Road lifting, misting upward into virgin forest, slowing. Atop each pass the world came to a standstill. And then a downhill list, the lightness of their load. Each summit closer to home.

"What's it like at the ranch, Dad?"

"Grasslands, prairie and mountains, free-roaming horses and even a few wandering buffalo. Foothill cattle." Trish's imagination took off as her dad described his homeland. "Enamel skies, sawtooth mountains. Not so much rain and gray as Spokane." At Lookout Pass the truck breached Montana, tamarack forests below and beyond. He downgeared and pulled into the chain removal pullout at the bottom of the grade, a rest from motion. Engine off, eardrums whistling. Wendel unstrapped Trish from her seat. They jumped down to a transfixed world—breezy trees whispering, pine-swept air blowing the world past them instead of them blowing by the world.

Wendel found the trail that led to Crystal Spring, a spring seeping from the roots of a time-gnarled pine, many a night spent here. Fat tree, lichenified stories embroiled in the bark. Trish bounced around the duff enjoying the forest softness. Wendel knelt to his belly and sipped the water from the spring.

Trish mimicked her father and crawled up to the flow, sucking water up her nose. This scared her and she cried. Wendel picked up his daughter and hugged her—rubber legs and rubber arms, tired and exhausted. Hard work being an all-of-sudden daughter, hard work for the both of them. He soothed her drinking accident, sobs disappearing into his chest, needed sobs, a lost year cried away. He knelt with her next to the water and carefully showed her how to touch her lips to the water. "Nose up, chin in." he demonstrated. "Knees and arms so, relax. Kiss the water." She puckered and kissed the water—outbreathing, then suckled some over her tongue, softly. Wendel wiped her face with his handkerchief, her eyes and mouth a miniature of Willow's but for Trish's sparking blue irises just like Dad's.

Wendel opened their satchel and pulled out the toy animals she'd stuffed inside. She set up a little ranch; twigs for a corral—mommy horse, daddy horse, baby horse. Wendel gathered wood, needles and kindling, a stick tepee ignited. Fire. After it burned awhile, Wendel put a small hole in the lid of some pork and beans and propped the can in the coals. Soon bean syrup welled into the fire, sizzling and hissing, the beans smelling as they warmed. Trish watched Dad sharpen a stick and place a little sausage on the end, roasting it so, careful, not too close. He set up a stick and sausage for his daughter. Trish gave it a try, carefully roasting, fat spitting. The forest floor was cool, the canopy flowing in a dulcet breeze, smoke drafting upwards, high and away.

Mabel had warned Wendel before he left that little girls' experiences with their fathers—however brief—mold the women to come. Wendel smiled and thought of Mabel's wisdom. Father and daughter finished eating and lay on their backs, trees asway. Trish hummed Indian stories, her keening young and ancient, part of the breeze, delicious song. Father and daughter grounded. They watched the trees sway for a long, long time, dozing and feeling safe on the forest floor.

When the Montana wind picked up, a limb snapped and brought them to their feet. Time to go. Trish picked a pebble from the bottom of the spring to bring with her. Wendel shaped up a walking stick. They packed their things and hiked back to the highway to hear their cattle mooing. Bum nickered.

"What's he saying. Daddy?" Trish believed her father to understand all animal languages.

"He's saying he doesn't like it all kitchened up with the bulls. He says, 'let's get rolling.'"

Trish looked at her dad, wrinkling her nose. "Kitchened? That's no kitchen, Dad."

"Sometimes in the kitchen means where you don't want to be. The Indians teach me funny ways to talk about animals. Ancient ways."

"So you think he wants out of there?"

"That's right. Out of here, anyway."

Wendel lifted her into the cab.

"Mommy's an Indian."

"She sure is," Wendel said, strapping her into the seat. "Just like yourself."

"What are you, then, Daddy? Mommy says you're not an Indian."

"Horseman, I'm a horseman among Indians. How's that?"

"That's good. I like horsemen. I like them among Indians."

Whatever he was, Trish liked her father, loved him like she understood she should love a father, more instinct than understanding. Wendel closed her door and walked around the truck.

"I'm an Indian horseman then," she said, as he climbed aboard his hi-riding seat.

"And I'm an Indian horseman at heart."

"Can't we both be Indian horsemen?" Trish asked.

"Why not?"

Trish smiled. A wave goodbye to the forest, a squirrel's staccato reply.

Rolling comfortably down the turnpike they experienced balance with their journey. The foray into the woods evened their world. Wendel gave Trish a whistling lesson. If not for dads, daughters would never learn to whistle. They warbled the miles until their lips dried. No Chapstick.

"Tell me a story, Dad."

"A story?"

"Yeah, one of those Indian stories from Browning."

"What about, 'Why Skeletons are Skeletons'?"

"No. That's too scary. Another one."

"Stars in the Sky."

Wendel told her the story: "Napi, or Old Man, was carrying a bag along the Old North Trail, the trail from the Asian landbridge down the Rocky Mountain Front of America, same place we're headed."

"Did Old Man come from Asia?"

"No. Old Man didn't come from Asia. Napi dropped him on the top of the world and he sorted of guided the people down this way."

"Hey, wait a minute. I thought Napi was Old Man."

"Well, kind of, but not really. I'm not even sure how they go exactly. Napi made Old Man in his image, and then Old Man went around making the rest of the things in the world, and Coyote helped. Only Napi created Coyote first, before

Old Man, or maybe it was the other way around, so there was sometimes trouble between them. Often. Who was in charge? Man or animal?"

Wendel didn't tell the story like Bubbles had first told it him, but for Trish his version was as valid as any. The oral tradition allowed for adaptation.

"Anyway, Old Man was busy at it. Coyote followed along and dogged Old Man because Old Man was carrying a bag over his shoulder, a delightful, good-smelling bag. Old Man walked down the Backbone of the World, down the Old North Trail, and Coyote with him. Coyote wanted to know what was in the bag. Coyote thought Old Man had some new kind of treat, because coyotes, like all dogs, are always thinking of what?" Wendel asked his daughter.

"Food," Trish said.

The things Trish remembered impressed Wendel. It seemed so long ago when he last told her the story. He continued: "Coyote tried to convince Old Man to let him look in his bag. To share it's contents. 'Nothing for you,' Old Man grumped, limping down the Old North Trail. Old Man had a hitchy way of going that aggravated Coyote, who slinked smoothly beside the ancient knower. 'Leave me alone or you'll be sorry,' Old Man warned. 'I'm busy tidying up the world. And tonight I have to tidy up the night.'

"'Tidy up the night, do you?' Coyote yodeled. 'It is I who tidy up the night. I do it with my mellifluous throat.' Coyote ululated. Old Man ignored Coyote's ululations and toted his load on down the Backbone of the World. Coyote above and behind, yodeling, the sun slipping out of the sky, falling behind the Backbone.

"The great shadow of night rolled over them. Old Man set

up camp in a cottonwood draw. Coyote stayed high and sang off the ridge, tidying the darkness. Night surrounded them— untidy, dark and moonless. Coyote set off a yodel bouncing between the walls of tight canyon, the echo of his yelps trapped in the canyon, back and forth, back and forth, echoing…perpetual. —Old Man figured coyote was up there yodeling, yipping all night, as usual. But no, Coyote had snuck down to Old Man, slunk into camp just in time to see Old Man opening the bag, peeking carefully, reaching in daintily, and coming out with a small glow in his fingers! Yes, something aglow. He carefully pasted a speck of the glow in the sky above. Coyote thought it might be sugar. It sparkled like sugar. He came closer, and unable to help himself, he tripped Old Man. Old Man dropped the bag, and its contents spill upward! — Stars, stars of the sky, spilling, spilled into the sky, spiraling all awry.

"'Look what you've done, Coyote,' Old Man moaned. 'You've spilt the stars in the sky. And they're all messed up. Some here, a cluster there. No rhyme, no reason.'

"'No,' Coyote said. 'Look. There is rhyme. A river runs through it, a bear hunts in the north there, and swan flies above us here.' They both gazed upward in wonderment, as would all men thereafter. 'All sort of reason, all the animals of the world,' said Coyote

"Old Man looked upward, forlorn Coyote had the last word in the arrangement of the stars. 'All the animals but Coyote are in the sky,' Old Man snickered. 'No Coyote in the sky. No stars able to depict that one, you.' But Coyote didn't care that he was not in the sky because he was here on earth where there was everything he needed.

"And so that's why the stars are spilled all across the sky like they are," Wendel said to Trish, finishing the tale. "Coyote spilled 'em before Napi could arrange them orderly like."

"There's no Coyote in the sky?" Trish asked, confused.

"No Coyote in the sky."

"But there is a Coyote in the sky, Dad. There is."

"You'll have to show me."

"I will Dad, I will. He chases the Rabbit in the Moon. Chases him all across the sky."

Wendel laughed, happy with the story, however much it changed with each telling.

"Sing me a song, dad."

"Hey diddle diddle, the cat and the fiddle, the cow jumped over the moon." A pause for Trish to imagine… "The little dog laughed to see such delight, and the dish ran away with the spoon!"

"Again."

"Hey, diddle diddle…" Cows. Moons. Coyotes. Rabbits.

Trish learned the song quickly, then sang glad tunes of her own. Dad loved her brave voice, her fearless soprano, the determination behind her singing. She coaxed him to join, "Come on daddy, sing with me. A huntin' we will go, a huntin' we will go. Hi ho the derry-o, a huntin' we will go. We'll catch a fox and put him in a box and then we'll let him go."

Let him go.

Miles rolled by, miles oblivious to the storytelling music makers. Each hour a fresh slice of Montana. Song and silence. Stories. The truck did not have a radio, the silence fine when the stories played out, the silence golden.

"Dad."

"Yes, Trish."

"What's Dharma?"

"Learning."

"Learning what?"

"Truth."

"What kind of truth?"

"Inner truth. Knowing who we are and how we connect to those close to us. How we connect with the world."

Trish looked at him wanting more.

"You know, doing what we're doing, travelling down the road with a load of animals and altogether loving it. Learning to enjoy our space. Sharing ourselves. Dharma is about seeking peace, least that was what I was thinking when I named him Dharma Bum."

Trish felt the peace. She accepted the name Dharma for their horse, but had trouble with Bum. She didn't like the word bum. She overheard her mother referring to Spokane street-people as bums, some of them Indians she knew from Wellpinit. She told her dad so, to which Wendel replied that they were good people who'd lost their way. "We have to be careful not to lose our way."

Nonetheless, she wanted to call the horse Chum. "Dharma Chum," she insisted. "It's Chum, not Bum. Chum like a friend, you know dad, his name should be Dharma Chum."

Dad agreed.

"We're chums, aren't we Dad."

"Chums is right, Honey. Dharma Chums."

The two felt good, eighteen wheels rolling north past Hot Springs, Montana. The convex thrill of hinterland highway took them east at Niarada, cattle country straight through to Elmo where the Big Arm of Flathead Lake elbowed into the land, the Lake coming into spectacular view.

"Ocean, Daddy. Is this the ocean?"

"Montana's ocean."

"Swim," Trish whooped. "We'll swim with the salmon."

"It's too cold, too big."

"Maybe for salmon," she said. "But not for me."

The lakeside roadgoing delivered them alongside delirious evening water, largest body of fresh water west of the Mississippi—Montana water. Highway tracked the shoreline lifting away between bays to sail over osprey cliffs. Geometric Christmas-tree farms, geometric cherry orchards, the road dropping shoreside again, glassy water reflecting their run, Mission Mountains doubled in splendor.

Trish watched until drowsiness overtook her, sleepfallen jerks catching Dad's eye. Better get her fed and to bed. Wendel slowed the rig, rolled down his window. Shorebirds and cherry blossoms. Trish sensed the change in air, lakeside air. "Dad?" She sniffed. "Where are we?"

"Montana."

"It smells great, Daddy."

"You're tired. It's time to camp."

"Yes, Daddy. Camp, let's camp." She'd camped before, but never in Montana with her Dad, not yet.

She fell back asleep with the thought. Wendel detoured into Kalispell and unloaded the horse and bulls at the stockyards. He threw some grass hay at them and flushed their tanks with water. He shored up Dharma Bum in a paddock for the night and unhooked the big silver trailer. They headed to Bubbles' cousin's place, Loon Raven, a Kootenai Blackfoot, a rare bird. He was trying to start a lakeside vineyard. By dark they found the place abandoned under the stars, Coyote stars. A watery darkness, a lonely shore with no tepee. Waves lapped cadence. Ricked Cherrywood waited next to a fire ring. Lakestone seats, a flatstone table in the open grass, the lake breathing air.

Wendel split cherrywood with a hatchet. He kindled and lit the fire, pine needles bursting to flame, yellowing their faces. A twilight breeze tattered the flames sending sparks over the water. Shoreline stars, phosphorescent waves. Trish snuggled into her Dad and slept, quickly slept... one year later slept, curled on the earth with her father. Wendel held her, staring from the fire to the water to the increasing numbers of stars— to her firelit face.

He pitched a piece of sapwood on the fire. After catching flame, it exploded, sparks percolating heaven.

Thoughts of Nancy began to percolate his skull. Just how rollercoaster could he make this journey by stopping to see Nancy?—or Nan, as Bo had known her. Wendel never heard her called Nan, one of those name changes to jumpstart a new beginning in life he suspected. "Nan." He practiced the word aloud. The sound surprised him, reducing the night to one-syllable. Another log exploded, Trish jerking, opening her eyes. "Daddy... go to sleep. Daddy." Wendel rocked her back into a dream and tucked her deep in her sleeping bag for the night.

They both slept.

Wendel woke to a different cant of night, the universe spun an hour or two further. He snuck out of his sleeping bag and chucked the coals of the fire, adding some small, and then larger wood. He looked up to the salt and pepper cosmos that cradled the world from above. He squirmed back under his covers and laid on his back entranced by the heavens.

"Dad?" Trish said, from deep in her bag, poking her face out to view the sky.

"Yes, hon. What?"

"Are we going to stop and see Nan?"

"Why do you ask that?"

"I heard you say 'Nan' to the fire."

"Do you want to go see her?"

"Who is she?"

"A friend."

"Like a girlfriend?"

"Why do you say that?"

"Doctor Dick wondered if you had a girlfriend. I heard him asking Mom."

"Sort of a girlfriend, I guess," Wendel said, what the hell. If it isn't Nan, the next woman Trish might meet would be Gretchen, the mother of his son. What sort of relationship would that be? She might as well meet a neutral women. "Do you want to stop and see Nan?"

"Sure," she said. "If you do."

Trish didn't second guess even Wendel's flightiest thoughts, something he wasn't quite yet used to. And wouldn't a visit with a woman be interesting? If Trish wanted to know her dad's world, women would be part of it. In Whitefish Nan had told him his heart beat with hers, always would. He remembered her words, he believed them. Gretchen's and Willow's sincerity seemed to have taken their separate and peculiar nosedives (admittedly as much his doing as theirs). Gretchen and Willow, the mothers of his children, mothers he knew better than to do anything other than appreciate. Could Nan's breast beat with Wendel's encumbered by kids and tormented by their mothers? And Nan only knew the half of it, the daughter half. He hadn't told her of Paddy, hadn't known then. What a life, what a serpentine life, his child asleep under the stars with him, a belonging existence, a feeling once known but not remembered, perhaps the sensation when his dad first camped under the stars with him, or his mother holding him as an infant, walking into the night.

Looked over by infinity he tucked Trish deeper into her goosedown sleeping bag, the fire softly flaming, listing with the waves—everything past forever present.

Above swam Coyote's cosmos, wet and blurred.

Chapter 21

MYSTERY MAN

Wendel woke to a starspun sky. The where-am-I?—I-am-with-my-child realization brought him into a delicious moment of living. He reflexively checked his pride and joy—she slept oblivious to darkness, secure in knowing her father slumbered beside her. He marveled at being with his daughter, seeing such vivid hope and imagination emitting from her without really understanding how it had wavered in himself. He examined the sky, constructing the menagerie above. Dolphin leapt toward the milkswept swan. A horned moon dimming the stars. Buffalo stampeding. Feathery green light illumined the eastern horizon. No, that's not east, it's north, not the coming of morning but the rare glimmer of springtime Northern Lights, a faint *aurora borealis*. He watched the light dance, appear and disappear, and with this found a version of rest, rest for the big day tomorrow.

When he awoke again, he sat up to take some deep breaths, breathing Bubbles taught him during their detoxification, techniques to locate sleep. He couldn't decide if he had slept yet. The starriness had quite possibly passed in introspection. He watched his breath rise, melting into the Milky Way above. The stippling aurora fluoresced the dew collecting on their sleeping bags and silvered the grassy reaches beyond. Wendel checked Trish snuggled deep in her eiderdown, breathing and comfortable. He rubbed her back, astounded at the warmness, marveling at the precise, delicate contour of her vertebrae. His bedroll was barely warm enough for the cold Montana night. He thought of Nancy exercising horses at Bo Triplett's stable, a side of her he'd not known. Bo wasn't one to let just any yahoo ride his charges. Who would have guessed Nan? Skier, lover. And now horsewoman, a talent he knew nothing of, but one that held great interest for him.

He opened his eyes, sky to daughter, watching her sleep. He couldn't ask for much more. Pegasus loped across the sky, collected. All the horses in the world loped across the sky, his sky. If he did sleep, it was interrupted by spells of bliss, childed bliss. He snoozed, woke and thought. Son, daughter, fathersondaughter, everyone's neurons hooked to stars in the sky. He'd been gone a long time from under the stars, too long a time. His heart pulsed and pushed, loving the life it nourished.

Sunshine. Trish poked at her daddy. Untold brilliance. His daughter, her nearness. Sunlight ripped off the lake, a wad of infinity. Wendel hadn't slept this late in ages, and never in his remembrance when camped in open air. Other than a kink in his back, he felt like a wish come true. He grabbed his daughter, who'd been up for some time, and hugged her. She pulled him into the day. "I've been waiting all morning for a hoolihan. Get and up and give me one." He stood, swung and flipped his little girl to his shoulders. She squirmed and giggled and kicked, ran circles around him until he gave her another, and another.

"Hungry, I'm hungry, hungry daddy. Let's eat."

Food. Kids need food. Men in the straightjacket of their

mind can easily go without, but kids need food constantly. Growth. Wendel found some canned food in the toolbox of the truck. In no time they had a fire snapping. Sun steamed the earth, fire and sun, father and daughter feeling fine. Sunshine and water. First spring grass. Whoo. Wendel fried up a can of corned beef hash with olive oil and wild onions, as well as rose hips Trish had knowingly harvested. He tucked the last can of pork and beans in the coals to heat up. The food cooked, slowly, and then they dined, hobo cuisine at its campfire best. Trish ate like a champ.

"More, Daddy. More."

Whatever Daddy liked she liked. Wendel carved the lid off the sooted bean can with his knife and spooned out the steaming beans. He scraped the last of the hash to her plate. He pledged to get some orange juice and fruit at the next grocery they passed. Fruit, she needed fruit, the little monkey. Rose hips weren't enough.

After breakfast they took to the lake. He stationed Trish ashore and dove in, cold stealing his breath, shocking good cold. Trish followed, wading after him, the surf soft and gleeful. Whooeeeee. He picked her up and took a shallow plunge with her in the crook of his arm. Yee-haw. They crawled to shore tingling and hopped into the shore grass which was good feeling to their feet. The water heating over the fire in one of Dharma Bum's buckets had warmed nicely. Trish took a soapy bath, an outdoor sponge bath! Back to the lake for a rinse. Oh, how the water perked her up. She looked new as a peeled egg, the sun drying her. He'd buy lotion for her skin when they stopped for the orange juice. Her hair, her hair. Long and tangled.

He squelched the fire with the bathing water. Stones hissed. They packed up and broke camp, heading out. Trish spotted a quick-stop store along the road. They went inside and grabbed juice, grape and orange, plus a quart of chocolate milk. No fresh fruit, only some blackening bananas, which she was not afraid of. They would have to do. Wendel spied a nice hairbrush and threw it in. Trish suggested M&M's. Wendel obliged. Outside they marched, supplied. He set Trish up at a picnic table with her candy and brush, and dialed Nancy from the phonebooth.

"Hello."

"Nancy, or is it Nan now?"

"Who's this?" A pause. "*Wendel*, where are you?"

"Thirty miles out. What's up?"

"Out of Whitefish?"

"That's right. How are you doing?"

"Long time no see, you tell me how you're doing first." Another pause. "I tried hunting you down after you passed through."

"I heard."

"It's been a year, Wendel. You talked like we might keep in touch."

"*I* did?"

"*We both did*," Nan said.

"Well, I'm in touch."

"A year later. Over a year."

Wendel recalled their lovemaking—the words attached to it, promise-making he'd not forgotten. Trish played before him. "I've been straightening my life out."

"Some life from what I gather."

"And you?" Wendel asked.

"I met your wife."

"Ex-wife."

The line fell silent, a silence with things going on. Nancy wasn't sure what to make of his predicament, theirs. Did he get rid of the wife? Had he been back to see her? Why was he on the phone to me just now?

"Triplett told me about your daughter. I think it's great. How is she?"

"With me."

"You're kidding?"

"No, she's right here."

"Wow. How long?" she asked.

"All summer."

"It's not summer yet."

"Well spring through summer, spring and summer, a long break before first grade."

"Coool…," she managed. More silence. Nancy thought back to her father when she was six. She couldn't come up with much. "I bet your girl treasures being with Daddy."

"I think so. She's a beautiful daughter."

"Not surprising. You're a beautiful man, Wendel."

He tightened inside. "It's nice being with her. I like it."

"When will I meet her?" Nan asked, anxious and open.

"You didn't see her at the track in Spokane?"

"No. No little girl around the stables the mornings I rode."

"Well, we're headed back to the Walking Box."

"Why didn't I hear from you when you passed through outbound?"

"I just didn't feel right, you know, wasn't sure how the trip would come down. Before I left I found out my dad was dead, you know. I'm still working through it."

"You didn't tell me about your dad."

"I guess I probably didn't. He wasn't around much during

those ski team days."

"Seems you don't tell me a lot of things."

"I tell you what I can. I myself got caught up with people not telling other people important things they should have told them. Blood things."

"So is everything working out?"

"Time will tell. More touchy business ahead."

"What touchy business? You bringing Trish back to the ranch?"

"That's part of it."

"And the other part?"

"Nothing, really."

"So you want me to tag along and play mom?"

"I didn't say that."

"Why didn't we work this out earlier, Wendel?"

"You knew I was at the Walking Box. Bo told you I was there. You could have called me a long time ago."

"I did call. Got through to Jesse James himself. Acted like it was some sort of joke, another woman calling Wendel Ingraham. Didn't he tell you?"

"I guess we had a lot going on."

"You and who had a lot going on?"

"The people at the ranch. Cow and horse things."

"What about people things?"

" — "

"Well... Spit it out, cowboy."

Wendel figured she was ready for child number two, but mother number two? "Turns out I have a son at the ranch. The boss's daughter, a high school girlfriend."

"You're quite the stallion, Wendel Ingraham."

"Cut me some slack, Nancy. I called to be nice."

"How old a son?"

"Eleven."

Silence. A tumbling inside Nancy, dreams tumbling, an urge to redirect the Wendel dream. She sighed. "I guess these things happen."

"To me they do."

More silence, a hum in the line.

"I don't know what to think about us, Wendel. Wives and kids scattered all over the country and you call me? You know I don't go for that Mormon stuff."

"Most women don't."

"That's putting it mildly. So what's the name of the boy's mother? I'll need to keep the details straight if I tag along."

"He's my son. 'Boy' doesn't sound right."

"Your son, then. His name?"

"Paddy," Wendel said. "Padrick. The mom is Ripley's daughter, a gal named Gretchen."

"Sounds like some gal."

"Hold it, he's twelve now. My boy, Paddy. Twelve." Wendel scratched his temple perturbed he'd lost track of his son's age. The vertical axis of time leaned on him. Trish ran around the phonebooth, laughing and leaping.

"So what do we do about all this?" Nancy asked.

"I guess we talk it over."

She did not answer.

"You need to meet my little girl before we go on, anyway. We'll stop by. We'll visit."

"You think that'll work?"

"Visiting? It might, you never know. It's worked before. We visit well, you and I."

"Some visitor, Mystery Man."

"I'm no mystery. Pretty simple, really." Wendel heard her sigh, the subtle call of some exotic bird. "So we'll stop by?"

"You've come this far. Why not?"

"Same place along the tracks?"

"Same place."

"We're on our way."

"Wendel means wanderer, you know," she said, holding him to the phone.

"Wanderer?"

"That's right. I looked it up."

"My name?"

"Wendel means wanderer."

"My mom had big plans for me, I guess—homelessness in the blood."

Nan loved going cerebral with Wendel. Conversation with him soothed her, metaphysical serenity. His voice restored in her a long-absent excitement, anticipation fuzzy with mystery. She continued, "St. Wendel, Pronounced *Ven-dl*. St. Wendel, patron saint of wanderers and wolves."

"Speaking of names, what's the Nan thing? I don't know if I can get used to calling you Nan."

"You can call me Nancy if you like. I was just trying to simplify my life."

"Seeing me might not be advisable in that regard."

"I'll be waiting." She hung up before Wendel could answer.

Butterflies escorted him out of the booth. Trish tinkered on the ground with street pebbles, tossing them at his truck. She was bored. Wendel squatted beside her examining her pile of pebbles and took a deep breath.

"Let's throw," she said. Wendel took up with her rock throwing. A marina lay below them, docked sailboats waiting

191

for the lake to rise, metronoming masts, a shifty sky. They walked to the water and skipped a hundred rocks into the lake. Trish wondered at the thought of skimming across the water, whisked away in a gust of wind aboard one of the sailboats.

When their arms tired and no more flat rocks could be found they loaded up and drove to the stockyards. The little girl threw flakes of hay over the fence trying to insure each bull had his own portion. Wendel put the thoroughbred on a longe line and jogged him in a big circle, both ways. Trish watched her father, his dealings with animals a great entertainment. She positioned herself beside him, moving with him, the horse jogging round and round, one way twenty times, twenty the other. She enjoyed her Dad's synergy with the horse, how his body language affected the horse's motion and direction.

"We'll be at Nan's in a half hour or so," he said. Fine with Trish, all fine with Trish. Wendel treasured her innocence, the thought that all women were once so interested in a father intrigued him. He cooled Dharma down, brushed and rubbed him, checked up and down each leg, along his back, looked into his mouth and eyes, and settled him back into his paddock.

Their rig crept through Whitefish, not your usual Main Street vehicle. They jumped to Front Street and motored along the tracks to Nancy's flat. Cha-clang ka-ching ka-boom, humping railyards close and distant, Trish awed by the sounds of trains. Nancy sat in a chair outside her house—not reading or knitting, but sitting and waiting. She smiled when they pulled up. They climbed out of the truck and moved slowly toward her.

"Nancy, this is my girl Trish. Trish, this is Nan," Wendel said, putting his daughter face to face with his old girlfriend. The new name worked. Nan. She shook Trish's hand and with her free arm gave Wendel a half hug at his waist, leading them into her quaint house where she a had a railyard lunch ready and waiting, knowing which sandwiches vagabonds like best. Nan had a special place set for Trish, a little doll perched beside it, a gift. Potato soup and beef sandwiches, one without onions or horseradish for Trish, extra of both for Wendel. Nancy bustled about her kitchen, waiting on them—tidying, clearing—nervous about her little visitor, moreso about the dad, not quite yet able to sit, relax, and take the father and daughter action in.

Trish asked questions, sensing they would soften her restlessness. 'What's this?' 'Where'd that come from?' She compared things in Nan's domestic world with those in her mother's, most things the same, some different, a new-house adventure becoming the visit to the friendly home where you're first treated like royalty—a long memory of discovery, a little girl on the road with her father, yes.

Inquisitiveness led to conversation, and the girls chatted good housekeeping, which quickly led to talking of life in general, a six-year-old talking about life like someone so much wiser and older, Wendel's six-year-old! After dishes, Nan presented Trish with a matching doll, a boy doll for the girl. This won Trish over completely. Wendel slipped to the sofa and stretched out. He spotted his sock from a year ago. It hung, tacked on the mantel like a Christmas stocking. He remembered losing it, how cold his foot got that night. He closed his eyes, daughter with him safe and happy... two socks on his feet. He wiggled his toes and dozed.

He awoke to silence—Trish vanished—the parental wham of kidnap panic glancing off him. He stepped outside, sleep not yet worked out of his spine, his breathing erratic. He brought his physiology under control and straightened up. He could hear a timbered exchange echo off the lakeside pine, happy voices bouncing delightfully. He spotted the girls on a swingset, swinging. Relieved, he sat to watch. Nan's legs pedaled in unison with Trish's, high they went, radiant sun off the lake.

Wendel strolled into their fun. Trish bailed out of her swing and ran to hug him. It took Nancy longer to unstring herself from the canvas seat. Wendel took Trish's hand. Nancy brushed herself off and joined up to grab her other, such nice little-girl hands. They skipped home, Trish swinging between, not enough flying on the swingset, Nancy and Wendel sashaying her up the street, Trish giggling.

"Time to head back to the ranch," Wendel said.

"I bet it's nice over that way," Nan said.

"You know you're welcome to come along," Wendel replied.

Nan looked at the father and daughter cheerfully. "She's wonderful Wendel, more wonderful than I could ever imagine another woman's child could be."

"What about you?"

"I'm game to happen along, nothing going on for me here for awhile."

Trish skipped about softly between them.

Wendel opened the door to her house, looking inside, everything readied for departure. "It'll be more than tagging along," he stated.

"I want to see that ranch," Nancy replied. "I want to play some more with Trish. I want to gallop the great Dharma Bum."

"Why didn't I realize you were into horse racing until Triplett enlightened me?"

"You never asked," said Nancy.

"All these years I been training at Playfair and didn't know you were in the racket. Where were you riding?"

"Longacres."

"Big time!"

"Small time exercise girl, big time track. No big thing, plenty of horses in the morning. All you had to do was show up, bright and early. I liked it well enough, made it easy to follow your training along, always fun visiting with the people who came over from Playfair legendizing you. They all had a story."

"Do your parents run horses?"

"A few—an aside. They wanted a big runner like everyone else. I spoke of you enough that they wanted you to train him. They sent me to Playfair to find you after I told 'em how we'd met up in Whitefish."

"Why me?"

"Good question. By the time you're famous, you're gone."

"You think?"

"It's true. Then that certain horse came along."

"The Bum?"

"The Bum. You made the horse a runner, a no-name into a real runner."

"I missed the best of it."

"You put him at the top. Everyone knows it was you behind the horse, even after you left they said it was you who'd put the bone on him. Sometimes leaving is what it takes to keep a horse running."

"We'll see if he runs again. I'm taking him home and turning him out."

"A change, however soft, is as good for a horse as it is a man."

"I like that thinking. Maybe I need the same change."

"Maybe so."

"Life under Chief Mountain is change. Chief Mountain or maybe Heart Butte," Wendel qualified. "Most people think I should leave Dharma at the track, leave him running."

"Huh? Look at the track, come on. You're doing the right thing. My information tells me you know how to get run out of a horse. You'll get plenty more run out of him, big run." Nancy smiled. "I'm willing to help."

"What do you think Trish, shall we bring Nancy along?"

"Yes, Daddy." She jumped and skipped about, graceful, horselike movements, singing.

Wendel smiled. "Better pack your bags."

"They're packed."

He looked at his daughter, trotting circles around them. "What do you think about all this?"

"Let's get going," she said, breaking into a canter.

"Legs," Nan commented. "Skier legs like her dad's."

"We'll go get that big horse and those little bulls and be back in an hour."

Trish gave her dad a sloe-eyed look, tilting her head.

"Can't you see she wants to stay, Dad? Go on ahead, yourself. I'll take care of Trish," Nancy said.

"So you want to stay with Nan, eh?"

"Yup," she said, cowgirl like, showing her pretty-please teeth. Wendel squeezed her shoulder, nodded okay, and walked to the truck. Taken back a notch, he took his time, reluctant to leave his daughter, feeling lost without her. How well did he really know Nancy? Well enough, he assured himself. Plenty

196

well enough, come on. He was losing his trust in women, clumping them together, knowing better. He climbed into the truck and headed out.

Grayness through town, westcoast clouds moving in.

He returned an hour later, bulls singing to the freightyard whistle. Wendel loaded his girls into the truck, Nancy and Trish a team of empowered sophistication. He stopped for fuel at a truck stop—the girls to the bathroom, then up and down the aisles, shopping for health food, disenchanted at how little was available. Topped with fuel and yogurt and oranges (a bag of popcorn) they headed into a moonlit forest. Diesel hum, pleasant hum, Wendel driving, Trish sleeping in the sleeper, the midnight world afloat.

Wendel yawned.

Nancy stared across the cab at him. "Time to stop and sleep?"

"Sleep? No. No stopping." Within two miles Wendel stopped. He tucked Trish into her bag in the sleeper compartment, and nestled down in his seat with Nancy on his chest. Rest of sorts. Kisses lurid little poems. He woke from a dream, one of those dreams before sleep, her hair in his face, her crisp hair.

"Lord Jesus Buddha Realbear," Wendel whispered.

"Did you say something, Wendel?" Nancy said, lifting her head, peeling open an eye.

"I'm a savage at heart, you know."

"Savage this," she said, sharing her breast.

"You're a brave girl, Nancy, tagging along."

"Ha," she said. "You'll think tagging."

"I'm a fool to bring you."

Nancy giggled.

"And you're a fool to come."

"Lay back, relax. Let see who's the bigger fool," she said, her voice velvet.

"Whatever you say, whatever you say..."

A sift of cold seized the lovers, their breath ice on the windshield. Wendel disentangled and resurrected himself to a driving position and hit the ignition. The same cold seized the engine, but this being a Glacier County outfit, the motor caught and rolled. Nancy mummered sweetly, music in her, and crawled into the sleeper with Trish. Wendel jerked the semi-tractor-trailer onto good ol' Highway 2. The Northern Lights pinwheeled green. A night train hobbling up the pass. Nancy's love on him. Wendel skinned the semi down the two-lane—horse, cattle, daughter, woman—rolling.

Nearing the pass the impossibility of a Walking Box return seized him. He couldn't stay there with this family. Life had been lived too fast the past few days for this realization to gell earlier. With Trish alone maybe they could have found a way to stay at Ripley's ranch, but with Nancy along it was out of the question. There were other places. Wendel had grown up on the rez. He had his hideouts. Palookaville seemed the best place to hole up, the sweetest summertime refuge he knew, solitude way up the headwaters of Little Badger. Brook trout galore, elk. Full-blooded Indians and crossbred cattle. They'd hole up with the Heart Butte gang—liberty and horses for all, free roaming herds—a place Wendel would be welcomed whomever he showed up with. No fences to mend in Palookaville, no hay to bale—life waiting... fish in the creek waiting. Foothills to ride, cattle to tend, mountains to penetrate. Horse country.

The Walking Box, Palookaville—worlds apart, worlds alike. Palookaville it would be, Wendel decided, Walking Box be gone, for now. Trish and Nan would surely thrive with the fringe Indians, Indians he'd first met at Rip's, Indians who'd left the Walking Box to never return. Palookaville, a pristine a place as any to summer a daughter, an Indian daughter. Room to roam, country to leg up Dharma, high country for a highborn horse. Indian heaven, especially to a Spokane Indian daughter.

Wendel geared down the Peterbilt to crest the pass, double-clutching fool he was, and climbed for the home country ahead. The Northern Lights waned over the Sweetgrass Hills, their last thrust of energy emanating from the sacred bosums of the plains, Sweetgrass Hills sheltering a past, holding onto native grass. Wendel pulled his chin over the steering wheel. The horizon of his birthplace beckoned another shot at youth, a last shot, but genetics weighed upon him and the parallax deteriorated. The Walking Box, his son, the Ripley household. And now Trish and Nan.

What cannot be remedied must be endured. The filigree of Northern Lights fell out of the sky once and for all. Wendel couldn't imagine anything ever being simple again.

Chapter 22

FIREMAN

Wendel motored into a new day, the aurora long-faded. Cresting a ridge, the sun's penumbra worked the eastern range. Solar flares leaped above the horizon, molten fire launched from a not-quite-risen sun. In all his years Wendel had never been witness to this sun-up phenomenon. Solar activity warping cosmic magnetism had been responsible for last night's aurora borealis and now the astral energy expressed itself as sunflares. Solar magma shot above the earth's horizon in a slow fluid motion, then suddenly, as if realizing gravity, rained back down in an even slower motion, splashing. Time and again. Until the first fist of sunlight breached the horizon and let loose true light.

The new sun illuminated the stretch of road between East Glacier and Browning, freezing the mountains to the west in white light. Wendel sensed an outside being, someone sharing the same scenery—an animal—and there Coyote scooted across the highway in front of him, here-and-gone Coyote. Wendel's new family slept oblivious.

Clouds sopped up the brilliant sky forty miles north over the Walking Box where Jesse James, Bubbles, Padrick, Gretchen, Mabel, Rip, and Diana quietly finished breakfast in the cookshack. Their thoughts flickered on one man, Wendel Ingraham, expressions reflecting a gamut of feelings. Paddy doodled the Walking Box brand on a napkin—a box over an inverted V. He smiled to himself thrilled his father was the unspoken center of attention. Bubbles hummed anciently, prayer for the travellers. Jesse picked his teeth knowing the score. Diana and Gretchen read their books. Mabel cleared the table. Rip scratched his chin. "Jesus Jesse, I hope those bulls are okay," he said.

"They're okay," Jesse replied. He didn't speculate on the critters' welfare, speculation in these parts had a history of inconclusiveness. The boatload of bulls moved somewhere down the line between the ranch and Spokane. This he knew. "They'll show up sometime today. Or tomorrow. Bubbles, are the corrals ready for the new bulls?"

"Corrals? Those bulls go straight to grass, cooped up long enough by the time they git here. No corralled bullies this day." He tossed his chin in the air ending such talk and continued his melodic humming, keening some would call it, wailing and rejoicing blended, a song of living to pass the time, for while Jesse sensed Wendel would arrive today, Bubbles *knew*. Those sunflares they'd both witnessed at the break of dawn told him so.

Bubbles had bottom grass waiting for the soft new bulls, a big smooth meadow up the river, long-rested; water, grass, and strategically placed minerals waited to alleviate the stress of their travels; nutrients ready and waiting, everything a spartan young bull would need or want after a 24-hour semi ordeal, 24 stretching to 48. Bubbles' taut fence would hold the yearling bulls until they recovered from truck lag. When their hormones resumed instinctive duty, he'd move them into

600 prime heifers.

Thoughts of the breeding season to come pleased Bubbles. He smiled at Paddy, who smiled back, now busy drawing horses. Not only was Bubbles in charge of delivering calves, he was in charge of beginning them, however much a mortal could, which is quite a lot these days. For the cattle's welfare it was best he managed both ends, and that he did, naturally. It made the Ripley ranch world more real, more understandable. Bubbles knew cyclic connectedness. The panorama of spring, the longing days, time itself enticing the fertility rights to begin.

Outside the wind picked up, a warm wind, a warm wind at last.

It was past midmorning when the sound of downshifting echoed into the home ranch. Mabel heard and looked out the window to see Bubbles Ground Owl outside cleaning the unloading chutes. He'd heard the semi coming minutes earlier, the ears of a ground owl. Rip and Diana had departed shortly after breakfast for a cowboy golf tournament, Gretchen and Paddy along with them. The family would be gone for three days, Rip's limit of absence from the ranch. Wendel had timed things right this day, timing a gift he'd received from Bubbles, a talent tempered and refined by Triplett. He rolled in shortly after Rip and company had rolled out. Their paths did not cross. Wendel came in from the south, the Ripleys leaving to the east.

The air blew clean, mountain fresh. A whirlwind scuttled a little army of last fall's leaves out from under the chute. The crisp leaves shivering in detention before scuttling back under. Mountains backwashed morning light. The weather had change in mind, the atmosphere carrying Trish and Nan into the aura of Wendel's Walking Box. Trish dazzled at the open valley, distant plains and not-so-distant mountains. Nan gazed across the native range to the edge of the world excited at the possibilities this life might bring.

Wendel backed the truck into the loading dock, Bubbles' signing facilitating a perfect coupling. The Indian opened the back door to feast his eyes on the Bum he had heard so much about—long stories told into the cold nights of winter, running stories, racing luck. The legends did not let the Indian down. The red horse nickered and stepped to Bubbles who led him down the alleyway to a spacious paddock, half in the barn, half out. The horse rested in his new quarters nibbling meadow hay. It felt good to be back. Horses never forget.

The white-faced bulls wandered out next. No prodding needed or electrification allowed. Bubbles casually lured them out of the truck, a good life ahead of them now, cornholing over. The bulls all had a good, long drink while Wendel saddled Dharma Bum. He moved the purebreds out of the corrals and eased them up the riverbottom to their new home. They funneled through the gate and fanned out running and bucking, sunfishing in celebration. Wendel walked his horse through the cattle. It was nice to watch them settle into the grass after their long trip.

Nan climbed the nearest hillside with Trish to watch Wendel and his bulls—land, cattle, and river shrouding their man. This vision of Wendel portrayed a sense of meaning and completeness for both Trish and Nan. Now they knew what he'd been doing the past year. Bubbles hiked up the hill and greeted the newcomers. Fresh faces on a windblown ranch in the middle of nowhere are always welcome. He walked the ladies back to the truck and carried their luggage and satchels to the red guesthouse, a pleasant place, a little house built into a rise above the floodplain. The Middle Fork of the Milk River hushed below the backyard in a lazy seep. A river named Milk because of its chalky alluvial hue—water carrying pulverized stone, eroded sealife. These clusters of refraction enlivened a milking effect—water muffled with earth.

Brook trout wallowed in the flow, occasionally drifting into tailwaters holding to feed, camouflaged by braiding moss. Northern Pike patrolled the stretches, big fish, carnivorous and cannibalistic, preying on their own dimwitted young as well as brook trout, young or not. These two species of non-native fish, brook trout and northern pike, had worked themselves successfully into a nature foreign to their ancestors, radiant adaptation Wendel hoped to emulate. The Ripley spread sustained cattle and horses in a similarly sympathetic manner. This land and the river and sky accepted all under it—native and non-native. Wendel wished his family to be part of everything. The strength of this country lashed strangers into its breast, lashed them into an unordinary survival.

Chapter 23

MIDDLEMAN

Wendel felt himself between dog and wolf, son and daughter, lover and mothers, land and money. They'd most likely have to leave tomorrow for Palookaville. The Ripley clan would need a good deal of distance to digest Wendel's latest situation. The Walking Box would get along fine without him, as it had for years. They could relax tonight, Nan and Trish fortunate to be able to experience Wendel's world in Ripleys' absence. The three hiked across the Milk and up Papoose Draw to the Big Flat. They sat in the fescue watching the sun regale Chief Mountain. They talked out their situation in the bent alpenglow, Trish having her say, Nan having hers, Wendel listening, nodding. Even with Ripley's gone the newcomers sensed the animosity, an oddness reflected through Wendel. It would be best to camp on neutral ground, beholden to no one but themselves and their horse. They all agreed on Palookaville. Life on Little Badger Creek would give them the best chance, an old haunt of Wendel's father, sheepherder in his youth, Forest Service and Reservation grass, borderland grizzly country.

Wendel would ride Dharma to the sheepcamp, leaving tomorrow morning. Bubbles would drive Trish and Nan, hauling along a truckload of supplies, enough to last a summer.

Darkness slipped off the Front like a slow-motion mudslide. They headed back, pupils dilating to the dusk, skipping across the twilit prairie, side-stepping down the draw to the cookhouse where Mabel had supper waiting. They ate their fill, taking in a Coyote story from Mabel Old Coyote herself—the coyote and horse story, their great race around the Sweetgrass Hills. They ate dessert—pumpkin pie topped with vanilla ice cream, the gourmet stuff. Outside the ranchyard was quiet, not a cow lowing, not a dog barking, not a coyote yipping. All the animals content. They walked along the river to the guest house. A sipping darkness. Tucked inside, they slept like gophers, three in a king-size bed, a dormancy to endure their spring to come.

Wendel slipped out by dark early the next morning, a last loop on the way downcountry to make sure all the Walking Box cattle were on their rightful grass. Bubbles left with Trish and Nan midmorn, Rip's pickup loaded with oats, tack, and miscellaneous commissary. They drove the ridge to Browning, the world unfolding. Bubbles pulled into the Indian Agency and stocked up on government commodities due him and his relatives.

Browning was a happy town with a happy people, happy Indians everywhere, Bubbles knowing everyone, giving them the smile, everyone extra-happy to see no wine in Bubbles Ground Owl, no wine at all. Nancy stacked in additional food from the grocery store. Loaded to the hilt, they rambled to the edge of the Reservation, another edge of the world— wilderness beyond, Glacier Park above. Bubbles entertained the girls with creation stories as they drove the Old North Trail south into the vortex of sacred light.

In the foothill distance, Wendel rode Dharma Bum through deep curves of land. He was happy to have missed all the hauling and loading of supplies, the trip through the bowels of Browning.

Because of the name Palookaville, Nan expected more, a ghost town perhaps, a few buildings, signs of civilization, the remnant foundations maybe. Quite the opposite, a natural serendipity, a creek bottom lush with life, flowing water and budding willows. Bubbles parked in the aspen-grove shade. The empty cabin a dwelling consumed by time and trees and cattle. Even bears had taken liberty. Bubbles suggested a tepee might be in order, and promised to bring one out and set it up soon. He busied himself repairing the corrals, constructing a suitable paddock for Dharma. Nancy wiped down the shelves in a coolroom next to the cabin, a spring creek dribbling through a stone trough. She laid away the commodities and groceries they'd picked up in town, the cool-rock refrigeration promising. Trish explored outdoors, chasing after the birds and gophers like a puppy—her curiosity antics dazzling Bubbles. She followed him to the corrals and watched him work. He answered all her questions about her new world as he sturdied up the corrals with baling wire and lodgepole. Birds, trees, plants, bugs, Bubbles knew it all. The two Indians connected, worldly wanderers connecting—springtime in sacred mountains, dream come true for a little girl. Bubbles absorbed her joy, the transfusion reviving his tired life, the cold winter nearly forgotten.

By late afternoon, Wendel joined his people, riding in on his proud-walking horse, Trish jubilant at his arrival. He dismounted, happy to make it. Bubbles tended the horse. Nan smiled, thrilled the wind had blown him in. They snacked, peanut butter on crackers, best peanut butter in the world, six gallons of government commodity peanut butter, twelve cartons of government saltines. Wendel insisted Bubbles stay, but no, work waited back at the Walking Box, Rip gone, animals to tend, animals and Mabel. He departed, bouncing across the old sheepwagon tracks in the truck, leaving the family to their summer, their only transportation a horse.

Wendel and Trish looked at Nan. "This is it, then. Our home, our summerhome," she said, hoping summer came sooner rather than later. Wendel set to work engineering some plumbing for their abode, diverting creek water through a pipe to the kitchen, resurrecting a long-since-used system. Nan tidied the cabin's interior best she could, cleaning the sink and arranging the pantry. They made it a home, crude but practical.

Bubbles returned two days later with logdepoles to erect the buffalo-hide tepee he'd promised, a bedroom for the family, a lodge. His arrival put a big smile on Trish. They raised the tepee in ceremonial fashion, stacking the lodgepole so, facing the door to the east. They soon had the ventilation flaps flapping in the high-flying day. The tepee gave the family living room, space to storytell when the weather was nasty, which could be often.

That evening Bubbles broke in the lodge by telling Trish his people's stories, his voice rhythmic, the fire breathing a good heat, coals glowing, words danced into images more colorful than reality itself. Smoke and flame enhanced Bubbles' living words, smoke swimming upward and out the top and into the night. Bubbles storytold into that night, feeding imaginations like wood to fire, worlds old and new flaming, coming alive. Trish listened and listened, as did Nan and Wendel, everyone falling off late, very late, sleeping into the next day lost in the great ancient dream of America before it was called America.

They woke and ate a great breakfast. Bubbles departed that afternoon, rejuvenated, the stories bringing life up in him, and in his listeners. Spring nights followed, stormy nights, tepee sleeping and wind. Clear nights, sleep-under-the-stars nights. Bison red-eyed and sharp-horned. The hunter chasing birds across the heavens. Swan, wings of grace, long neck of eternal flight. Fish breaching, horse loping, bears foraging the Pathway of Souls.

Nights aglitter, nights alive, Trish as skybound as her animals, the sky constellated to her liking, a sky ruled by Coyote. She pointed him out. "Right there, see! I told you coyote was up there." And, indeed, coyote was there, big and brave. No one could argue with his slink across the sky.

Summer suns bridged the nights, high-flown suns melting the frosty rime of Glacier daybreaks. Summer birds returned daily, hourly. Loons, hawks, seedbirds and bugbirds, great flyers all—bluebirds, bats, and golden eagles—a world aflight. Trish growing an inch.

Nan exercised Dharma each morning, rider extraordinaire (downhill legs and an uphill heart, good wrists and fingers). Wendel guided his daughter into each day, brushing her hair, braiding the hair, always the hair (Trish refused to allow it cut, hair black as her mother's once was). Wendel rolled up the three tepee bedrolls each morning, and moved into the cabin to prepare a hearty breakfast. Nan showed up hungry after her morning gallop, olive-oil venison broiled with sage and juniper, buttermilk hotcakes. Wendel the chef. Hearty lunchtime soups and salads. Elk roasts and prairie turnips for dinner. Life was good.

Visitors stopped by to visit and to eat—Big Badger Indian

families moving small herds into the mountains to summer grass, people proud of their cattle, following the lead of their cattle-drive kin. Stories told, up and down their family trees, Indian and Cowboy. Teddy "Blue" Abbott bringing in the first cattle herds, their great-great grandad. Chief Many White Horses a great-great on the Blackfeet side, killed in battle by a Crow arrow, a mortal wound to his neck. Wendel and Trish and Nan listened to the history. Old worlds unfolded before them, the cattle moving into the mountains.

The spring that flowed through the cooler room kept fresh the quarters of game and harvests of roots the cattle movers bestowed upon them for helping move the cattle along their grazing way. They needed more horses to help properly, two more at least to explore the woods where elk birthed and grizzly patrolled, three more to take pack trips to the valleys where wolverine ruled large and low, king of carrion. They settled for stories and heard the wolf howl more than once.

Spring leaned into summer and caught a heavy snow. Sun followed and the world exploded. Where a pair of gophers had lived, twelve heads popped out of the earth, chirping. Fishers fished for their fish-loving young who waited patiently in the nook of a tree. Badgers burrowed for meat to feed their earth-loving broods. Lynx stalked about, hungry for their babes, never telling where their kittens might be.

Porcupine and skunk went on with their solitary lives.

The land flourished. Indians trailed through more cows and calves. Bellowing bulls echoed cattle calls into first light, wildflower meadows came alive, hooves trampling lightly. Grass, the fat of the land. Brooktrout. Whitefish. Elk, good meat, lean and tart and chewy.

More snow weighed in the second day of June, heavy snow.

Nancy, Trish, and Wendel relaxed late into morning, their snow-darkened lodge weighed down. When the afternoon sky cleared they emerged, their green world white. Wet snow, spring snow, soon a snowman rolled up and piled tall, soon the sun setting, heat going down. Full moon rising, Strawberry Moon, strawberries ripening under the snow. Stars faint, snowman glowing in the moonlight. Snowman freezing, cold driving the girls to bed.

Wendel sat staring into the firepit flame hoping to read a portent of horseraces to come. Outside, moon brought snowman alive. The fire weakened. A chill drove Wendel into his bedding for a restless night.

Two mornings following Wendel awakened well before sunlight. He started a fire in the tepee and went to the cabin to cook the girls a pancake breakfast. The crackling fire woke the girls. They rose, bundled warmly, and went in to eat. The snowman stood frozen, camp robbers pecking the potato ears. After breakfast they saddled Bum to travel to Big Badger and meet up with Frenchy, Wendel's longtime friend—bareback childhoods shared two decades ago, their horses captured off the edge of the Milk River world, caught and tamed and rode into summers they thought would never end. Twenty years later Frenchy tamed the same horses, edge-of-the-world cayuses, fine horses.

Wendel led Dharma Bum out of camp, Trish and Nan riding atop him double. Wolf light, the frozen trail slippery under his feet, Dharma surefooted, his feet gripping the ground underneath. Their predawn procession entered the forest where the trail softened, quiet going, softer and darker.

CRASH!

Dharma stopped in his tracks, pricking his ears, readying his body for flight. A rush and rumble ahead, a scramble before them, something manlike and big, rocks loosening under the feet of the beast. Timber snapping. A muffled woof and then nothing.

All the light belonged to the moon hidden behind a cloud above them. Wendel held still. Dharma sniffed. The world stopped.

Quiet.

The animal stopped, eyes a faint spackle in the forest dims below.

Bum held fast, his two startled riders braced atop his back. He sniffed again, snorted. A deep smell—wetdoglike, musky—a taste as much as a smell, heavy and close. A bear, Old Mister Griz, they'd crossed Old Mister Griz's path. The cloud slipped by and the moon lit his forest. He huffed and stood, rising gracefully, phosphorescent before shooting away, disappearing into a labyrinth of lodgepole. His smell lingered, a strong smell, then faded with a breeze.

Dharma whinnied. Everyone resumed breathing, Trish and Nan tongue-tied, Wendel winded, the beast manlike, human when he stood, possessed of a bipedal knowing. They moved on and up the winding trail, hushed and lucid. Sunrise greeted them as they crested the Big Badger ridge, light and clarity welcome and warm.

Farming stared back at them from the plains, precisely rectangled, Mother Earth turned inside-out, scarred deeply and forever—monoculture strips, sterile strips—all the distance broken by farming, tillage taking the entire history away from the land, depriving it of any future. The fury of the bear's rush across their path remained in Wendel's head. He imagined a feral being, a wild Bigfoot, he imagined the beast's wildest thoughts, what it might think upon reaching this rise to witness the farming, knowing innately how it haunted his survival, the beast becoming scared, running into the mountains to avoid it all, a beast crazed by the farming. Bigfoot, bear or man?

Sunrise fired the mountains behind them. Cold air moved up from below, valley-chilled. They headed down the ridge, three people and a horse, the breeze subsiding, a cortege of silence escorting them downward, downward to Big Badger, a river fed by a hard rain the day before. An owl hooted as Dharma Bum switchbacked down the steep trail. Wendel stepped aside at the river and grabbed the saddle as Dharma and the girls crossed the flow. He hung tight when the horse dropped off to a full swim. Water rushed over them, pulling Wendel downstream, he kicked and found Dharma's tail and held fast. The horse pulled them all through and scrambled up the far bank. Wendel dragged to shore, wet and slippery as an otter, the girls still atop the horse. Some river, Big Badger. Snowmelt cold. Wendel walked out of the canyon without a word, the trail climbing upward, the steepness warming him.

Above they came to a flat, then water, a lake called Mitten, a glacial pothole carved out of the plateau above the river. They crossed the thumb of the Mitten, swimming through a hundred yards of saddle-high water. Trish hugged Nan, Nan holding her knees to Dharma Bum's neck, Wendel dragging behind, clinging to the horse's tail (practiced now). They swept through algae-topped backwater, slowly lifting out of the water. Wendel and the horse dripped off their wetness on the alfresco plant life at lake's edge. Campsmoke scented the air, burning alderwood leading their way to camp. Frenchy Rising Wolf worked horses in a corral, flaxen manes and flashing tails, a light dust rising into the morning.

"HorseMan. Welcome. I see you there, camped over the ridge. One week I watch from Slippery Hoof Pass. Good to see you up close. Quite a crew you've brought along." Frenchy eased toward them through his horses, the band milling to gawk and whinny at the wet, red horse.

"Greetings, Frenchy. I brought my family to meet you."

"You came to get horses."

Trish slid off Dharma into Frenchy's outstretched arms.

He held her to the sky. "This girl, she has blood."

"Salmon blood," Wendel said.

"What's your name, little one?"

"Trish."

The braided Indian cocked his head at Nancy. "You're not the mother."

"No, no I'm not. I'm Nancy."

"And you put up with this rascal?"

"Which one?"

"The both of them."

"Yes. Don't know why, but I do."

"I know why you put up with them."

"Tell me, why?"

"They're fun, aren't they?"

"That they are," Nancy replied.

Trish giggled. Nancy laughed. "How'd you know?"

"I know who's fun in this world. I tell by the eyes. Wendel and I once had summer after summer of fun luring ponies off the Big Open, always fun in his eyes when we ran those ponies, always fun."

Frenchy ran a clear discharge out of one nostril of his sculpted nose, and furthermore seemed unaware that it ran. Wrinkles worked from the corners of his eyes over his high cheekbones to long tall ears, a rich darkness to his skin, sparse whiskers, a solid body supported by a wiry frame, age in the bones, sag to the skin around his neck. He unsaddled the visiting thoroughbred and turned him into a roped section of pasture he seemed to have ready and waiting for the arrival of such a guest. His own horses nicked and neighed, curious about the newcomer, displeased their handler was handling *him*. Dharma ignored them, ripping into the tender mountain grass.

Frenchy led the visitors into his tepee. A cooking fire, alder coals, a slow burn. Wendel took off his wet clothes. Frenchy left to his old sheepwagon to find him a fresh change. The girls sat on the boneback chairs at edge of the fire, leaving Frenchy his big willow-wicked chair, seat of honor. Smoke worked upward, swimming to the vent at the top of the tepee. A shard of sunlight danced its way through the oblong door.

Frenchy returned with legging leathers for Wendel, and a Hudson's Bay woolen vest. He set a basket of frybread near the fire and hung low a bag of spring water. Nan drank from the buffalo horn dipper that floated atop. Trish drank as well, cherishing the ladle. They gnawed on yesterday's frybread, happy to be sitting and eating, calm and warm. Frenchy sat quiet, appreciating his visitors' contemplation. His family lived in town in the high school complex, his wife a teacher. They would move up when school broke for the summer.

They rested and ate some more. Frenchy in the know of their need for horses, no need to talk. Nothing mentioned of possibilities. French was happy to sit and listen to Trish's relentless chatter. He poked about the lodge, finding little gifts he'd collected from old times and the prairie. Smooth rocks and clever twigs, arrowheads, a carved realbear, a sacred buffalo stone called an iniskim—powerful medicine, an ancient fossilized vertebrae that looked like a miniature buffalo. Trish talked and played with the relics, enchanting everyone in the tepee.

Rested and fed, they rose from their morning council and went to inspect the horses, droop-headed in the risen sun. Frenchy caught some up. For Trish he selected a pinto pony, a black and white Chincoteague named Skunk. For Nan he sorted off a grulla dun, Bjorni, an Icelandic gelding who quickly settled to Nan's calming hand. This was a special horse, as were all Frenchy's horses, but this Bjorni had two extra gaits, a pace and a tölt, the fabled running walk of the Icelandic breed. For Wendel, French threw a hoolihan loop and caught a leopard appy, a white horse with liver colored spots, a livered right eye giving the horse mercenary appeal. "Pony horse for a pony pal," he said, nodding to Dharma in the distance. Frenchy handed Wendel the lead rope and squinted back at his remuda. For a packhorse the Plains Indian selected a quiet sorrel with big feet and thick bones, stout withers.

"Thanks, French. I'll have them back this fall in tip-top shape for roundup. What do I owe you?"

"Did you bring the floats?"

Wendel unfolded an elk leather satchel from the saddlebags and arranged the dental files from Playfair. The annual ritual began. He went through Frenchy's band, one horse at a time, performing needed dental work. Most needed little attention, a swipe here and there, retained deciduous teeth popped off. Their grazing life promoting dental soundness, silica plentiful in the native grass. Wendel found some nasty points in the older stock, smoothing and evening their aging arcades. He removed wolf teeth and deciduous caps from the youngsters.

When he finished sun topped the day.

After a pemmican lunch he worked through the feet of the band, his patience relentless, shoeing the weak-footed stock, trimming the hard-hoofed, finishing the day's work by sunset. Trish relished the day, her dad slave to the horses. She made friends with the only foal in the bunch, a newborn filly, relating to her lot in life, the two communing as youngsters, learning much of the bigger world around them. Nan calmed the horses for Wendel, brushing them down while they waited, reassuring them, organizing the shoes and nails, trimming some feet herself. Frenchy coaled an elk roast through the day, which they dined upon into the evening. Fresh frybread. At nightfall the entire crew tucked into the tepee and slept soundly, Frenchy snoring across the grove in his sheepwagon. A good day.

Morning came clean, a deep night, no din penetrating this paradise. High pressure, a buttery sun. The four saddled up and rode to Mitten Lake. They crossed the thumb and switchbacked to Big Badger, speckled trout finning a bottomless hole, Mediterranean blue. No glaciers headwatered this stream like the Milk, fewer particles of continental demise, older mountains, less erosion. They crawled off their horses and touched their lips to the blueness—looking, sipping, Trish now a pro at surface drinking, the ritual a ceremony. Refreshed, they remounted and rode on to explore Frenchy's world. Trish sat in front of her dad on his horse through rough climbs and water crossings. When the trail smoothed she hopped back aboard Skunk. They rode cross country to the Two Medicine, an even older river, and explored the South Fork. Elk thistles with their pink blooms, the horses snatching stickery bites as they walked the trail. Their appetite for something so sharp amazed Trish. How could they lip and tongue and chew thistles that pierced her skin with ease? The valley flattened into an open bench that rose above the river, horse-going a pleasure.

They stopped at Jackson's summer camp and put the horses to graze in the pasture he'd constructed, dead-now-Jackson, bucked off, his head hitting a rock, twelve dudes and a cook watching—Jackson, their guide, dead. Bad deal. Frenchy came in and hauled him home draped over a packmule, his wrists strapped to his ankles under the mule.

Frenchy fetched frybread from his saddlebag. He started a little fire in the fire ring to warm the grilled buffalo tongue he'd brought along, tongue marinated with prairie spices. He cut the tongue into thin slices using a flint knife and made sandwiches of sorts with the frybread, spring in the air, the scent of summer to come. Sun off the mountains. Birds in the sky. Good food, tasty.

Trish watched the Indian. His subtle actions told of his power. His learning came from the flight of birds, the coursings of rivers, the night auroras. He emanated wisdom, connected with the land. Frenchy didn't need to talk to communicate, but when he did speak, his audience drank up every word, crows even known to listen in, Frenchy a great converser with crows.

After lunch, they mounted and rode on, all day riding, following the Two Medicine River downstream, out of the mountains onto the plains. Nan mastered all five gaits of her Icelandic Horse, the running walk her favorite. The gait was said to pleasure women riders immensely, this tölt, and Nan smiled all day long. They rode south down the Front through foothill plains. At Badger Creek they followed the sapphire flow upstream to Mitten Ridge and back to Frenchy's camp, completing a sacred loop.

Everyone empty. Nightfall. Trish fell asleep in her daddy's arms. Frenchy finished with the horses and took Nan to the root cellar, wild meat and cheese—stoneware containers of bread-dough starters. Mortifying grouse, feathered but drawn, their eyes x's. A hind quarter of elk gracefully aged, strung by its hock, cheese-clothed, the room ferric. Shelves of preserves and syrup—chokecherry, huckleberry—jams and marmalades.

Frenchy fished some strips of marinating meat out of a crock and grabbed a bowl of bread dough and bottle of jam. He fired up the sheepwagon cookstove and left the dough to rise. An hour later they gathered in the tepee to eat fresh frybread with strips of sage-flavored meat, indigene fare served in turtle shell dishes. Trish rallied to eat a helping of meat and some jellied frybread, tepee-cozy, feelings of belonging. Frenchy left to bed down in the sheepwagon. He could soon be heard snoring, snores interrupted by disturbingly long pauses of silence, silence followed by furious gasps for breath. Later in the night Nan heard Frenchy coughing hard for a long time, hackneyed gags to dislodge imprisoned phlegm. She woke Wendel. He told her of Frenchy's childhood lungs, lungs scarified by fire, pneumonia picked up at a BIA hospital. He was there being treated for smoke inhalation from a fire he started atop the Two Medicine pishkun, a misdirected ghost dancer trying to bring the buffalo back. He'd fasted for five days—delirious. He sat spinning wood. Wood to fire. Wind. They found him lying in the middle of scorched earth the next day, feet black, feet burned. Lungs burned. The fire burned to the edge of the cliff and died. Thirteen years old trying to call the buffalo home with fire. Hospitalized, seared lungs infected. A week later rain thrust a trillion fronds of grass out of the earth, the tender green buffalo grass. One buffalo arrived while Frenchy lay in the hospital hacking.

No one knows how a lone buffalo showed up to graze the new growth. Some believe it crawled out of the Two Medicine River where all buffalo once lived in an underground world. Perhaps a friend of Frenchy's dumped him there to show the world Frenchy wasn't so deranged after all, to show how fire indeed once brought buffalo out of the earth. Old Man was a friend of Frenchy's, and so was Napi.

Frenchy in the hospital, waiting for buffalo, waiting to breathe.

One buffalo grazing the fire-wrought green.

The next morning it was time to head back to Little Badger.

"When are the races this year?"

"Indian Days. July."

Wendel talked summer racing with Frenchy, rather he discussed it with himself as Frenchy didn't have much to say. Frenchy was the quiet one. He listened and looked and sized up Dharma. He knew Wendel had a runner sound of leg, long of wind, and big of heart. How the horse would brook the reservation gruel would be a thrill to witness. Could a month of mountain work strengthen his bones enough to handle the native turf, tone his muscles to last three heats, lube his joints enough to stay sound?

Strong bones already, taut muscles, thick joints. Altitude would thicken his blood, the prairie would strengthen his feet. A conditioning game, here as elsewhere. Indians and horses, men and horses. Wendel Ingraham and Dharma Bum. Frenchy escorted the trio and their band of horses through the mosswater of Mitten's thumb. He said goodbye in the native tongue, peace with the world. Wendel's family arrived home around noon, a string of colorful horses.

Horses and solitude put them in the wandering mode. Each day they explored the wild reaches that surrounded them, each day a different direction; fringe of the world, elementary truths, mountains bridging plains, a beauty few knew. Blackfeet purgatory. Sacred ground. Warrior headwaters, headwaters guarded by sundance skeletons.

Trish became child of the land, dancing under the sundance lodge she discovered up the draw. Wendel told her about the Dolly Varden trout who spawned the chill headwaters over the Continental Divide, inland salmon. They'd go visit them when they spawned, late summer, if she was still around. Trish relished her existence, loving life with Dad and Nan, air and water, trees and fish. She loved how they paid close attention to the clouds and moon, how they observed the activity of birds and wildlife. Each night the sun set further north, a new sunset each evening. Nature beheld them.

Riding the high country they spotted the Summit wolfpack, daddy wolf bringing food to little ones, mama nursing, Trish happy to witness the wolf family life. She knew her dad and she knew her mom, she understood her place in the world. Wendel painted her the past she didn't remember, his version of her past, his remembrance; days when Willow, he, and Trish rode as a family, were a family. He recalled the day of her snowy birth on the Spokane Reservation. Trish listened intently to her dad as they sat together propped against a time-wrinkled cottonwood tree. "You were born when the first star of the night began to twinkle. No doctor, just an Indian midwife and your mom's great aunt."

"Were you there, Dad?"

"Oh yes, of course I was there. We had your mommy bundled

in soft flannel sheets on a big bed. The house, a drafty old ranch house in a draw above the Columbia River, is gone, burned to the ground later that winter. You were born in October, the Last Buffalo Moon, October fifteenth. Snow fell, wet snow, heavy snow, big flakes catching the day's last light, magic. A horse—Ease the Pain, a two-year-old we raised—stood alone in the pasture with his tail between his legs waiting to run a futurity in Yakima he never ran. You took his place. You were our futurity, little one, our future."

She listened carefully. Dad told of her birth at sunset, halfway between the fall equinox and the winter solstice, nearly five years ago. A night with a new moon, which meant what it said to her, new moon, not no moon, "How could new moon mean no moon, Dad?"

"It just does. I don't know. Your mommy cried when she first held you, sobbed and sobbed."

"Was she sad?"

"Oh no. Happy, happiest Indian in the world."

Wendel told how he was the proudest man on the reservation. How he cried. Her reservation birth secured her a place in the Spokane Nation, Native American despite the blue eyes gleaned from her fair-skinned papa. A priest arrived three days later to say a Sunday mass. He baptized her on his way through, immersing her in the spring that whisked through Ease the Pain's corral.

Trish begged to hear the story again and again, a story her mama hadn't shared. She wanted to know about salmon and why they no longer ran up the rivers of her people like they should.

"How does a fish run?"

She wanted to know about the mighty Columbia River,

and where was the spring she was baptized, where did it run? She wanted to hear again about the waterfalls where ancient people harvested salmon, her people. Why did they dam the river, crippling the migrations that sustained her people? Wendel had plenty of stories, some of them Indian, others just stories of times past, storyteller Dad. He told of her first step at eleven months, a step across a shedrow on the Playfair backside after Bum won the Spokane Futurity. How her first word was Bee, Bee for Bum the horse. How she sat on Bum before she could walk or talk. Dharma Bum.

Nan did her part to mend the split-parent business, a process that salved her resentments regarding Wendel's previous philanderings. Each Sunday she rode along with Trish the three miles to Marias Pass, a smooth, safe ride excepting one big bad bog where they had to tightrope logs to get through. At the Summit Nan dialed the rest-stop payphone to phone Trish's Mom in Spokane. Trish took over when the phone on the other end began ringing. She talked weekly with her mom, assuring her she was safe and happy in her father's care. Mountains towered over the talk. The hustle and bustle of Highway 2 traffic sometimes muffled words. An occasional train made conversation impossible. The phonebooth didn't sound like the wilderness location Trish described. Wendel accompanied her at times, the summit reminiscent of his railbear ride.

Once a month Father Dan prayed up an outdoor mass near the 'brakeman' summit—east over the ridge on the South Fork of the Two Medicine river. Rocky Mountain splendor, blue sky, continental pyramids hove in granite and limestone. The Holy Trinity.

Sun.

River.

Earth.

Wendel, Nan, and Trish joined Frenchy and his family for the services. Horse travel to the service became ceremony itself, millennial nomads travelling the Backbone, a high mass, communion, alpine feasting and dancing, drumming into the night, South Fork of the Two Medicine flowing. Prayer and drumming, frybread and elk. Mushrooms and tubers. Chanting. Smoke. Singing. Drumming. Eating. Wailing. Nightfall, nightriding, moonriding. Sometimes waiting all night for sunrise, sometimes riding home into the darkness, other times fire-talking into the Monday sunrise. Here Mondays were nothing, stories everything. Stars fading, sun rising. Storied horsemen riding home.

Chapter 24

GAMBLING MAN

Management fell into disarray back at the Ripley spread. Cattle strayed into the grizzly zone with increasing indifference. Big bears took down three calves and crippled a cow below Goose Lake—range Wendel would have kept the cattle cleared out of had he been tending the grass, country too deep for Jesse's range rocket, too thick for even his cow dogs.

Bubbles, well Bubbles thought it fine that realbear dined on Ripley veal. Whenever he got the chance he pointed the cattle realbear's way. The aspen grass was good, the predation hard to detect. Wolves and coyotes took care of the realbear leftovers. Ravens and magpies loosened bones from their plundered carcasses. Endangered varmints packed them away. Death gone, flesh ingested, blood-stained grass licked clean. Bones shared with all the world.

Jesse knew of the griz trouble when a couple cows showed up at the east gate tight-bagged and bellowing—sore, swollen udders—unsucked and unhappy, their calves most likely dead, realbear dead. When the missing-calf information reached Rip he blamed other two-legged thieves, neighboring Indian ranchers, their stealthy cattle-thieving ways at work in the backwoods at night against whitemen again. True enough, in years past a calf was nabbed here and there for spiritual purposes, a ceremonial tongue relished, a hunger for meat sated, perhaps, and what better to nourish an Indian's carnivorous hunger than a whiteman's beeve. But this summer it was Griz, no doubt in Bubble's mind, nor Jesse's. They'd witnessed Mother Nature's thinning ways in their time on the Walking Box. Displaced park bears took what they needed to survive, travelling where they needed to get it. Their prowlings through the Rocky Mountain foothills made ranchers crazy, thoughts of bear devouring their carefully bred stock. The first fear came from sheepherders, oh boy did those griz love sheep. Sheep don't do well in bear country, sheepherders neither, a lot of dead bears and a few dead sheepherders. Quite a lot of lambchops.

But these days sheep were gone like the buffalo, so Walking Box bears settled for calves. Twenty or thirty calves lost to predation out of a herd of four thousand was a small price to pay for the best grass in the world, a bargain by anyone's standards but Rancher Rip's. Most of the victims were the weak and slow-witted, the sick and injured. The bigger part of the herd, the more-than-healthy others, became keen to predation. Survival hadn't been bred completely out of them. Mostly, but not completely. Rip's cattle tempted the bears, who helped themselves to the less survival-oriented individuals; the unlucky, the unaware. Survival of the fittest helped improve Rip's herd whether he admitted or not. Bears were not all that bad for the operation, not at all. The Walking Box foothills offered refuge, aspen draws, fens and lakes, diversity without people, sustenance and nourishment, mental and physical—a space free of tourists and wildlife biologists, space for realbear to roam freely. Great spreads of willow thickets, Milk River floodplain grass, prime picking roots and berries, sweetgrass.

A pack of wolves followed the bears helping them strengthen

the animal world, predators hovering along the elk and cattle, stalking alongside—picking off dyers and lungers, calves that didn't get a good start, older cows taken to their limit on the spring journey to summergrass, the weakhearted, brokenmouthed gummers—age and time taking a toll, the bears and wolves helping them reach their Maker peacefully. Altitude sickness or larkspur poisoning occasionally killed a cow or calf. Wolves dined. Bear. Cattle. Elk. A grass and meat circle, man outside the loop, Bubbles witness to it all, difficulties on the horizon with another turn of the century around the corner.

The wildlife who shepherded Rip's stock flourished while Bubbles headed the other direction. With Wendel gone south, he weakened. He needed storytelling to survive, listeners who listened, stories passed one way and the other. Mabel was there to listen, occasionally spinning Bubbles her own tale, but he needed more, or he thought he did, fresh listeners to know his stories, to carry them on. He'd connected with Paddy, and connected deeply, but the boy had up and left with his mother, Gretchen packing their bags one sudden day, swept off again to Iowa Bob, her off-and-on marriage, and who knew how long this time?

The Walking Box Ranch—outdistancing culture, both white and Indian—had stranded Gretchen like it stranded Bubbles. Her options were few. Live it or leave it. Gretchen left. Bubbles stayed. Most who remained were cowboys, cowboys not quite enough Indian for Bubbles. They listened to his stories and appreciated his connection with a past culture, but they weren't so much into that sort of thing as they were into today's world. The cowboys lived to move cattle and they moved them with their horses. Bubbles' romantic notions of the past didn't tune into their notion of modern cowboying. Bubbles felt the cows should move where they wanted to graze and that the cowboys shouldn't worry so much about herding them around. He felt the men should be haying, preparing for the winter lingering in everyone's future, cow and elk and wolf and man in these parts all owning the same memories of winter. Bears slept through the winter, the perfect adaptation to this country. What a life, no memory of Milk River winter, no winter memory at all, winter a dreamworld for bears. Other than the grass the cattle grazed, none of the cowboys had an interest in the deeper nature of the world. None showed the reverence for Bubbles' stories that Wendel and Paddy showed.

Bubbles and Mabel stopped by Palookaville the next day and informed Wendel of Paddy's departure. Wendel endured the news in silence. Mabel explained that Padrick had wanted to stay, to spend some time with them in Palookaville. Mabel loved Padrick, a fine young boy—a fine young man— reminiscent of the young Wendel, full of energy, ambitious and kindhearted. A good eater. Good with horses, a keen eye. An inherited fondness for the land, a fondness the Walking Box land would someday need. Mabel relayed the particulars of Gretchen's departure to Nan—womanly info: sure enough, the arrival of Trish and Nan had sent Gretchen into a huff. Emotionally discontent, she high-tailed it away with Padrick, skedaddling back to Iowa Bob. Bubbles had managed a word with Padrick before he left, explaining his dad would be around for him when he returned. Pad reassured Bubbles he would indeed return when the time was right, mother along or not. For now he felt obligated to follow his mother, son duty, he called it. She needed him. He went along, did what he could to keep her melancholy in abeyance.

Iowa Bob offered more of the high society Gretchen figured she needed. Iowa did not always provide enough though, just like the ranch hadn't provided enough of something else, neither place enough for Gretchen. Iowa Bob offered a different security, though, one having nothing to with land or animals or sky. Civilized security, a certain urban luxury.

Mabel shared the skinny on the Iowa husband with Nancy—a good man, a business man, but, of course, an insecure man, a lover suspended while Gretchen explored the possibility of restructuring a life with Wendel. Nan listened to Mabel's information about the husband, sensing Gretchen's lack of heart about either man. Before leaving this time, Gretchen told Mabel that she was going to attend college in Iowa to become a writer. Writing was thin stuff for a woman raised on the oral tradition. Mabel thought of corn-fat hams when she thought of Iowa. What the hell was there to write about in Iowa?, whole damn earth turned inside out—Iowa, pure monoculture: corn and more corn, cornpone Iowa.

Gretchen assured Mabel she would return someday to record contemporary life in this, her homeland, writing to sustain the Blackfeet culture, to transcribe the oral tradition. Mabel had heard that story before, but wished Gretchen luck, nonetheless. Educated Indians left the reservation to secure diplomas with which to survive, if not prevail, in a whitewashed world, while their culture dwindled in their absence. Some returned, educated, only to leave again, dismayed at the lack of progress, unable to resurrect their derailed culture.

Mabel Old Coyote understood departure. Buffalo departed to never return, well, almost. Why would the best minds of this latest generation ever return? All Indians waited for someone—something—to return, a ghost dance in each and every one. The scourge of changing cultures, a life cobbled together from a longlost past. However unknowingly, Mabel participated in the change, feeding cowboys to herd cattle, cattle that replaced her buffalo, the twilight of the Great Plains, the flummox of Manifest Destiny. Bubbles listened to all her talk and slipped away, losing his grip on reality, slipping differently than Gretchen or Paddy, differently than Wendel.

Bubbles and Mabel returned to the world of the Walking Box, people coming and going. Leaving. Gone. Gone with little to return to. All the buffalo gone save the little herd grazing the perimeter of the Walking Box, the herd that had nearly trampled Rip, a man saved by Wendel's dad, a gone father, forever gone, buffalo gone. Jesse James was approaching an end as well. The motivation Wendel had instilled in the ranchhands was thinning in his absence. Jesse drank frequently—a heavier, more dysphoric drinking than before— dark trips to Babb, Jim and Coke all night long, cocaine after-hours, grumpy and caustic in the morning, shoving work down the help's throats, bent out of shape. This had all happened before, this come and go, this ebb and flow of alcohol. The Walking Box took its toll on its keepers.

Even Rip watched his world disintegrate, disintegration he'd learned to accept in his age, accept as part of ranching, disintegration to give his own personal disintegration company, all things disintegrating over time. He let Jesse worry about the fences, grass, and cattle, yet Jesse didn't worry. Younger days would have found Rip Ripley in the middle of everything, knowing every cow, every loose fencepost, doing most all the work himself, a desperate scramble to keep things held together. He looked over his world and understood, finally, that all that scrambling didn't change much. Left untended, cattle herded themselves, cowboys or not. Feed them all winter and they head out in the summer and come home in the fall to be fed all winter again, a lifetime of ranching boiled down to that bit of wisdom. To distract himself Rip concentrated on golf. He mowed himself a chipping green in Diana's backyard. He popped away at the little white balls, tapping them into a hole he'd burrowed with a post hole digger. Golf by day, awake by night, time backwashing—whitewashing. Up early chipping and putting, tapping the ball in—his joints stiff, his back aching, the buffalo incident settled deep into the marrow of his bones.

Wendel's dad had saved Rip's life, and lost his own life doing so. Rip thought about this a lot these days. It had become apparent Wendel was aware of his father's death by now, but not the exact circumstances. A riding accident was all anyone ever said. How it might have happened, when and where, and why?—those things Wendel didn't know. Everyone was afraid to tell him how his dad had lost his life, gored by buffalo as he saved Rip from being trampled, buffalo stealing Rip's grass, tearing down his fences and stealing *his* grass, Wendel's dad helping Rip run the buffalo off his land, a horse accident.

Mabel had immediately informed Wendel's mother when her estranged husband was killed nearly six years ago. She left the mother to tell the son. But by then Wendel's mother had become a drinking woman in the saddest sense of the term. Even she didn't know if she'd ever told Wendel about his dad. Maybe she conveyed it in her way, maybe she had phoned Wendel, or tried to, but Wendel, knowing her stupor, did not hear or would not listen. Refused to understand. Wendel unbelieving, unbelieving of anything by then but the Playfair marathon series, the Walking Box a shameful childhood by then, a dead dad too much to absorb, a journeying dad easier to hang on to than a dead one.

The Walking Box, Wendel Ingraham and Rip Ripley, a running history. Rip in desperate need of manpower to run his ranch, horseback manpower, management horsepower. He needed cowboys and he needed Indians. He needed Bubbles to hang on, he needed Jesse upright, mostly he needed Wendel Ingraham to take the reins of his empire. Wendel was gone, Bubbles and Jesse hanging by the thinnest of threads, neither very well with the world, neither walking upright. Badtooth Gene would never leave, but there were not enough like him. Bunkhouse Chris smiled through it all, another run of ranch seasons, his long life the Walking Box, Bunkhouse Chris; time himself.

Rip knew Wendel. He knew Wendel's space and he knew Wendel's heritage. He owned a part of Wendel, even if Wendel wouldn't admit it. Rip investigated all the reports of the fancy red horse that Wendel had brought home to his reservation roots. He investigated the rumors of his talent, researched the records the horse had accumulated, and found a lot of truth to the much-storied horse. Dharma Bum wasn't completely foreign to Rip. He'd bred the mare that produced such truth. Wendel ended up with the filly, not a gift, but payment for an impossible job accomplished, an impossible job bringing home Rip's cattle that had strayed into Canada during the last long drought. A job well done, an international job, an illegal job. Frenchy kept the filly after Wendel left, grew her up and bred her to Journey Mad Plume's California stud, The Kootenai Kid, a double-tough miler, producing Dharma Bum.

Rip had a canny understanding of the reservation fascination with horses. Knowing his own horse fascinations, he understood Wendel's fascination, his horse-split mind, his thoroughbred sensibilities. Yes, Rip knew Wendel, he thought he did. The Blackfeet were getting Two Medicine fever, horserace fever, the only passion left for a buffaloless people, horseracing the last replica of buffalo running, running without buffalo now, running long and running true, chasing after dreams other than buffalo, the same dream as buffalo, the great dream of glory and fame, tribal respect. Rip didn't successfully maintain a ranch in these tribal reaches without a knowledge of the buffaloless peoples' tribal passions.

A special horserace could resurrect his reservation dilemma and set his world straight, his outer world and his inner world. Nothing like a horserace to inspire reservation excitement, like an ancient buffalo herd drifting within encampment's reach. A horse race, properly orchestrated, would bring Wendel back to his ranch, and thus convolutedly lure the cowboys and Indians home where they belonged, the only place they could ever belong if they'd only just accept the fact that the upcoming century didn't mean ranching would end, or even change. Horsemen still had their place on the plains. His horses seeped class. He needed men to ride the horses to chase the cattle round. Rip knew blood, he knew passion. He knew the reservation horses and the reservation horsemen, he knew the Indians within his reach.

Thoughts in order, a race foreordained, he caught up his best runner, Milk River Chinook. He trimmed the horse's feet, brushed him down, wondered if Wendel had floated his teeth—of course Wendel had floated his teeth, he did all the horses' teeth. Wendel did teeth whenever he was here, and hadn't been gone long enough for any grazing horse's teeth to get bad.

Rip looked his steed up and down. He had always known everything about an animal just by looking, but these days he was having his doubts. The horse needed muscle and bone work, he was right about that. He felt the horse's legs, got each limb in his hands like Wendel'd taught him, flexed the appendage about, each joint separately. He felt the muscles of his horse's back, checking for tone and soreness, the muscles of the upper legs, the shoulders and gaskins. The muscles felt good. He palpated Milky's throat, that ever important throat, deliverer of air, of oxygen; distance running hinged on the horse's throat. Rip himself felt fine. He brushed his horse down, got in touch with the horse by brushing. He pulled the mane and tail, trimmed the hair in the ears, clipped a bridle path, all in sweet horse time, all the time dreaming of a big race.

He considered his competition. He'd studied the *Form*. He estimated Bum to be soft, a city runner, Playfair bush. Spokane bush. Ha. This was Blackfeet Indian Reservation bush. Wild bush. Ha, ha. The gruel of three one-and-a-half mile sprints would be too much for a Spokane runner. Ha, ha, ha.

With thought hard in his head, Rip jumped over to the cook house and had Mabel send the moccasin telegraph out to retrieve his much-favored trainer, Matt Saddle, a Blood Indian who knew Milk River Chinook inside and out, knew his heart and knew his bones, knew how to get every hoof of run out of the horse, a fine horse indeed, a runner needing his trainer. Rip knew that much about horses, he knew Milk River Chinook needed Matt Saddle.

Across the rez, Wendel lay awake half-nights looking at the same stars Rip might see as he stepped out to his putting green in the Great Plains darkness. Horses galloped both their heads. Marathon running, reruns, runs to come, long runs, turf. Stars.

Wendel loved endurance running. Distance—endurance outdistancing speed. Rip loved speed. Wendel understood the fallibilities of speed, the lamenesses brought forth. Distance and longevity is what Wendel admired, the horse's more noble nature. Know your horse, know your opponent's horse. Know yourself. Know your children—what more important than a world with children, an ongoing world, horses and children seeking continuity with earth and sky.

Nightwrestler. Summer heat, sheets kicked into a python roll that tries to suffocate and strangle their sleeper. Nightwrestling Rip tossed and turned until he conjured just what stakes young ol' Wendel Ingraham needed to keep himself and his children happy. How could Wendel's happiness benefit his ranch? What did Wendel need (or think he needed) to bring his own personal dream together?
Wendel needed a ranch.
If he didn't need one, he wanted one. A ranch of his own, that's what Wendel Ingraham needed, that's what he thought he needed. Wendel needed a ranch to keep his life continuous with his children's, the great dream of ranching. This Rip knew and he happened to have just such a ranch, a slice of his big ranch, a thorn in some respects—out of the way, rugged country, open, vulnerable to winter, more vulnerable than his Middle Fork, the South Fork downwind of Starvation Ridge.
The more Rip tossed and turned and wrestled with his self-orchestrated python, the stiffer his night-ridden body became. Both cattle and buffalo had taken their toll. Every nook and cranny of his sorry carcass had been stomped, hooves and horns all-knowing of him, dents penetrating every inch of his hide. He'd paid the price for his aristocracy. Done the time, felt the

trauma (the hooves and horns), older now, unable to whip the ranch into shape like he used to (alone if he had to). He and Diana had worked the place stranded together many a year past. Gone years, months long gone, the ranch too big, too complex now. They needed Wendel, knower of the Walking Box, the Old Walking Box, a Walking Box that clicked, Wendel, knower of the cattle and of the land, father of their grandson, antagonist of their daughter, she his antagonist, *they* his antagonist. Family, ranch, blood. Cattle and grass. Buffalo.

Some nights Rip tried to tell himself he didn't care who ended up with the ranch when he was dead and gone, his daughter the rightful heir… but it took a man to run a cattle ranch, a white man at that, white to make the land produce, solvent and manifest. He told himself this fallacy knowing good and well Diana ran this ranch, Indian woman, good a rancher as any man or woman, Indian or white. Rip failed to picture his daughter running the ranch, he pictured a man at the helm, her husband perhaps, Gretchen serving him up the land, the man commandeering it, but Iowa Bob was not so inclined.

Wendel Ingraham more or less wished such a life, more for his children than for himself. Rip knew his wish (he'd once wished it for himself and the wish came true after he married Diana). He knew that Wendel didn't want Trish stranded in Spokane, or Pad cornponed in Iowa. Parents want their children with them, children of the land, something about having your children with you on the land, native children on native land.

What better to lure Wendel to the Walking Box than a chunk of land for his own? Who better to ensure the continuity of the Walking Box than Wendel Ingraham? Married to his daughter or not, the father of her child. Fathers and sons, fathers and daughters, Rip crazy with time and age, obsessing about the continuity of the empire, a phony empire, yet real with the land and cattle and nature and horses and mountains and god damn it all, what a lot of empire.

Ripley plotted, nights shortening, days lengthening, his horse legging up, he himself easing Milk River Chinook into a conditioning routine, longeing. Lope in the air, dust in the exercise ring—horserace in the head, ranch on the line. Summerhome the place was called, a place left each winter, a ranch Wendel couldn't resist, a life he needed (oh, again if he only knew it, only knew it), a ranch life, a ranch-of-his-own life, a Summerhome life. The little ranch to the south on the South Fork, deeded land when the allotments sold a century ago, Whiteman land, a dispensable part of his bigger world, a little ranch, the Bird sisters' Summerhome, an adopted white boy inheriting the land and selling it to Rip, whiteman reservation land, ancient, swaled, first ranch on the reservation some say, a ranch past its time, land needing a family. Wendel Ingraham needing land.

Rip, rejuvenated with future thought and horserace hope, did his yoga stretches as demonstrated on Canadian TV at 5 am each morning and began galloping his racehorse, day in and day out, galloping, conditioning Milk River Chinook, a deep-winded runner, triple tough, Rip an old rider, an old man, tough, wiry, old. White in color and thought, Indian by association. The drumming of the feet galloping, drumming the earth, Rip drumming over Squaw Flat, Chief Mountain shouting run, Milk River Chinook running, Rip riding. Day in and day out. Horses didn't come in green off the range and win two out of three, one maybe, but never two out of three, not down Two Medicine flat. Nope.

To his muscle-torn relief word came down through Medicine Hat to Mabel that they'd located his trainer Matt Saddle, holed up somewhere in Canada, holed up in a bottle, but now headed home.

In Palookaville, Wendel's family rode horseback through worlds unhindered. No rush to live any other life, no rush to be any other place. Centered day after centered day. Time in the clouds, hoofbeats to the flow of water, the unattached life, life disconnected from electricity, blackout deluxe. They loved the country, the wildlife. If love was understanding the beauty of something, loving the beauty of this land, then Nan and Trish loved Wendel Ingraham, a beautiful man, misunderstood but beautiful.

Nan loved his compassion towards things, towards her, the compassion about feelings; not much on sharing his own feelings though, not much on that, not his deep feelings about her, no. I understand, I understand him. But what did she know about love? He? Ha. What did anyone know? His daughter flowed through their relationship like a spring. The country, the horses. Towering mountains, towering high. Too good to last, too towering, she knew it couldn't last, but wished it somehow would last, dreamed it would last, life in love in the mountains in the spring, an untroubled void. Fevered.

One fine day Frenchy came with news.

Spring did not last, lenticular clouds in the sky, summer wind down the front.

The Métis rode in on an afterthought of light and caught Wendel off guard. "Good day brother."

Wendel jumped. "Frenchy!" His eyes lit. "What brings you

over the ridge?"

"Horses."

"Horses?"

"One at Rip's, the other here." Frenchy nodded to The Bum.

"Horserace?"

"Horserace. Big race, stakes race."

"Which horse is he taking after me with?"

Frenchy smiled.

"Milky?" Wendel asked, wincing at the word, the thought.

French nodded, yes. His black eyes wet.

"What are my chances?" Wendel asked.

"Good."

"That's all? Good?"

"Good enough. Anything can happen up there."

And anything could.

Frenchy recited the details, told the story of the horserace in the making, a horserace orchestrated by Rip, Rip a great stakeholder in this land of big stakes. Wendel listened to Frenchy explain the stakes. He felt his life distilled to a horserace. Stakes race. Ranch on the finish line. Bird Ranch on the finish line. The Bird sisters' old dreamranch, Ripley's now, some knew it as Summerhome in the old days. The Bird. Frenchy murmured goodbye in Blackfoot and thinned back into the breeze that brought him, disappearing south, coming and going in such a fashion to cause wonder as if he'd been here in the flesh at all. Here or not, his words remained. Rip had put up stakes, a chunk of land for anyone who beats Milk River Chinook. Of course Rip would get to keep the horse that beat him in exchange for the sweet-swaled riverbottom ranch, as Rip knew the only horse that would try to beat his Milk River Chinook was Dharma Bum.

Frenchy had told Wendel all. Milk River Chinook, Matt Saddle back to train the runner, a wizened Blood from the old school, a maker of great racehorses. Matt had trained some beauties, horses with great names: Duck Lake, Freezeout Ridge, Croff Lake, Count Coup, Great Red Hope, a proud string, a long line of winners, horses with bottomless wind—a route man same as Wendel Ingraham. Matt Saddle, rollercoaster man, rollercoaster Indian, glory to gutter, plains to pity, ranchlife to clubhouse, alleys to winner's circles. Wendel never crossed his path on the racetrack, Wendel coming later into the horse game, on the rise as Matt went on the slide.

Matt Saddle, horseman, legendary wins with Milk River Chinook in provinces all over Canada—Calgary, Alberta; Saskatoon, Saskatchewan; Winnipeg, Manitoba; Vancouver, British Columbia, derby money, commonwealth wins. Wins in America as well, Arizona, Turf Paradise; Mexican wins at Caliente in Tijuana. Matt Saddle, a distance man outdistancing himself, returned now to condition Milk River Chinook once again.

Frenchy's words remained floating on the wind, details blowing back and forth across the landscape of Wendel's mind. Bum would have his work cut out running down Milk River Chinook with the Bird Ranch on the line, five sections of land on the South Fork of the Milk, three sections of river bottom, two more atop—real range, bunchgrass range. Bottomland and topland. —House. Barn. Hayfields. Native country for keeps if Dharma Bum beats Milk River Chinook. A horse for a ranch. Fair enough horseracing, a horserace for a life, his son *and* daughter taken care of. Summerhome bottomland, bunchgrass foothills, milky river. If someone *had* to own such Milk River sweetness, it might as well be Wendel and his Indian children.

He phoned Rip from the summit pay phone the next day after Trish talked to her mother.

"Rip, Wendel here."

"Wendel, we miss you on the ranch."

"Sounds like it. Let's talk."

"Land, Wendy my boy. Land. If you beat Milky the Summerhome spread is yours."

Wendel hated to be called Wendy by Rip and he hated being called boy by anyone, especially Rip. "Free and clear?" Wendel asked.

"Well, yours in your lifetime, Paddy's later."

"That's a nice gesture, Rip. You expect me to run a horse race for your grandson's inheritance?"

"How about if Dharma beats Milk River he's mine, but the ranch is yours."

"Not my horse to gamble."

"Whose then?"

"My daughter's."

"Your daughter's?"

"She's entitled to an inheritance someday."

"Not in the case of Summerhome."

"No deal, then. That's deeded land, you could easily turn it over to me. No deal, Rip, unless it's mine on paper to pass on as I please," Wendel said, his voice sharp.

"No deal then?"

Wendel did not respond. He gazed at his daughter running around the pine duff. She was playing hide-and-seek with a squirrel she'd made friends with over the many trips to Summit.

"Chance of a lifetime for you. Don't let it slip by."

"Free and clear. The Bird Ranch mine to do with as I please if I win. Otherwise no race, and no horse afterwards if I win. Dharma stays with my daughter, either way."

"Can't do that."

"You're not risking a thing, just someone to work the Bird until your only qualified descendant grows up."

"He's your son for chrissakes."

"And Trish is his sister."

"Sorry."

"Fine. If you change your mind let me know." Clunk.

Wendel suspected Rip would change his mind. He'd dealt with Rip a large part of his life, Rip had the racehorse jones as bad anyone, ranch isolation crazies a man about horses. Wendel knew Rip. Rip had bred his horses to race. He had to run them and Wendel knew he had to run them.

Sure enough. Rip sent word over the next day with Frenchy: Bird Ranch Summerhome free and clear if the Bum beats Milk River Chinook. But. If Dharma loses Wendel becomes obligated to Rip to run The Walking Box for the next ten years, a paid indentureship to train Paddy to eventually take over the Walking Box reins. Best two of three races, one-and-a-half miles each. Two Medicine straightaway. Wendel succumbed to the concession and agreed—the moccasin telegraph shot back to Rip like lightning.

The horsemen readied their horses.

Chapter 25

MOUNTAIN MAN

The big race was scheduled for mid July after Indian Days, nearly a month away. Wendel took Nan's place longeing Dharma Bum. Every other day he cantered the horse on a long line, around and around, thirty minutes one way, twenty the other. Again. Then a long walk. Walk, walk, walk. Jog. Jog, jog, jog. More cantering. Rhythmic hoofbeats wearing a circular racetrack in the meadow. The path deepened, the horse thickening. Nan and Trish watched. They picked up rocks that worked out of the sacred circle of horse training ground. They piled them up, little cairns marking the inner limits of the course.

After lunch each day Wendel rode Dharma into the mountains, up the mountains. Every drainage of every mountain needed exploring, and each was in its time. He conditioned the horse, working every leg and muscle through the summer light. By evening, Wendel galloped the horse. He gauged the horse's progress by the depth and recovery of his breathing and heart rate. Suns set to the cadence of canter. Wendel tended to Bum's feet and legs daily, rubbing tendons, oiling hooves, working joints, and massaging soles. He gave Dharma Bum backrubs while the horse ate the delicious summer grass.

On the next phone foray to Summit Wendel called Mitcheltree. "We got our race."

"Better than I can say we got here."

"I could use your help."

"Can't come. I've got a stable of horses to tend," Mitch said.

"Find someone to watch to 'em."

"Who?"

"Doc Dicky."

"I'll ask."

"Ask nicely," Wendel said.

"When do you need me?"

"First two weeks in July."

"You might need Doc, there too," Mitch said.

"Why's that?"

"Patch up those sticky joints on Bum."

"No sticky joints. Doc'd best be not around."

"You mean you'd rather not have Willow around?"

"Her either."

"It's their horse too, ain't it?" Mitch asked.

"In some legal-technicality sort of way, I suppose."

"They'll be coming. Willow's been goin' nuts with her daughter gone."

"How'd they know?"

"Journey Mad Plume told everyone at Playfair. Big news for a place without racing. Sounds like a big race any way you look at it."

Wendel pictured the prairie crowd of indigenous humanity, the horses racing across the native turf, the dust and sky, the smell of the prairie.

"Who's riding Bum?" Mitch asked.

"Who do you think?"

"Not you?" Mitch knew Wendel had planned to ride before he asked.

"Who else? I'm staying pretty light."

"I'll bring Akifumi, he's been riding the horse all along."

"Not across a prairie. This isn't Playfair's bullring."

"What do you weigh in at these days?"

"Okay, bring Aki." Wendel gazed at the pyramids towering above him. "See you in July. Bring tack."

"We'll be there. Bye." Mitcheltree hung up.

Wendel dialed up Willow for Trish. Better talk to her myself, he decided. The horse race had him pulsing.

"Willow?"

"Wendel? How's Trish?"

"Fine. The Bum's going to run here. A rez match, land at stake."

"You'll ruin him."

"I don't think so."

"He's not that tough," she implored, almost crying.

"He will be."

"What about Saratoga?"

"Not going."

"I forbid you to run him on *that* reservation," she shouted.

"I thought he was mine."

"The paper's haven't been transferred. If you run him there he's coming back."

"Fine. He's running here first."

"We're coming to get him then, and Trish too."

"No."

"Yes, Wendel, she's coming to live with her mother where she belongs."

"Here, you tell her." He lured Trish from the forest and passed her the phone. As he walked away he heard Trish excitedly tell Willow every blissful outdoor detail of their last week.

Wendel took a stroll through the squirrel kingdom. Road clatter penetrated the grove with the dreadful throttle of hill-climbing combustion. Willow had got to him. Hadn't resolved their separation as well as he'd thought. She sounded anxious—tweaked and determined to retrieve Trish and Bum. When Trish finished talking Doc Dicky intervened on the phone to mediate, vet he was. After a few minutes Willow agreed to let Bum run. She and Doc would come watch the big race. Afterwards they would return to Spokane with Trish. Wendel had another month with his daughter. They'd make the best of it.

Chapter 26

WEATHERMAN

The following week it rained, Montana monsoon rain. Early summer rain. Cold rain. Cold, cold rain. The skywater filled a dry niche the wind had sucked from the earth. Roots eager to nourish redirected the rainwater into the grass and leaves, sipping it into needles and flowers, sipping until the plant life could sip no more. Water welled, welled to flow off the land, seeking its way to lower ground, chasing gravity, pooling up and rushing down. More clouds arrived from the Pacific sassy with wetness, a wetness full of lies and misconceptions. High pressure trapped the clouds against their mountains. More rain. Little Badger Creek swelled, slate-grey anger, insatiate water tearing at the land, silt hauled beyond.

This chilling, wet world trapped Trish, Nan, and Wendel, trapped them in their Palookaville encampment for a week, trapped them until a wind vanquished the clouds and night froze the water in place. They woke to blue transparence, a rime upon the land, land veiled in ice and hoarfrost, an iceland which Nan's little horse Bjorni embraced. The sun's rays embellished refracting crystal, the prairie a million tiny knives. Trees presented blooming ice-castles. As the sun rose the ice melted, coalescing a thick dew upon the trees. Dew became drippings, drippings became splashings, followed by sporadic showers of release. Water evaporated, the day melted, heating and steaming.

The liquefying prairie published a mist that hugged the land, a mist unwilling to rise. Above the mist—clarified air, a thin atmosphere bearing infinity—a cobalt sky. Sun dogs howled on either side of the sun—stifled rainbows barking their colors. Sunlight set Trish free. She ran circles around the racetrack, around Dharma Bum basking in the infield waiting for his muscles to soften, muscles stiffened by the week of rain. He patiently waited, waited to run off accumulated spleen, red blood cells accumulated by time, time replenishing his blood depleted by all the mountain training. Dharma Bum waited to race—sensing he would race soon, he waited. Wendel and Nan watched Trish dissipate endless energy. They watched Dharma Bum wait.

As the day warmed the horse tired of loafing and became anxious and heady. Wendel walked him for two hours before Nan galloped him through the muddy swirl of soup the training track had become. Hooves slung gumbo mudclods high into the air, flying mudclods that entranced Trish. Flying mud. Sunstruck mud. The horse harrumphed around the track in a collected gait chomping at his bit, lolling his tongue. His tendons and ligaments snapped strong and taut, powered by muscles conditioned and enduring. His joints flexed in fluent synchrony, his body melting with the day, melting into the harmony of run, spring melting into summer.

By the end of June—the land already dry again—a plume of dust rose from the horizon. From the top of Hat Mountain Trish, Nan, and Wendel watched Mitcheltree roll toward their camp pulling a three-horse trailer, longest, skinniest horsetrailer in the world. Squealing wheels rolled its length into their camp. He unloaded a horse, a thoroughbred who would become Dharma Bum's galloping partner, a relaxed chestnut, big-boned, supple-muscled—Corporal Trim, a Playfair allowance gelding. He then unloaded barrels of nutritious feed and bags of rice bran, boxes of wraps, amber bottles of leg oils and cure-alls. Brushes and combs. Tack, bridles, Sherwins, tongue ties, bits, racing plates, nails and stickers, blinkers; everything needed to outfit a horse to race and win. Hammers and files and nippers and floats.

Wendel's family ran down the mountain to greet him. Mitch smiled at their excitement and shook Wendel's hand. Trish poked about all the intriguing racehorse supplies.

"Good to see you Mitch. Thanks for coming."

"I wouldn't miss this. Never."

When Mitcheltree finished organizing, he looked to the mountains. Not a building or person in sight. Paradise surrounded him, a welcome paradise rescuing his sanity from a winter of Spokane drear. What a place for manège. His inquisitive horse came alive when Dharma and the Frenchy horses ran up to inspect the newcomer. The Corporal huffed and snorted, measuring his fresh new world.

Wendel looked over the abundance of feed and supplies. "Where to next?" he asked Mitch. "You have enough leg paint and feed to chase horscraces all across America."

"You got that right pal, it's Saratoga or bust. Willow has a house rented there and three stalls reserved. Doc came through with connections, pulled some strings with a regulatory veterinarian he went to school with at Cornell, some hi-tone woman horsedoctor running the show these days. You're listed as trainer; Saratoga, just like you always dreamed."

Wendel rubbed his forehead.

"I'm licensed as assistant trainer, so you wouldn't even necessarily have to come along," Mitch added, sensing Wendel's reluctance. "Dharma Bum's earned enough to stall at Saratoga. We're all set to go there, come August."

"The Travers?" Wendel muttered.

"Well, we'd have to win some big races between here and there to qualify for that one, but that's one of my contingent plans, the Travers, sure. There are plenty of lesser races, though, allowance and handicap action right up Dharma's alley. We plan to pick up some better horses along the way."

"Some better horses?"

"Kentucky breds, you know. Bluegrass stock. Horses bred and fed for bone."

"Nice plan," said Wendel.

"You're coming, ain't ye?" Mitch asked, flabbergasted by Wendel's reluctance.

"I've dreamed of it."

"No shit. You're the one put the blasted idea in everybody's head."

"Did Willow say if the papers were changed to my name yet? Bum was supposed to be transferred back to me. That's what the divorce papers I signed said, or I thought they said."

"She didn't say, but Doc hinted that the Bum's still in her name. I think Willow might still be pulling that horse's strings."

Wendel felt like she was pulling his chain. "So the papers aren't changed yet, then?"

"Perhaps not," Mitch said, scratching his chin, digging around for a cigarette. "I think maybe they want you to reconsider some things, in fact they want you along to train the horse, I believe."

Wendel didn't take a shining to this plan to become Willow's handmaid. He stared at Mitcheltree, stared through him seeking more information.

"More than that I think they want you out of this place you're at here, they don't think it's right for Trish. Basically, they're working you into a hostage deal, I think. Trying to, anyways," Mitch explained, seeing Wendel's distraught reaction.

"I'm staying here."

"Why so?"

"Look around."

"But Saratoga in August, that's all you used to dream about."

"A notion, a stray dream," Wendel countered. "Something bigger than where we were at at the time. That was all Saratoga was, Mitch, something bigger than Playfair, a pretense for motivation, nothing based in any sort of reality, sort of a joke really, dreams of running down the bluebloods at Saratoga when we had trouble winning at Playfair."

"You never had trouble winning at Playfair," Mitch reminded him.

"Still a pipedream, come on, Playfair to Saratoga."

"Well it ain't no dream no more, Wendel Ingraham," Mitch squawked. "It's done materialized and we're going through with it. I'm going through."

Wendel reimagined the dream—Playfair through Palookaville to the fabled Spa, yes, that was it, pulling horses all through America, winning races along the way, driving them through all that green corn all the way to that leafy Saratoga backside where horses are handwalked to cool out, handwalkers waiting everywhere to walk the horses, grooms and trainers and owners handcooling horses. Something about handwalking the horses made Saratoga desirable to Wendel, most desirable, a high standard for horses.

Wendel knew better than to get ahead of time. Triplett taught Wendel to focus on the race at hand, to run only one race at a time, because dreams always beckoned, future races. Wendel remembered the last horse from Montana to win the Kentucky Derby—Montana born, bred, and trained—a horse named Spokane who came along after the Civil War. Funny how things Spokane haunted Wendel, this Spokane the horse that walked to Kentucky from Montana, running one race at a time all along the way, arriving at Louisville to nab the roses by a nose. One race at a time he won the Kentucky Derby. All this before Wendel was born, before his father was born, before his grandfather, all the way back to his great-grandfather's time, this great-grandfather a Kentucky horsemen before the advent of the automobile. The one thing that sifted down from that great grandfather, the thing that stuck, was his famous saying that it *took two hundred years to become a good horseman*. Well, for nigh two hundred years horses had been running in Wendel's family blood. Although there had never been land or money, fame or fortune, there were always horses. He envisioned Saratoga Springs, a Saratoga silenced and stunned by a long odds victory, a Wendel Ingraham trained entry.

A red-tailed hawk screeched and brought Wendel out of his Saratoga stupor. He inhaled the pine-needle breeze. He stared into the deep mountains hoping to find solace there, his mind fissured as the backbone of the world. Mitch loitered about, walking through the horses, picking their feet, talking to them, reacquainting them. Feeding, rubbing, checking. Liniment in the air, memory coming to Ingraham, the deep training at Playfair, the seed of that Saratoga dream. The idea of hitting the road to Saratoga gnawed at him. What about his children?

Racing horse races around America is no home for children. What about August? August in Montana is as august as it gets. He tried to set the Spa thoughts aside. He needed to focus on the Two Medicine race. Trish ran by, notching another lap through life. A little dog followed her. A dog! Mitch had arrived with a puppy he'd found abandoned at the Browning Town Pump. Wendel grabbed Trish and picked her up. He'd been so wrapped in Mitch's arrival he hadn't noticed the dog she'd wished for so long. She squirmed away from her father and took off with the Indian mutt, a proud Australian Shepard-Border Collie mix, lots of chrome, a blue merle with a blue speck in one of her brown eyes, a smart dog, a cow dog, a cow and horse dog. The puppy checked him back into the Palookaville reality. He looked around for Nan. She was off again, off on another of her rides, she'd taken to tölting her Icelandic Horse deep into the mountains, fast.

Days to come found Mitch and Wendel and Nan training their horses onward. Mitch ponied the Bum for a half hour each morning warming him up, soft miles early. Afterwards Wendel and Nan galloped around the track, their horses paired, Nan riding Corporal, Wendel atop Dharma, vice versa. Corporal Trim proved a game horse, going head to head with Dharma Bum every step of the regimen. Losing her place at the center of attention, Trish found solace with her puppy, Lick, who bestowed Trish with an additional set of ears and eyes to unravel the world about her. The two experienced the endless phenomena of summertime Montana. Trish talked to Lick and Lick listened. Nan tölted the Icelandic and rode, galloping her life along as best she could. Everything in this wild life funneled to a horserace. Everything. And yet it all still seemed right.

A week before the big day Nan and Wendel left Mitch and Trish and Lick at camp. The two rode their mounts the eighteen miles across the prairie to the coulée above Two Medicine River, site of the race to come. The track was swale smooth and rock free. A few badger holes lurked, mostly on the fringes. An artesian underflow of mountain water rendered the meadow surface soft as English turf, and a spring flowing into a beautiful pool of drinking water for horses and folk alike. Rains had thickened the course, a verdant run of ground, over which Nan and Wendel wasted no time, racing their horses as they arrived. The emptiness of the big open exhilarated them, their competition diligent and intense.

The tromp of hooves across the primal land took Wendel away, well away—hints of how it must have been chasing buffalo horseback, a two-hundred-year window of horsemanship fun. Their horses ran well, Dharma and Corporal, as far as they could tell they ran well, for in this world there was nothing familiar with which to compare, no clocker, no tote board—no semblance of any racetrack they'd ever known, real or imagined. After two heats, they quit. The horses held up well and recovered quickly. The equestrians sat high on their animals as they ambled home in an ancient manifestation of chivalry. At the river they stopped to water and rest their thoroughbreds. Nan unsaddled the horses and brushed them down, allowing them the rich riverbank grass. Wendel had brought a pack rod. He put it together and flyfished. He caught a mess of fish to bring home. They saddled and mounted and rode on, detouring over the foothill steppe to Mitten Lake to visit Frenchy at his pony camp.

Fat cows with sturdy calves grazed the park below Mitten.

Twilight, the cattle silky in the leafy light. Frenchy's band of horses milled and snorted about the blind corral, whipping their tails and stamping their feet, anxious for turn-out to graze with the cattle. Frenchy stopped, caught up by the vision of Dharma Bum trotting in, the gait supple and springy. He noted the horse's big chest, his long hip and perfect bone; impossibly perfect bone. Soft nostrils breathing air down a big throat. Good eyes. Shapely black feet. Everything about the horse pleased Frenchy's eye. The sight lifted his animal heart. Long neck, full mane, relaxed carriage of tail. A fluent suspensory apparatus levitated the horse's pasterns at the perfect fetlock angle. Solid sloping shoulders, prominent withers. Dimpled knees. Bright eyes. Discerning ears. Awareness. Spirit. The horse glowed. He emanated run. Sunlight reflected off Heart Butte and lit Dharma Bum. Wendel stepped off. The horse ripped away at the lush buffalo grass—varip, varip, varip—music to his admirers' ears. Corporal Trim looked no less a horse. Wendel and Nan held their horses while Frenchy released his remuda from their lodgepole corral. They loped by going to grass fast as they could run.

Chapter 27

HORSEMEN

The Sun Dance passed and the following week race day arrived. Rejuvenated Indians came from far and wide. They travelled up and down the Rocky Mountain Front departing from the trailers and flood houses that had replaced the tepees of their native Plains. The people gravitated toward the Two Medicine course, a crisp July morning, the atmosphere suffused with prairie aroma. Rip arrived bright and early with Milk River Chinook, a full crew escorting the horse along. The polished Ford truck and aluminum horse trailer reflected the bright morning sun as it meandered up the panoramic Two Medicine River Valley to reach the racetrack swale. Mabel and Diana and Bunkhouse Chris prepared a camp near the finish line. Jesse James erected a Powder River corral they'd hauled along.

Matt Saddle unloaded Milk River Chinook and readied him to run, letting him graze the perfect summer grass while rubbing him down. Old Bunkhouse Chris painstakingly erected a canvas tent to keep the food area shaded and cool. His rectangular construction contrasted pyramidal tepees rising distant, lodgepole triangulations poking above the horizon. Sacred paintings of animals unfurled on tepee walls. Sun worked light and wind worked motion upon the animal medicine, bringing a past into the present.

Many races were scheduled to run in addition to Rip's match races with Wendel. Entrants arrived in trucks and horsetrailers. Less affluent others rode to the track bareback, color descending upon the racecourse from far and wide. In the far distance under the shadow of Heart Butte, Wendel rode Corporal Trim down a long hogback ridge. Daughter Trish rode Dharma Bum beside him, her dog Lick holding a wary-eared trot to the horse's big heels. "You're gunna win, Chummy, you're gunna win the big race," she repeated, patting the horse's neck. Nan followed atop Bjorni, her faithful Icelandic.

From the dusty reaches of trailworn foothills, stock trucks and trailers twisted through ruts and badger holes making their way to the racetrack that sat up above the river in a great coulée of grass. Mitcheltree pulled the three-horse trailer behind his pickup and camper, swaying down the dusty road. He searched for his crew from Spokane.

Akifumi Cato—Wendel's jockey and haiku master—and Triplett had arrived earlier, spending the night in the East Glacier Park Hotel demonstration tepee after their long train ride from Spokane. They hitched a ride to the track with Harold Mountain Chief first thing this morning, and now walked aimlessly through the horses and Indians, strangers to this world.

"Looks to be some race," Cato declared with a crooked smile. "Never seen anything like it."

"Ain't Spokane," Triplett said, watching colored horses with near-naked riders prance by. "Ain't Playfair."

"Are all these racing horses?" Cato asked.

"Most. Things are loose here, Aki. This ain't no regulated affair, no pedigree papers required. Racing here is pure. Raw and pure."

"How so?"

"Anything goes. First horse to reach the finish line wins." Triplett smiled.

"What does that mean?" Cato asked, "that they all get elephant juice?"

"No, no drugs here, no horsedoctors on this backside. No milkshakes, no morphine. It means the soonest horse wins, but not necessarily the fastest. Indian running rules."

"Indian running rules?" he asked. "What are they?"

"You want to know the Indian running rules?" Triplett asked with a smile.

"I do," Cato replied.

"You sure?"

"Sure I'm sure! I'm riding in the big race aren't I?"

"You are," Triplett agreed, smoking, looking down at the little man's excited eyes, smiling.

"Well. Tell me the rules," Cato demanded.

"There ain't none."

"What?" Cato asked.

"No running rules. None writ anyhow."

Cato rubbed his forehead and pulled his head back to watch the shifty sky.

"Everything okay?" Triplett asked.

"Everything okay," Cato answered. He wandered out on the prairie to be alone, lost in thought with no place to hide, wondering just exactly what it was that Triplett and Wendel and Mitcheltree had gotten him into. This didn't seem to be about money, not like racing everywhere else was about money. No money at this venue, he thought, no money at all. And he was right. Land on the line perhaps, or so it was rumored, but no purse money. Good thing Mitch had offered him a flat fee to come all this way and ride, a hefty fee.

Several Indians became interested in Akifumi. They followed him out on the prairie. There was no place to hide under this big sky. Young girls and boys were drawn to his black eyes and burnished complexion, comparing his skin with their own. Triplett mingled with other Indians, older people, his bronze skin aglow, a smile with pride. He was related to a few of the locals through his Kootenai grandmother, and visited anxiously with them. People walked and rode about dressed in traditional garb, others paraded by in cowboy attire, everyone jovial, smiling or singing—horses in hand, horseracing in the air.

A hand painted sign declared NO DRUGS or ALCOHOL ALLOWED. This was to be a dry meet, as were most things tribal were these days. Despite the rules a few jugs always made it through the disheveled assembly of native horseplayers, but it was seriously frowned upon. Sun worked through intermittent clouds. The wind blew, but only softly. Song and dance rang over the land, the smell of sweetgrass, the wonderful drumming of hooves everywhere, little sprints and warm-ups, races here and there. A general conviviality. Darkskinned babes riding ponies about like they were born atop a horse.

Arriving from Spokane, Willow and Doctor Dick pulled through the running horses in a long low car, a Lincoln Town Car. They stepped out and walked nervously about, lost until Triplett spotted them and settled them in with his clan of relatives where Willow's Spokane Indian heritage earned her a respected place of honor. The moccasin telegraph had informed all that Willow was the Spokane mother of Wendel's daughter Trish, whom they all knew well by now. Akifumi fell in with another clan. Adopted as some longlost Mongol brother, he

259

ate and smiled, chatting with the teenaged girls and beautiful young women that had lured him into their circle.

On a far horizon Wendel's string of horses slowly closed the distance to the festivities. Nan rode behind the father and his daughter, a strange space to inhabit, she thought, becoming absorbed with the faint footfalls of horses running across the hills afar. The rhythmic bursts of hoof-tossed dust carried up by the light wind enthralled her. The panorama made it clear what drew so many to the ceremony, the horse inspiring a rapt quality in man, all the drumming and singing and riding and racing had a place, and that place lay ahead of them, waiting, a place in geography and time she believed, something for everyone she hoped. They crossed the river, Wendel and Trish trotting now toward the racecourse, Nan maintaining her Icehorse in a brisk tölt.

It was Nan who first spotted the woman coming toward them, running toward them. Willow, who had spotted her daughter riding in, sprinted across an open mile of prairie. By the time she reached Wendel's horseback family she had winded herself. Wendel dismounted and handed Corporal's reins to Nan. Nan said hello to Willow, but Willow was unresponsive, breathless, drawn to her daughter who slid off Dharma into her arms. Willow hugged her girl. "How have you been my little mouse?"

Trish pushed off her mother's shoulder to look her in the eye. "Fine mommy. We're gunna watch Chum run!"

"I know, my sweet. I know."

"I have a dog." The dog sat at Willow's feet waiting for acknowledgement. "Her name is Lick. Pet her mommy. She wants you to pet her. Go ahead."

Willow was flustered, her composure strained. She expected

260

her daughter to be more infatuated with their reunion. She looked up to Wendel. "Didn't you tell her I was coming?" She stood above her daughter, exasperated. Trish tended to her dog.

Wendel didn't reply. He had been telling Trish of her mother's coming every day the past week, ever since he was informed of the date of Willow's anticipated arrival, the day Wendel dreaded, this day. Trish knew her mother was coming and when she was coming. She was overwhelmed by the day, the race they'd prepared for all summer—happy enough to see Mom, but that meant it would be the end of summer with Dad and Nan. The circumstances of divorce conflicted the child, and it grieved Wendel that such was so. He kept quiet. He understood Willow's anger, the same anger he felt from time to time, a tearing sort of anger, a ripping apart of something sacred, of a child born of two parents.

"What have you been telling her?" Willow demanded insecurely, fearful of some slander told to her daughter about her relations with Dr. Dick. But there had been no slander, none intentional, at least. And Wendel still did not respond. He had learned to listen rather than reply, always best to listen, to absorb a mother's tension, understand split rather than react defensively or inappropriately. Gretchen had taught him well, and in a short period of time.

Willow took Trish's hand, about-faced, and walked off toward the tepee village tugging her confused daughter along. Lick followed, subdued by her change in ownership. Wendel rested his arm over the seat of his saddle and leaned against his horse. He sighed and watched them walk away, dreading this summer with his daughter gone. After a talk with Nancy, the same talk they'd had each day regarding Trish and her mother, they mounted their horses and followed. Nan gazed to the billowing sky. She prayed the sun shine on them all. And the sun broke through and shone. Nancy truly felt part of it all despite the turbulence around her Wendel.

The great gathering absorbed arrivals from everywhere. People and horses, all colors and all breeds, highborn and range born, halfblooded and full. The Ripley setup attracted the well-heeled crowd, Indian and white alike—neighbors, relatives, and friends, people who wore boots. A big spread of food was put out on long wooden tables, roast beef and homebaked bread, salads, cheeses and creams and butters, sauces and juices, desserts and fruits. Diana and Mabel reclined in lawn chairs in the shade of the Featherlight horsetrailer, pleased to watch the visitors eat their fill. Any and all were welcome at the Walking Box tent, but not all came, some less welcome than others.

Morning races ran, planned and unplanned, everything in between. All the running and racing warmed the crowd to the melodrama ahead. A murmur drifted through the throng when Milk River Chinook left the Ripley encampment with grandson Padrick in the irons. Everyone thought the cool and collected Wippert kid, Rip's indentured rider, would ride, but Rip upped the ante by putting his own grandson on the Milk. Lost child of Wendel, Padrick had appeared out of nowhere, smuggled back from Iowa with his mother, Gretchen, who lay low amidst the Ripley congregation. Wendel took a deep breath and greeted his boy at the starting line of the first race. He wasn't surprised Rip had staked his own grandson against Dharma Bum, a gesture befitting of Rip. At least the boy was mounted. Milk River Chinook was a solid horse, a runner Wendel knew and feared, a welcome challenge any other place and time. But now with his son in the irons he felt stung from the setup, and stung badly—a coagulation in the chest, blood pain, family pain, the worst kind of pain, conflict he'd about had enough of. After all the pre-race cogitation and contemplation, how did he manage to overlook the possibility of running against his son? He should have known, should have known Ripley better than he did.

Akifumi Cato sat atop Dharma Bum waiting for instruction from Wendel, who didn't have much instruction to give. Ride your race, you know the horse. Aki nodded, no sweat. The horses pranced, throwing their heads, switching their tails, tugging at their riders, ready to run. Horseplayers looked and gestured at one another. An excited group of red men mingled about waving colored ribbons in the air, someone occasionally picking out a ribbon and giving it to someone else, placing bets in some mysterious Indian axis heretofore unraveled by even the most progressive anthropologists, Indian time going vertical. Horseracing gone spiritual. Harvey Old Man—grand master of the here and now—called Rip's race to order. Wendel managed to sign Akifumi to save some horse early. Aki nodded, straddled atop a lunging Dharma Bum with nothing like a Playfair starting gate in sight. An Indian on a bright paint horse loped down the racecourse and cleared the track of anxious spectators. Akifumi and Paddy circled away to come back around, ready for the start of the big event. Beyond the excitement Akifumi chatted with Paddy, tickled at the resemblance the boy had to the Wendel he knew so well.

"Did your dad tell you about haiku?" Aki asked Paddy.

"The short poetry you mean?

"That's it."

"A little, I guess."

"I taught him some of that, you know. Got him into the essence of the far-east stuff."

263

"Yes," Paddy nodded, "He's tried east on me, tried to teach me the way. I'm not yet sure if I understand what it's all about."

"No one does, it's just that you seem a natural, you and your horse there. You have a nice handle on him, I can tell, a haiku handle—nature and human nature and horse, that certain mix, the discipline and structure required, the respect and understanding needed to run and win."

Paddy smiled. "I'm glad you see that."

"It's beyond science. The nothingness between yin and yang, you know," Aki went on.

"Somewhere between dog and wolf, right? That zone between tame and wild," Paddy replied, squinching his nose.

"Something like that." Akifumi smiled, but with a crooked brow. "Slightly different from wild, though."

"Perhaps not so different in these reaches." The starters waved the horses to the line. "Good luck," Paddy said.

"You too," Aki responded, thinking between dog and wolf.

They came round to the starting line, handlers pairing the horses side by side, holding them together, pointing them down the track, and stepping back.

A *free* start.

The jockeys nodded to one another. Old Man yelled "Ok'i," the Blackfeet word for now, meaning in this case now is the time to start racing your horse, and off they went, poof, gone— hooves digging in, turf flying, two blood horses running away at the drop of the word Ok'i—the starting gate in this part of the world a word.

Dharma Bum won by five lengths going away. A solid run. Akifumi breathed a sigh of relief, safely through another horserace. But the race did not end at the finish. On the outrun Dharma Bum dropped a front leg into a badger hole and stumbled badly, nearly going down. The agile Dharma recovered okay, but the bobble threw Akifumi's head into Dharma's poll, nearly knocking the rider out. Akifumi woozily steered Dharma Bum back to Mitcheltree's trailer, and abruptly fell off the horse, hurt. His mind swam, his muscles burned. The head bump was too much. Akifumi was out for the day, a likely concussion.

Despite losing the first race, Paddy rode Milk River Chinook like a buffalo hunter, proud and fearless. He spooled his horse back around the foothills, cooling off alone beyond the fringe of activity, waiting for the next race, hoping to ride better, faster. Aware that Aki was probably unable to ride the next race, Pad came up with a bold quick-start strategy for the second race—catch whomever is riding the Bum off guard, get a good jump and keep the dirt flying in their face. Paddy slowly cooled and watered Milk River Chinook, he rubbed the horse down for over an hour while more races ran, wild horseraces. With the buffalo vanquished, it was the next best thing to chasing down the great herds.

Nan, witnessing Aki's head-bump, trotted down off the hill to offer her riding services. She was by now certain that some destiny had delivered her to this prairie. All her horseracing experience boiled down to this one day, this prairie meet, this next race. Nan felt delirious at the thought of joining in the fray atop Dharma. Wendel had no qualms about putting her up, so despite Aki's injury, the second race shaped up nicely.

Paddy and Milky reached to the top of their game. As planned, they jumped out to a sharp start and held the lead. When challenged, Milky handily held off a late charge by Dharma Bum. The going was a little rougher than Nan had anticipated, and she failed to persevere. The clods of dirt had given her body and face a beating. The reckless running behind was too much.

She collected Dharma and brought the great horse around, cooling him softly. He felt good to her coming back, but she'd lost any desire to ride the final heat. Not a lack of confidence, now, but fear of bad karma that could arise getting between Paddy and his father. This last run was no regular horserace, this was the rez derby, and it had boiled down to father versus son, whiteman versus indian, although not necessarily the whiteman and indian one might think.

Nan shared her reluctance with Wendel, and he understood her horsy butterflies. One more race would decide all, and it was only he who could dignify that burden, Wendel up against Paddy, father and son in a horserace, Dharma versus the Milk. It had been a long afternoon, but the summer days on the Blackfeet Indian Reservation were known to be long, long was expected, the late-lingering summer light embraced. Dust in the air refracted last light, carrying the slower light aloft, a redness into the western sky, a big sky with a gone sun.

Wendel found himself in the irons against his son.

Nan limped back up the hill to watch. She understood how Paddy must feel. One race and she was hammered. It would be the boy's third. It took a horseman to ride three of these, and she supposed that of all horsemen, a teenager could probably weather it best, a soft-boned, loose-jointed kid like Paddy, like she was a decade ago. Gretchen fretted. Diana consoled her daughter, attempting to calm her as best she could. Mabel watched as Mabel always watched. Bunkhouse Chris lingered about, pale and wobbly, the heat of the day and blitz of racing taking a toll on his ninety-some odd years. Mabel urged him to the shade to lie down, but he insisted on standing at the edge of the track determined to guard his place to witness the finish of the *grand finale*. Enlivened by the excitement, the old man held his ground near the finish line.

From her perch on the ridge, Nancy watched the familiar old pickup meander up the long swale from the river to the racecourse. It weaved and swerved, stopped a time or two. It was Bubbles, seemingly fallen off the wagon. She smiled from the ridge above it all, a grand and beautiful spectacle, horses and people at their utmost, if not their finest.

Willow couldn't watch, worried of the toll this silly spectacle could take on Dharma's precious legs. Trish and Lick waited mid-course with a tassel of Indian girls, Trish talking, Lick wagging, girls giggling.

The sun had fallen into the mountains by the time the big race began. The crowd buzzed, fervent anticipation waiting to explode. Prairie people, a prairie handicap. The finish line attracted a crowd, and Bubbles arrived to join the expectant horseplayers, chiefs, and fancydancers, but they sent him stumbling down the course toward Chris, who tried to contain the delirious Indian. While at the other end of the track, the race began:

"Ok'i."

The horses broke clean and even, Wendel in the middle of Dharma, his son folded atop Milk River Chinook. A rich silence settled upon the prairie, silence save the hooves, two horses' hooves pounding the tired day's earth. Quickly the pounding escalated to a fury, the fury of acceleration. Dust burst up behind the horses, their nimble footwork a lovely crescendo that settled into a rhythmic roll. The horses throttled down the ancient swale, fatigue setting in early, the third long race of a long, hard day, men pushing horses to their limits, loping down the turfway, spectators boiling about the racecourse fringe.

From Nancy's position on the hill the race transcended time and motion—a dreamscape of how things are when ancient peoples gather on ancient landscapes with their animals in hand. And here the riders had their horses in hand, fingers to reins to bit to tongue, melting into their mounts, becoming horse, uncanny stillness in their motion. The horses carried the men and the men carried their horses, carrying their heads, atop them yet carrying them forward. Nancy watched the father and son ride, her vantage unique. Watching them ride was like watching water flowing over rocks in the river, horses flowing out of hands. The riders fingered their taut reins, an occasional head cant to assess the other's position. The horses' heads bobbed, swinging more deeply and heavily as the race progressed—nostrils flared, ears cocked, ears ready for clucks of encouragement from their cavaliers, horsemen dashing their horses across the native land, collecting their strides, collection to gather inertia for the finish, to save energy.

They gallop, onward, slightly downward, hooves sending cups of turf through the jubilant air behind. The halfway mark finds both riders holding their mounts, saving heart and lung and legs for the finale—a game, a waiting game, a riding game both father and son privy. Wendel glimpses aside and manages a wink as he passes little Trish. Lick wiggles and waggles next to her, whining and fussing. Trish quiets her pet with a touch of her hand. "Come on, Chummy, come on," she urges as the horses bolt by, stirring the quiet evening air. "Come on, Paddy," she shouts.

Neck to neck, stride for stride—son glancing to father, father to son—the horses leg it down the course. Padrick rides Milk

River like a glove. Wendel eases up on his reins letting his horse take over. Dharma holds just off Chinook, drafting he holds, the finish coming, Dharma pulling aside Chinook, even now, Paddy looking over at his dad, the look Wendel would never forget, his boy bearing down, digging his horse into haiku awareness. The time has come and the horserace is on. Paddy's energy ratchets Wendel's mind to all the riding they'd done together on the Walking Box prairie, none as aggressive as this. His son gives Milky a tap with the quirt and the horse catches a higher gear. Dharma surges to the challenge, surges late to the challenge. The two steeds charge beside one another, close beside, hooves drumming the world.

With three furlongs to go the dual livens, a horserace materialized, perfectly matched opponents grinding it out. Pad urges his mount on, forever urging him on, on and on. He holds a lead by the thinnest of margins. A quarter mile to go. Dharma, a saved horse—a horse saved by the HorseMan—is cut loose. Stampeding now, horses stampeding nose for nose, eye to eye, forging over swale land. A furlong to go, both holding tight to the other, one a nose ahead, then the other. Back and forth, up and down, struggling, struggling downward, struggling through a flashing world. The crowd rises to witness the finish, a finish coming quickly, the end of three races coming quickly … the end of a long time coming quickly.

Out of nowhere and everywhere Bubbles stumbles onto the track with Chris astride his back, they lurch in front of Dharma, a scary proposition for a hard-running horse. Dharma Bum shics sideways and bumps hard into Milk River Chinook. The sidelong force jars Pad off the top of his mount, throwing him inward toward his father, inward and downward. Paddy hangs between the racehorses amid their furor. Pinned between the two thoroughbreds at forty miles an hour the boy clings to the side of his runner, Milk River Chinook running flat out, boy falling, falling nearer the fracas of hooves below. The horses know horserace and they continue grabbing for the lead despite the spillage. Paddy disappears between the horses' torsos, Wendel—in one desperate swoop—grabs his son by the shoulder and throws him back atop his mount. By the time Wendel gathers his horse, Milk River Chinook and Paddy win the race by half a length.

Wendel and Dharma drifted by the finish, rock and earth stinging them, rock and earth from the apt hooves of Milk River Chinook. Wendel caught a glint of Rip Ripley's gold tooth as he rode by. The crowd frenzied around the man. Rejoice collided with despair. Dust rose from the dimming earth, a lavender dust. A plume of drummed-up dust, dust of the world, buffalo dust. Risen dust. Race dust. Wendel forged through the dust, chasing after his son.

They carried their horses beyond the racecourse swale, letting their mounts take them far beyond it all, carrying them into a coulée reaching to the river, a coulée beckoning them. Paddy stood high in the irons, huffing over the rush of his calamitous victory. Twilight reddened the wet horses, sweat-thinned skin displaying every line of muscle, every slope of bone. Wendel caught up and congratulated his son. It had been a horserace every leap of the way.

Mountain shadows cast across the prairie. The ancient odor of grass.

"You're quite the horseman, son. I'm proud of you."

"You saved my ass, Dad. You really did."

"I was thrilled to be there for you." Wendel laughed. "I can't believe Dharma bumped you. It was a hell of hit—Milky went out from under you big time. You were flying, son, flying between horses."

"Didn't feel like flying."

"I don't know what held you up." Wendel wiped his brow. Paddy had lost his breath. He couldn't talk, anymore. They slowed to a trot. Then a walk. When he got his wind back he told his dad, "I didn't want to fall. I hung on to you, your stirrup. Didn't think I'd ever make it back up. I remember your leg right there and seeing the earth whiz by. My other hand full of mane."

Paddy drew in a big breath of evening air. Wendel tingled, sweat burning his eyes. The horses blew. They eased and began sneaking bites of sweetgrass, finally stopping to graze. A cortege of silence cradled them, a long awaited cortege of silence, silence save their horses ripping at the sweetgrass—varip, varip, varip.

"Next thing I know I'm back on top winning the race. What happened?" Paddy asked.

"Someone fell onto the track and spooked Dharma. I'm not sure, but I think it was ol' Bubbles. Bubbles with Bunkhouse on his back, for chrissakes."

"Our good old Bubbles?"

"Who else? Seemed Chris might have been trying to keep Bubbles in line somehow."

Paddy looked back toward the racecourse.

"Let's keep riding," Wendel said, knowing what his son was thinking. "I'm staying out of it. It's Rip's race, Rip's all along."

"It's not fair dad. You would have won. I felt you surging. Dharma was on to a strong finish and you know it. My horse was tapped out, finished."

"You seemed to keep him going pretty well."

"Not that well. I could feel Dharma coming on. I saw it in

his eyes, in yours. And then there were people on the track, our people. You should have won, Dad."

"We'll never know," Wendel said.

"I'll know," Paddy said. "I know how much horse I had, and how much horse you had."

"It's runner beware, son. Grandpa Rip's a little shrewder than I."

"Maybe," Paddy said. "He's older."

"So just how was Ohio?" Wendel asked, changing tack.

"Iowa," Paddy said. "I was in Iowa. It's good to be back, Dad. Good to see you."

"Good to see you, son. What a way to get back together."

"No ranch of your own then, eh Dad?"

"Nope. No ranch of our own. Not the Bird anyway. Someday though. Someday maybe we'll have our own outfit, a small cowcamp somewhere."

"Is that possible? Grandpa Rip said something like that could never happen. Not these days. Said to get a ranch you had to marry it, marry it or inherit it."

"He did, eh?" Wendel smiled. "Well he forgot the old-fashioned way, working for one."

"He said a man couldn't ever work enough in three lifetimes to buy a ranch. Besides, the bet was you'd run the Walking Box for him if you lost. You and me."

"I thought you were set up in Iowa with your mom."

"I told her I wanted to stay here. With you. I told her it's time. She knows I don't like Iowa. I'm back. I'm here aren't I?"

"You're here all right, horseman deluxe. What a ride. I still can't believe you kept afloat."

"You pulled me back astride, that was it."

They headed over a ridge and fell into a crease of the Great Plains, the Old North Trail itself, its ruts enhanced by dusky light, the Old North Trail that led the first men down into this new land, land aging now. To the south Heart Butte thumped blood into a lilac sky. The Rocky Mountain Front lay before them, Glacier panorama, the world surrounding them, landscape beholding their existence.

They rode along the bluff—Paddy taking the vistas in. They dropped into a draw that led down to the Two Medicine River—wordless, the sort of quiet riding they'd treasured the summer before, cadence of horsebeat holding them up.

By the time they made it through the riverbottom cottonwoods their horses had stopped blowing. The flux and spin of a horserace released the father and son completely to this world. At the river they watered their mounts, allowing a few gulps at a time, easing the cool into their horses' hot bellies. They heeled the horses deeper into the river, the cold flow soothing their hooves and legs, clopping downstream to the deep hole, a bend in their river, flow carving bedrock into a deep black pool.

They dropped their horses ashore, trusting them to have the hunger to stay and graze, and took a good look at one another—father son. They shed their riding clothes, plunged into the river, and let the flow carry them down and away. The water took their breath, cooling their lungs, rinsing them free of the raceday grime, a welcome cold.

Running races didn't matter like it used to an hour go... enough racing, enough for this day—swimming a grassland river adequate fulfillment, water calming their senses, diluting the electricity of the race. Nighthawks zigzagged the river's sky. Paddy dropped under the current and breaststroked upstream, eyes open. Wendel tripped and splashed, going to his knees trying to keep up with his boy. Last twilight found them atop the rim of the big hole. From the sedimentary precipice they dove into the deep water, repeating the rush over and over, each dive deeper into the hole. When the river lost itself to darkness, they dressed and caught up their mounts and rode out of the riverbed. Mountains sawtoothed the last light. A little band of Indian kids loped out to greet them. Hoofborn clouds of dust floated starward capturing the sorrel light of fevered bonfires, a celebration of prairie life. Bareback children whooped about—some only four or five years old—running circles around the festivities.

Trish loped out of the maze atop Corporal Trim. The moon waited to rise, patiently. Constellations ran roughshod over eternity. Swan flew straight above—humanity swallowed by sky. Nightfall overwhelmed Wendel and his family. He was grateful for all the people who'd gathered to live the life they knew best, everything and everyone connected, men and animals, fishes and birds, grass, trees and stars. Unmistakable connection. His son rode before him, man now, his daughter beside him, woman to be.

Their horses became reluctant as they approached the flaring bonfire. Drumming layered the flames—songs to vanished buffalo, to starved Indians, sparks chittering the heaven and hell of time. Wendel's family dismounted. Paddy tied Milk River Chinook to Rip's aluminum trailer. Trish and Wendel tied their horses to Mitch's trailer. The horsemen unsaddled and rubbed their horses down and fed them clean green oats. With their animals comfortable and content, they made their way to Rip's barbecue spit where a hindquarter of Limousine beef roasted. Badtooth Gene carved red meat, blood red.

Wendel shook Rip's hand—no ranch, but plenty of ranching ahead.

Bubbles had departed, burdened. Bunkhouse Chris sat up on his cot to stick up for Bubbles, saying it was one of those things that couldn't be helped. Bunkhouse regretted his misfired attempt to fend Bubbles off the racecourse. Perhaps he shouldn't have tried to keep him away. Perhaps Bubbles just wanted to watch the race like everyone else. Maybe some things are just meant to be, or rather not meant to be. Bunkhouse Chris understood Bubbles Ground Owl's appearance to be foreordained, woe be he to alter such a sacred rhythm as Bubbles'. The horse medicine man made his appearance as medicine men still do. Chris laid back down on his cot and looked up at the Milky Way, pathway of souls, soon his pathway, he thought. He lay there, entrenched in eternity, his toothless grin innocent as a newborn's.

Trish couldn't keep her sleepy eyes off her firelit father and hero brother. Lick hung close to her, nuzzling in response to Doc and Willow's overbearing possessiveness of her. The Spookalooians had humbly endured the entire day's races and proudly doted over Trish, basking in their reunion with her. Despite Dharma's loss—which they considered insignificant— they'd come to like her Grandfather Rip. His storied world of horses and cattle and land drew them in. What a man. They also very much admired Milk River Chinook, and like good horsemen, were graceful losers, thankful most of all that Dharma hadn't been crippled.

Lick whined and panted anticipating where she and her little master might be headed. Nan visited with Frenchy as they rode the transparent night on the top of the ridge, walking their horses slowly, now. Frenchy knew Wendel and thought him worthy and told Nan so. The night dissolved with the rising moon. Fires dwindling. People slept or left, heading home every which direction. Wendel suggested that Doc and Willow turn Dharma Bum over to Mitcheltree to train for the rest of the season. Doc agreed that Mitch deserved to take the horse to Saratoga Springs, thought the horse might now be fit enough to handle the east coast traffic. If someone deserved the Saratoga nirvana it was Mitcheltree, the survivor who hadn't yet had the wind completely knocked out of him by the racehorsing game.

Willow and Doc walked to their Lincoln Town Car.

Wendel hugged his daughter good-bye.

"I love you, Daddy."

Trish then hugged Padrick, her brother. She turned and left, walking to the car, her dog tight at her heels. Her mother and stepdad pulled her and the dog into the long low car and wheeled off across the dark prairie for Spokane. Wendel watched the automobile scrape along. Billows of disturbed dust collected lost light and surged about their chassis like a nightmare, the Town Car carrying his daughter away.

Wendel and Mitch, Paddy and Nan standing under a hovering moon.

Saratoga twinkled in Mitch's eye.

Wendel thought about ranching the Walking Box under Rip. He'd have cows to pasture and horses to ride, a son to school, wild country to keep wild. Ownership couldn't matter. Moonlight flooded the country, fishcolored moonlight. Ownership of a chunk of this range by a human, one human, any human, was as ludicrous a whim as horseracing. The departure of Trish ached. Wendel would never become accustomed to having children whisked away. He put his arm around Paddy, the son he'd never hugged until now.

There wasn't much left to say. Wendel wanted to ride home horseback with Nan, her turn finally come. Paddy climbed in the truck with Mitcheltree and the two horsemen drove to Palookaville for the night. The young man fell asleep not far down the road.

Wendel and Nan.

Each time Nan looked Wendel's way through the day he'd sported a different demeanor, his biography revealed in a series of relationships. By first light Trish pervaded his consciousness and molded his antics, then came the women who burdened his soul. His mother considered, a father passed on. An ex-wife to contend with, a daughter, a son and his mother, his son's grandfather and grandmother. Seemed everyone but Nan had flowed through Wendel's life today. She mounted Bjorni. Wendel swung onto Dharma Bum, two souls homeward bound with nary a word. They let the universal beat of their horses' footfalls take them home. A quiet wind clarified the atmosphere and allowed the stars to sparkle.

Moonlight lit their camp as they rode in, Mitch and Paddy long asleep. They unsaddled, rubbed their horses and put them to grass, netherworld of stars above, a world they'd come to love like one another. They flopped in the tepee. Without Trish, an emptiness cried out. They folded into each other and loved and slept—peace settled within them.

In the morning, when the towering darkness slipped off the edge of the world Nancy informed Wendel she was returning to Whitefish.

"I'm leaving today," she said.

"Leaving?" he replied.

"*Empire Builder* drops me off not five blocks from my home."

"The *Empire Builder* never delivered me to any home."

"That's 'cause you've never had a home. But now it's settled. You do."

"Indentured servitude, some home."

"A home nonetheless."

"You like that I have a home?"

"Yes. I do. I like that you have a home, indentured as it may be, but isn't it said, Wendel, that a man's home is his empire?"

"Somewhere it must be said."

"Well then, I'd say the *Builder* did deliver you an empire after all, this empire, this homeland." Nancy waved her hand across Montana. "Good thing the train runs through it right to my doorstep. Maybe I'll see you sooner rather than later, this time."

"I'm thinking sooner," Wendel said.

Nan looked at him with her steely blue eyes. Moisture glistened the surfaces. She put a cool hand behind his neck and pulled her man to her, she pressed her lips to his and kissed him long and willing. He needed time to add everything up, and so did she, and the time to add everything up had arrived. It had been a fine summer, all those horses they rode.

278

Chapter 28

EARTHMAN

That afternoon Mitcheltree drove Nan to the train station at East Glacier with Dharma in tow. He was heading to Saratoga Springs, New York via Shelby, Montana. He sported a smirk as wide as the Chinook Arch. He had a new tooth, an Indian tooth carved out of ivory, elktooth ivory the denturist fixed up in a flipper for him, a sweet smile, gap gone. Owners wouldn't think he lacked class anymore just because he lacked teeth.

Wendel and Paddy saddled up and cut cross-country to see Nan onto the train. They beat her and Mitch to East Glacier, arriving at the depot just in time to see Bo Triplett and Akifumi Cato hobble through the flower gardens that led down from The Big Hotel to the Amtrak Station, each man hobbling along in their peculiar crippled way. They'd stop to rest occasionally, looking back to the mountains, or maybe up to the sky, and always to the flowers. They reached the trainstation as Mitch rolled in with Nan.

Wendel and Nancy took a walk through the linear flower garden. By the time the departure whistle blew they knew they would hook up again soon enough, they just didn't know when, or where, and didn't fret about it. When they did meet up, they knew things would be solid for once in their lives.

Nancy joined the train-travelling horsemen heading west over the Continental Divide. Once aboard and seated beside Triplett and Cato, she wrestled down a window and waved goodbye to Paddy and Wendel.

Mitcheltree headed east with the Dharma. Saratoga here we come.

Wendel and Paddy stood together as the train pulled away, no longer the passengers they had once been. Their horses waited next to the tracks, waited to carry them home.

Two days later Wendel and Paddy rode to the summit from Palookaville to use the public telephone. News at the Walking Box was that Bubbles had not returned. No one knew where he was, although they all had their fears. Last he'd talked to anyone was just after the big race when he'd told Mabel he was leaving to retrieve the horse medicine bundle. Wendel and his son rode back to camp, quietly they rode, Trish's voice missing, squirrels wondering why.

Badtooth Gene showed up the next day to tell Wendel and Paddy the news. A railroad engineer had found Bubbles dead in the railyard the day before. Wendel left for town to see if could help with his friend's passing. Bubbles' sister had organized everything. Against a wish apparently only Wendel knew, Bubbles was going to be given a graveyard burial despite his preference for six feet up some cottonwood. Wendel could not change things, did not try. He was not family and he was not Indian. The graveyard was not his choice.

Indians had melted into America, been forced to melt into America, now buried like their conquerors. In many ways Bubbles had refused to melt, and Wendel knew this as well as anyone. He thanked realbear for those who did not accept the new ways, for those who wished for a timeless return of buffalo. Wendel looked over the vast plains to the north and east, and upon the backbone mountains south and west. He thanked this world for Bubbles Ground Owl, knowing this world would be different without him.

As the sun fell, Wendel went to the railyard where Bubbles had snatched Wendel's broke-down life off a freighter over a year ago. Badtooth Gene had helped bag up Bubbles' body and told Wendel of the exact site of his last breath. Grass was still pressed into the earth where Bubbles had lain lifeless. Wendel stood and felt the wind. He touched the earth where Bubbles had expired. It somehow remained warm. The spot was hemmed in by corrals on one side and traintrack on the other, where neither mountains nor prairie could be seen. Wendel looked up. A line of oil cars sat long and round on the track, their sides stained with the jaundiced drip of yellow crude. Behind him the splintered stockyards creaked in the breeze. A lone whitehorn Hereford bull bellowed and pawed cloven hoovesfull of dried dung into the wind, a wind rising.

A new bouquet of graveyard flowers blew by—their plastic warped, their color faded by summer sun, faded the color of death… A broken wine bottle lay nearby, shattered green glass held together by the label, a label picturing a gloriously clad Indian, Chief Thunderbird Red, the image torn, the paper redsoaked.

The following day Wendel and Paddy rode horseback to the Holy Family Mission graveyard along the Two Medicine River. They worked their way down from the ancient piskans that beheld the valley. A dirge of wailing greeted their arrival. Mabel and Bubbles' sisters and their women clan of friends keened most beautifully, ancient notes sent into the wind. On and on they wailed, on and on. Father Dan preached everlasting life, every other word blown away.

When the spoken words ended, gravemen began lowering the coffin into the earth. The wailing resumed, primeval howls ten thousand years old.

Bubbles began his final descent.

Then everything stopped.

The wind stopped. The wailing. The coffin stopped—a grave too narrow for the redwood coffin. Having been dug into the river bedrock spawned by the last ocean that flooded this land, the grave could not be widened with shovel or pick, as it was rock held true. The backhoe had departed, and nothing was available to widen the tomb. Wendel considered Bubbles' secret desire to be buried above the earth, this grave-jamming his final refusal to melt. Wanting closure, the mourners pushed and pried and crammed the unwilling coffin into the obnoxious bedrock. One end fell to the bottom. The other end was pushed a little deeper, below the ground they managed it, deep enough to cover up, deep enough but mostly upright, Bubbles Ground Owl buried standing on his head.

The crestfallen crowd of relatives, ranchhands, and clergy wandered away in their blowing blackness. Wendel grabbed a shovel to help the gravediggers cover the diagonal casket. He tried to wedge Bubbles a little deeper, but the ancient bedrock held tight, poising the sarcophagus upright, forces of nature working hard to squirt Bubbles Ground Owl up and out of the earth, he himself willing it in death.

They began pitching dirt. Paddy, for the first time, helped bury one of his people. They shoveled and wind returned, big wind. Bubbles' wind. Wendel's spade clinked into a bottle of

Thunderbird Red stuck in the filldirt piled beside the grave, carefully hidden by Mabel Old Coyote. Tied to the bottle was the horse medicine bundle. Wendel removed the bundle and handed it to his son. "What's this?" Paddy asked.

"It's the power. Bubbles' horse medicine bundle. Yours now."

"Mine? But there has to be a transfer."

"He told Mabel he wanted you to have it."

"But I don't know how to use it."

"It will come to you in a dream," one of the gravediggers said.

"What sort of dream?" Paddy asked.

"Bubbles will decide that. He will come to you and you will know horse."

Paddy held the bundle up to the sun.

Wendel set the bottle aside, and finished filling the grave with the Piegan gravediggers.

Paddy kneeled to the ground and set the bundle carefully in the grass next to another small-marked grave.

"Dad," he called.

Wendel looked over from his shoveling.

"Look at this."

Wendel walked to his son. The gravespace beside the medicine bundle was marked a with temporary gravemarker weathered and rusted and small, nearly obscured in the prairie shortgrass. The first name was difficult to make out, but the last was clearly theirs. Wendel squatted and brushed off the tarnished marker. James Willard Ingraham it said.

"Your grandfather," Wendel said.

"Your dad," Paddy replied.

"I didn't know he was buried here," Wendel said.

"I didn't know he was dead."

"I should have told you. Others should have told you."

"We'll have to get him a proper stone."

"We will," Wendel said.

The two resumed filling Bubbles' grave. Wind paused to let a coyote hark a lonesome elegy. The gravediggers and father and son stopped and listened, keeping an eye on the grave. An airpocket behind the casket gave way. Loose gravedirt moved, sucked down to an emptiness below. Wendel opened the bottle of reinforced wine and threw the top into the twirl of hourglassing soil. Time took the cap in and time took it down. Wendel poured the wine on the sifting dirt, but wind spattered the redness across the prairie.

Wendel held the almost empty bottle to the sun. Wind sucked one last song out of the screwtop hollowness. He imbibed the gulp that remained—swirled it around his mouth and spit it onto the last toss of gravedirt.

Earth consumed the red liquid.

Epilogue

MAN

In his Sand Hills Bubbles dreamt the horse dream, he transferred the story of his people to Paddy, who dreamt the same dream that night as he slept with the horse medicine bundle...

In the dog days no one owned land, or grass, or anything earthly—no one and everyone. And then the horse returned. Life changed. The continent changed. Your bundle began its journey.

Our Blackfeet mastered the horse like whitemen mastered the wheel. Horse enabled Indian to reign supreme over hunting grounds far and wide, guarding safe the range that sustained the eternal herds of buffalo. The grass, the rivers and streams of the sacred beaver that supervised the water world below. Blackfeet, horse-raiders of the Great Plains, captured all the horses they needed, and more. The horse came quickly, standing time still for two centuries. Horse's arrival erased millennia of foot travel. A great love came together, Indian and horse, the beginning of the end of North American man.

Smallpox followed the horse, and after that whiskey, reservations and railroads, a prairie people transgressed.

Buffalo disappeared, extinct by Manifest Destiny.

Then Indian knew nothing, understanding nothing but

buffalo. An unfathomable disappearance, seas of buffalo once forever upon the plains forever gone. Migrations and endlessness vanished, the mirth of living departed. Time itself returned, and with time the horse remained.

The horse medicine bundle is the last connection to the bountiful past when all young Indian men became horsemen. Keep it safe, Paddy. Pass it on. The old Indian men knew the horse like you will know horse. Horses and buffalo were all we ever knew, all we wanted to know. With buffalo gone, we were left with horses. And in the end the horse people encountered snow and cold, no meat and little else. During the winter of 1884, the buffalo vanquished, a third of the Blackfeet nation starved to death, six hundred native souls starved to death under the care of America's Army and Indian Bureau. Foodless starving dead reservation Indians, glandered horses and Indians starving… vanquished.

But we survived. Horse became our memory of buffalo, our last connection to ancient ways. The horse became the beginning and the end. After the starvation winter we surrendered. Chief Buffalo Heart, my great-great grandfather, knew our people would be exterminated if we did not submit. Hungry and starved—buffalo-dependent, buffalo gone—we submitted, but we remain horsemen. With nothing left to embrace, we embraced our undoing, we embrace the horse.

The horse medicine bundle is yours. Use it sparingly. Pass it down.

Asleep a boy, awake a man.

About the Author

Sid Gustafson lives in Bozeman, Montana, with his children Connor and Nina where he writes and practices his natural approach to veterinary medicine. He is the author of the novels *Prisoners of Flight* and *Horses They Rode*, as well as the guidebook *First Aid for the Active Dog*. Dr. Gustafson is also an assistant professor of equine studies at the University of Montana-Western. He was born in Montana, as were his parents and children. Information about the author and his books may be obtained at www.sidgustafson.com.

Praise for Sid Gustafson's *Prisoners of Flight*

"This is a haunting book. It is refreshing to come across a literary account of The Real Thing—so graphic, so poetically rendered."
   The Independent

"Gustafson manages both an economy of words and a compelling lyricism. There is much that is satisfying about *Prisoners of Flight*."
   Washington State Magazine

"The book's imagery and sparse, elegant language pulls you through. Linguistic gems pepper almost every page."
   Bozeman Daily Chronicle